The
SLAUGHTER
MAN

CASSANDRA PARKIN

Legend Press Ltd, 51 Gower Street, London, WC1E 6HJ
info@legend-paperbooks.co.uk | www.legendpress.co.uk

Print ISBN 978-1-78955-0-573
Ebook ISBN 978-1-78955-0-580
Set in Times. Printing managed by Jellyfish Solutions Ltd
Cover design by Rose Cooper | www.rosecooper.com

Cassandra Parkin grew up in Hull, and now lives in East Yorkshire. Her debut novel *The Summer We All Ran Away* was published by Legend Press in 2013 and was shortlisted for the Amazon Rising Star Award. Her short story collection, *New World Fairy Tales* (Salt Publishing, 2011) was the winner of the 2011 Scott Prize for Short Stories. *The Beach Hut* was published in 2015, *Lily's House* in 2016, *The Winter's Child* in 2017 and *Underwater Breathing* in 2018. Cassandra's work has been published in numerous magazines and anthologies.

Visit Cassandra at
cassandraparkin.wordpress.com
or follow her
@cassandrajaneuk

For Becky, Ben, Holly and Rowan
Wishing you a long and happy ride on the merry-go-round

PART ONE

SEPTEMBER

CHAPTER ONE

She's at her sister's funeral, and she knows she's dreaming because the heads of all the people there have been replaced with the heads of birds.

At the front of the church, the vicar's surplice is made soft and welcoming by her enormous pillowy breasts. When this day happened for real, Willow had briefly laid her head against them, in that first naked moment when the vicar turned her soft sad gaze towards her and said, *I'm so sorry about your sister,* and her words turned a key inside Willow's chest and the grief she'd vowed to hold onto tumbled out like coins, splashing and crashing in bright sharp tinkles onto their laps. Now, the slick green head of a mallard turns its open beak towards her and she glimpses the tongue, flat and disturbingly human-looking. She wonders why Reverend Kate wears the head of a male duck. Perhaps it's the sardonic commentary of her unconscious on the customs and practices of the church. She can see its beak stretching and relaxing with the rhythm of its speech, but she can't hear a word. The church is entirely silent.

In the pew three rows behind her, a cluster of students from college – the college that used to be *theirs* and is now, unbearably and irrevocably, only *hers* – sit glossy and silent. Girls and boys alike wear speckled starling-heads, their sharp jabbing beaks turned downwards as a mark of respect, and not because they're looking at their phones. Beside her, her mother's body shudders with tears, but above her shoulders the raven's head remains expressionless and silent. In real life, her mother had reached down and taken Willow's hand and stroked her fingers and whispered, *I'm sorry, I'm sorry, I'm so sorry,* over and over and over, senseless and endless, until Willow's fingers were tingling and sore. Perhaps the bird-heads are masks. Perhaps the people wearing them are trapped inside, their whole worlds reduced to the simple need to breathe. Willow wants to reach up and touch her own face, see if she too has been forced to wear one, but her hands are too heavy to lift, and so she sits and waits for what she knows must surely come.

When this happened for real, Laurel was carried into church in a white coffin with a satin finish and fiddly gold handles. Willow had looked at the coffin and thought in disgust, *How can you possibly have picked that one? She wouldn't want that one, she'd want a black one, we both would. God, if you pick one like that for me…* and then the horror of her thoughts crowded in so fast that she could hardly breathe for guilt. She was imagining her parents picking out her own coffin. She was dreaming of her own ending, of going down into the darkness to join Laurel. She was imagining death as an escape.

A change in the light tells her that the men are coming in with Laurel. There's no coffin tonight. Instead her sister rides still and flat on the shoulders of four men. Three walk with the strength and synchronicity of professional undertakers, and wear the steady gaze and long, wise beaks of ibises. The fourth, his red-topped woodpecker head incongruous and gaudy, is her father. He holds tight to Laurel's ankle, buckling at the knees occasionally as he forces himself to perform this last duty. Willow wonders if he'll fall, and if Laurel will fold and crumple as she falls with him, or if she'll be stiff and rigid, like a plank of wood.

The procession lacks dignity, the ibises unbalanced by their fourth companion, his head and suit mismatched, his pace out of step with theirs. Willow had wanted him to be with her and her mother, and she was fairly sure her mother wanted the same thing, but her father had insisted. Just as on the day of the funeral, he's so stricken with grief he can hardly walk. Just as on the day of the funeral, Willow thinks how much better it would have been if her father had been in the pew with them.

Then she glimpses her sister's head, which is also her own head, sees the face they've both been wearing and looking into since before they came into the world, and wonders in panic, *Is it me they're burying today, or is it her? Which of us is still alive and which of us is dead? What if I'm not Willow at all, what if I'm Laurel and I don't know it? What if she thinks she's me? What happens then?*

The three ibises and her woodpecker father reach the front of the church and lay Laurel down on the altar. It's been swept clean of crosses and candlesticks, and covered in a sheet of thick blue-tinged plastic that blurs the gold thread embroidery of the altar cloth beneath. The ibises step back and melt away. She will not see them again. This is the first sign.

Wake up, Willow thinks. *Wake up. This is your last chance. Do it. Do it now. Right now. Wake up. Wake up!* And she's not sure if she's talking to her twin, or herself.

She knows what's coming next because she's had this dream before. The congregation, each wearing their bird-heads, stand, slowly and effortfully as if they're wading through water. She doesn't want to join them, but this is a dream, and she's given no choice. She wants to hold her mother's hand, but her mother is just ahead of her now, second in the long chain of people that's forming up behind her father, whose bright streak of red feathers glow like a beacon in the spray of sunlight, shooting through the window to splash across Laurel's closed, silent face. This is the second sign.

Wake up, Willow thinks. *This is a dream. You don't need to stay here. Wake up and get out of here. None of this happened. You don't need to be here. It's only a dream.* She closes her eyes, fierce and tight. When she reopens them, she can feel the rustling that comes from the excited agitation of the thousands of tiny feathers, covering the bird-heads of the congregation. They've begun to clack their beaks in anticipation. This is the third sign.

The minister stands behind the altar, behind Laurel's body, and raises her hands in blessing. Her father, the first in the queue – the head of the family, she supposes – mounts the three shallow steps to the altar, raises his hands for a moment in imitation of the minister, then bends from the waist and plunges his head down, down, down, into the soft cold belly of his daughter. When he turns his face to the waiting congregation, his beak and feathers are covered in blood.

No, Willow thinks. *This isn't what happened. I won't let this be what happens. This is a dream. I won't let it happen.*

Her mother next, stepping up to the altar with quick steps, soaring on a wave of air created by the swift eager movements of those who wait behind, as if instead of clapping their hands, the congregation are urging Willow's mother onwards by moving their arms like wings. The gesture of blessing. The dip. The pause. Her mother's face, birdy and bloody.

Willow should take her place at the altar now, but she's not wearing a bird-head. The vicar bundles her over to one side, a swift kind gesture that nonetheless has the seeds of exasperation in it, as if Willow is a small child refusing to leave her offering at the Harvest Festival, or clutching stubbornly to her small silver coin for the collection plate. Helpless and sick, Willow tries not to look as one by one, the congregation take their turn at the sacred feast, each bird in its turn, the raptors and the seedeaters and the water-birds, the ones who hunt and the ones who strip the carcasses and the ones who live on honey and nectar, each dipping their faces and raising them again, eager but not impatient, knowing there'll be enough for everyone.

Stop, she thinks. She wants to scream her thought aloud, but her throat and mouth are stopped by a mighty weight that she doesn't dare try to push aside. In this dream, she's always voiceless. Her inability to speak is increasingly leaching out into her real life.

Don't ask them to stop, the vicar tells her. There's still no sound, just the kindly angling of her mallard head towards Willow's face, and words that unspool in her mind. *This is Death. We are all Death, every one of us, and we all need to eat. Would you rather they ate you instead? That could happen very easily. They'll probably find it hard to tell the difference between you and your sister. After all, you're the same, aren't you? You're the same. Separating you from each other, that's going against Nature.* And then her gaze turns over Willow's shoulder, and Willow has the sense that beneath the mallard-head, the vicar is smiling. *Ah, look who's here. He's come to call for you after all. It must be because you're an identical twin.*

And standing in the doorway of the church, Willow sees the most terrible bird of all, man-sized and man-shaped and dressed in black, with its blue-black head smoothly feathered and a thick stabbing beak like a crow and bright pitiless eyes that see everything, everything, the firm young flesh of her body and the strong marrowy bones beneath, the bright leap of blood in her veins and the glistening throb of her heart. The Death Bird sees all of these things, and then he looks inside her head and sees her thoughts, and she knows she invited him here. She's wished for him to come for her, and now she can't send him away again.

There are words tumbling in her throat – *I didn't mean it, I don't want to die* – but they won't be enough to set her free. Words only have power when they're spoken and she can't speak now. Her voice is locked away for ever, and she's going down to join her sister in the darkness, and the congregation will eat her body and she'll never see daylight again. The Death Bird holds out a long pale hand. All the flesh and feathers have fallen from his head; now he is wearing a bird-skull.

He's come for you, says Laurel from the altar, and this is new, because usually in this dream Laurel is voiceless, too. She doesn't dare to look because she doesn't want to see what the congregation has done to her, but still it's Laurel's voice, the voice which is also hers. When they were little and recorded themselves performing plays or reading stories, they would sometimes be unable to tell which of them had spoken which words, who had taken one part and who the other. *He's come for you. You have to go with him when he comes for you. That's what happened to me. Now it's your turn.*

But Mum and Dad, Willow thought helplessly.

But I miss you, Laurel pleaded. *And you miss me too. Don't you? That's why he's here. Because you miss me. We belong together. Please don't go out of here and leave me behind. I can't bear it.*

If she could speak, she could set herself free. She could tell him *No,* and send him away. But she can't speak. She can't even hear herself think over Laurel's pleading voice, and she isn't even sure that she wants to be rescued, because after all, Laurel's right. They belong together, and their sudden cleaving into separateness has made a wrong place in her soul that will never, ever heal. The thought of the long years stretching out before her, the long barren decades of life where she'll walk alone into the world with an empty place beside her, seems like too much to bear.

I'm going to die in my sleep, she thinks. *My heart's going to stop.*

And then in the place between two heartbeats, the place between life and death, she tells herself, successfully this time, *Wake up!*

She wakes, sweating with fright, tangled in sour-smelling sheets, warmed only by the damp place between her legs where she's wet herself in the utter terror of her dream.

You're disgusting, she thinks wearily, and climbs out of the bed so she can take the sheets off.

She pads as quietly as she can down the corridor to the top of the stairs, cautious even though she knows her parents won't wake. She spies on them just as they spy on her, all of them secretly watching each other for signs of illness or weakness, and she knows this is one of the rare-but-increasing nights when they've both taken sleeping tablets. They must finally have begun to trust that Willow won't die in her sleep because they weren't awake to watch over her. Or perhaps they're giving in to the inevitable truth that, if they don't begin to look after themselves in some rudimentary way, they'll die too. Despite the pain they would all (if they ever dared speak about it) describe as *unbearable*, they all still want to live. The shame of wanting to survive makes it hard for them to look at each other.

Downstairs in the utility room, she fills the washing machine with sheets and pyjamas, then switches it on. Back upstairs, there's a damp patch on the mattress.

Newly clad in fresh pyjamas, she considers her options. If she puts clean sheets on a wet mattress, it will soak into them and she'll have to change them again in the morning. If she turns the mattress over, will it dry in the dusty gloom beneath the bed? Or will it simply fester and degrade into ammonia, making her room and everything in it stink? She could sleep on the floor. Perhaps that's what she deserves. But she knows she has another place to go.

She stands for a few moments at the threshold, her fingers tracing out the shape of the name on the door. *Do you still want those names on your doors?* their mother had asked a few months before Laurel's death. She'd been on one of her periodic decluttering missions, when comforting piles of detritus were swept out from corners and banished, and no possession, no matter how sentimental, was safe from her assessing gaze. *Yes,* they'd answered simultaneously, and when their mother tried to persuade them – *You're going to be eighteen next birthday, do you really want your names on your doors still? Really?* – their father had come to their rescue. *Come on, let them keep their doorplates if they want to. What harm does it do?* And now, perhaps, no one would ever dare to change them.

Knowing that she's trespassing, she creeps inside. The bed is still made up, the litter of clothes on the floor mundane and comforting. When she presses her face into the pillow, she can smell the shampoo she and Laurel both used each morning, taking it in turns for the first use of the shower. This ought to be a terrible place, a place she can hardly bear to enter, but the bed welcomes her, the shapes in the darkness feel familiar, everything feels familiar, the duvet folds over her like an old friend. She closes her eyes, knowing she's reached a safe haven.

On the edge of sleep, she realises something terrible. This room she's in now feels familiar because it's *her* room, which she stumbled out of not two hours ago, her body seeking out the comfort of her sister's place, her mind wandering through the border country between waking and sleeping. It is Laurel's bed she's left wet and unmade. Laurel's pyjamas, taken from Laurel's drawers, that she's fumbled her way into. And this is not the first time. When her mother and father wake in the morning, it will be to the discovery that their surviving daughter has once again left her own bed and crawled into the space that should be sacred, marking her territory like a badly behaved cat before slinking away. She's losing the boundaries between herself and her dead twin. The shock sends her out of the bed and over to the mirror where she can gaze at the face looking back at her.

My bed, she thinks. *My room. I'm in my room. This is my room. This is my mirror. This is my face in the mirror. I'm Willow.*

She tries to say the words out loud. If she can say her own name, here in the dark where no one will hear her, she'll know she's all right. It's very hard to get the words out, but after a short fierce effort, she succeeds.

"I'm Willow," she says to her reflection, and is startled by how hoarse she sounds. It sounds as if she's been screaming into her pillow for hours and hours, the way she sounded the first week after Laurel died. As if she hasn't been able to speak at all now for several days, not at school, not on the bus, not to her parents, not even when her mother begged her to *say something, to just try, please, sweetie, just try, you're safe, nothing bad will happen, you can talk to us,* and she tried and tried to force the words out, but they wouldn't come. Then her mother had wept, loudly and helplessly, all the while repeating *I'm sorry, I'm sorry, I'm being so stupid, I'm sorry,* and Willow had wondered if things might be better if she was dead too.

"I'm Willow," she repeats, trying to make her voice softer and more human. "I'm Willow. I'm Willow. My name is Willow. And I'm still alive."

She sounds as if her head has been replaced by a bird-head, ready for her to take her place in the church and join the congregation.

When I wake up I'll be able to speak again, she thinks. *Things will be better in the morning. I'm not Laurel. I'm Willow. I'm not dead. I'm alive. I'm taking my A-levels next summer. College starts tomorrow, and I'm going. Tomorrow, I'll do better.*

The face that stares back at her looks as if it doesn't believe her.

CHAPTER TWO

For a few days, she's able to defy herself. For a few days, she actually manages to do better.

Better sees Willow onto the bus, through morning classes and all the way to the college canteen, with her sandwiches and her apple and her drink and her bag of crisps. Some days she's so consumed with guilt at still being alive, and at doing something to make sure she stays that way, that she can hardly swallow. Some days, she's so furious with the world that she eats every bite and then buys half a dozen chocolate bars from the corner shop and eats and eats and eats until she's sick and dizzy with sugar, until she thinks a single mouthful more might split her open, until she has to kneel on the floor by the toilet bowl and use every ounce of her willpower to hold onto the contents of her stomach, because some things cannot and should not be undone and she won't allow herself the release of vomiting. But today she can eat normally, one bite after another, steady and careful, with pauses for mouthfuls of Diet Coke to wash it down.

Perhaps what she said to herself last night was true. Perhaps from now on, she'll do better. Maybe this is the beginning of her slow climb out of the pit, back towards normality.

She's sitting with her lunch and trying to focus on this thought, the idea of being normal. Maybe she'll be able to speak in English this afternoon, join the discussion on *Othello* out loud and not simply in the empty places in her head. She's aware of the arrival of a cluster of girls she knows well and used to be friendly with, but she only vaguely registers the new face in the centre of the group, her expression one of frantic effort and furious concentration, the outsider trying to find her place as quickly as possible.

"… food's all right, but it gets really busy and you can't take plates or cutlery into the student lounge, so most of us bring sandwiches and eat in the lounge, and just buy snacks in here."

"I've only got money today. Sorry. Um, I can eat in here, and then meet you in the lounge afterwards if you like?"

"Don't be daft, we'll sit with you. You get some food and we'll hang around and wait for a table…"

"Um, that one's almost empty…?" That faintly artificial uncertain note. She already knows there'll be a reason for the table remaining almost-empty when every other table in there is almost-full. She's not suggesting they sit there. She only wants to know why they can't. Willow feels envy clutch at her guts. *She* used to be able to do that, used to be able to express almost anything she wanted with the smallest modulations of her voice. If only she could speak, if only the hand at her throat would *just let go*.

"No, that's Willow Tomms." Ellie-Mae's doing her best, but it's hard to talk quietly when there's so much ambient noise. Willow keeps her gaze facing carefully forward, not wanting Ellie-Mae to know that she can hear. "It's really awful what happened. She had an identical twin sister called Laurel, but she died last term, right before the holidays – she wasn't, like, noticeably ill or anything, it was really sudden – and now Willow has really bad social anxiety and she can hardly talk."

"She's really brave coming back," adds Georgia hastily. "None of us were expecting her to make it. I don't know what I'd do if that happened to me, I'd…"

No, you wouldn't, thinks Willow scornfully. *You wouldn't die. You'd keep going. Because that's what you have to do. You have to keep going.*

"God." The new girl's voice falters. "God, that's... that poor girl."

"I know. It's so sad. She's in our English class this afternoon, but she probably won't say anything. She used to be really clever as well. I tell you what, if you've got money do you fancy chips from the chip shop? There's a good one just round the corner, we've got time." They drift away again, leaving Willow behind.

She wonders about going after them, trying to find her feet in the group once more, but what would be the point? Of course they left her behind. This is where she belongs now. This is who she is. This is who she'll always be. She'll never again be *Willow the identical twin, no-that's-not-Laurel-that's-her-twin-sister-Willow, yes Willow, what did you want to say?* Now she's only ever going to be *Willow whose twin sister died, Willow who doesn't speak any more, Willow who we all know we have to be nice to but we don't really know how to do that so we sort of leave her alone and hope that's enough, Willow who used to be part of the gang but really, how can we keep including her when she doesn't speak?*

The new girl is the first, but there will be many others. And the more people who know her in her silent, twinless form, the more impossible it will become for her to make her way back to her old self, until one day there'll be no one who knew her when she was whole and had a voice, and she'll never be that girl ever again. This silent girl, who sits alone in the canteen and who frightens others by her very existence, is who she is now.

She thinks, *I will not be scared of this. I won't. I'm going to get better. I'm going to get better. I'll be able to talk this afternoon in class. I will.* She thinks, *oh God, oh no, I'm going to wet myself.* She stares hard at the table and clenches her fists and forces herself to hold on. After a minute, the feeling passes.

She stands and pushes her chair beneath the empty table.

She tries not to notice that everyone around her tenses up, just a little. She puts her lunchbox back in her bag. She takes her coat off the back of the chair and puts it on. Then she walks out of the canteen, pushing against the flow of traffic even though that's against the rules. She walks the wrong way down the one-way corridor, waiting for someone to step in and send her back with a stern warning, perhaps even a sanction. But nobody does.

She walks out of the canteen building and across to the admin block, and waits for someone to stop her as she passes through Reception. The staff behind the desk fall silent for a moment as she passes, but still nobody stops her. *I'm the invisible girl*, she thinks, and for a moment Laurel's there beside her, her companion in the few acts of mischief they undertook on the days when they rebelled against their good-girl labels, and she thinks, *Hey, Laurel, how about that? You turned me invisible*. She can almost hear her sister's laughter.

Stop me, she thinks, and pushes through the doors and into the pick-up area outside, half-filled with cars even though it's the heart of the school day. *Stop me*. She passes two teachers, who look at her apprehensively, but do not speak to her. *Stop me. Say something to me. Try to stop me*. They let her pass without a word. She crosses the car park. *Stop me*.

One more step and she'll be outside the bounds of the college. *Stop me*. This is the last moment before she can change her mind. Once she leaves the premises, she'll never find the courage to come back again. The staff aren't stupid; plenty of them have watched her as she leaves. They must know what she's about to do. They can tell the difference between students leaving to go to the shops, and students leaving to do something they shouldn't. The one time she and Laurel had tried skiving off from classes, sneaking out of separate entrances to avoid drawing attention with their doubled nature, they'd been casually intercepted before they'd even reached the street. It had been both scary and comforting to discover how closely watched they really were.

Stop me, she thinks, and takes the step off the car park and onto the pavement. For a moment she shivers, and wonders what she's done. Then she feels a curious sensation, a physical relief, as if a real and tangible weight has been lifted from her shoulders. Perhaps what has left her is the last shred of her reality. Perhaps now she's truly invisible.

She turns and heads towards home. The world feels strange and slowed-down. Normally she would be on the bus. It's going to be a long walk, but on the plus side, she'll only have to walk it once.

Just try to stop me.

Time-wipe. She's blinked and missed a chunk of time, but it's all right, if she concentrates hard enough, she'll be able to fill in the blanks. She's in her room. (A moment of panic: is it her room? Yes, definitely her room, the room with *Willow* written on the door.) That means she must have made it home. She's put on her pyjamas, leaving her jeans and t-shirt in a crumpled heap on the floor at the end of her bed. When she reaches out a hand, her t-shirt feels cool to the touch, so she must have been home for a while. Is she hungry? Not really. Is she tired? She's not sure. How long does she have until someone finds her here? Perhaps they never will. She stretches out on her bed and closes her eyes.

She's begun to slip into the welcome darkness of sleep when she hears the front door bang open, then slam shut. Then, her mother calls her name up the stairs. She can hear the panic in it, the semi-rational terror of a woman who's already seen into the abyss and now knows for certain that there's no bottom, it goes down and down, a place you can fall into and never climb out again. A woman who knows there's no end to the amount of bad luck the universe can contain, and that having one dose of it does nothing to inoculate you from receiving another. "Willow? Willow, are you there?"

Her mother's voice has been made desperate with love.

Willow feels her own heart swell with love in return. This is the moment. This is what she needed. This is why she came home. It's not a backwards move, it's a step towards recovery. She *has* to call back, she has to put her mum out of her misery and let her know she's all right. She can do this. She will open her mouth and she'll be able to call back.

She opens her mouth. Her lungs fill with air, the words are there in her mouth, every muscle of her body is willing and eager. *Mum, I'm here, I'm fine.* What's wrong with her that she can't even let her mother know she's safe? She could do the second best thing and go to the door of her room, fling it open so that her mother will hear the sound, stand wordless but visible at the top of the stairs. She's all right, she can do this, she only needs a minute to get herself together.

"Willow? Willow? Are you in here?" Her mother is rushing up the stairs now. "Willow! Sweetie, please, I'm not angry, I just need to know you're okay." On the landing. "Willow, please…" The door opens, and there she is, fear aging her, so Willow can see what her mother's going to look like when she's an old woman. Or is it simply the change that came over her the day Laurel died?

This is what she's been waiting for. This moment when her mother will come to her and find her sitting in her room. She knows Willow's run out of college and come home; she knows Willow's ignored the frantic messages on her phone; she knows she sat still and silent as her mother called her name. Now, in this moment, her mother – who studied for years to understand how the human brain works, who spends her days fixing people who have to live with the almost-unbearable – will find the way to fix her.

What will it be? Perhaps her mother will be angry. *You heartless little monster, how could you do this? How could you leave college and not tell me where you were going? How could you sit there and listen while I called your name? Right, that's enough. I've been holding off, letting that other doctor do her best, but it's time I took over. This is what you're going to do, and you'd better bloody do it, Willow, or else…* Or perhaps she'll be softer, more tender. *My poor girl, I'm so sorry, I thought you'd do better with treatment from someone external but now I understand… and I promise I can fix you. This will work, I promise it works. I only waited because it's hard and you've been through so much already…*

Either of them, she thinks to herself, *either of those is fine. Just tell me what to do. I'll do the work, I promise. I don't want to be like this for ever. You're our mum, you grew us. You're a grief counsellor, for God's sake. You're supposed to have the answers.*

But what she sees in her mother's face is what she always sees these days: fierce unending love mixed with hopeless confusion. Because her mother does not have the answers, and does not know how to fix her surviving daughter, and they are both lost.

"Oh, sweetie," she says helplessly, and presses her hand against her mouth. "Oh, sweetie. It's all right. It's all right. We'll be okay. It doesn't matter. It's okay." She sits down on the bed beside Willow, puts her arms out and draws her into a fierce tight hug. "It's all right, my little one, I promise I'm not mad. We'll sort it out with college. We will. I'll talk to them. Tell me what you need and—" She stops herself, and Willow hears the echo of the advice she's overheard the psychiatrist give both her parents at the end of every appointment: *Don't put any pressure on her to speak, try not to make her feel guilty.* "We'll get all of this sorted."

But how? Willow wants to ask. *How can we get all of this sorted? You don't know and I don't know, and Dad's got no idea at all, and who else is there in the universe who can help?* And for a minute, before she pushes the thought away, she thinks of the Death Bird that waits for her in the place where she goes to when she sleeps, of the congregation with their hungry beaks. *That would fix it. If I died, it would all be sorted then, wouldn't it? You wouldn't have to look after me any more. You wouldn't have to look at me walking around wearing Laurel's face. You could just... wallow in your grief.*

No, she tells herself fiercely. *I don't want to die.*

But then, Laurel hadn't wanted to die either.

And besides...

She's losing time again. A blink, and a night and a morning have passed and she's at her desk that looks out of the bedroom window and over the garden, staring blankly at the work her teachers have sent home. Another blink and she's lying on her bed, exhausted even though she hasn't left the house, hasn't even showered or dressed, and has spent an hour at most on her school work. Another blink, and it's long past dinner time and she's hungry. Did her parents call to her to tell her it's time to eat? She searches back in the archives, trying to find a clue.

Her father's been at home every day since Willow left college. He doesn't trust Willow to keep herself alive. Willow would give anything to make her parents understand that they doesn't need to hover and twitter and peck, dropping scraps of food into Willow's mouth whenever they get the chance. They don't need to worry. She's going to be all right. She only needs to be left alone for a while, to be left in silence so she can finally understand, finally *hear* what's going on in her own head.

Has she slept through dinner? She's done this before and they've let her, but they've also saved her some on a plate to go in the microwave. Her stomach growls. When she tries to stand, she feels weak and shaky. It's like this now: she's not hungry and not hungry and not hungry, for hours and hours and hours, until suddenly a switch flips in her head and she's starving. She ought to go downstairs and find whatever meal her parents have ready for her, but the hidden packet of biscuits is closer and easier, and she crams six chocolate digestives into her mouth, one after another without pausing. She could eat more – could happily eat the whole packet, and then sink back into sleep with her teeth coated in brown mulch and her breath sweet with sugar – but she forces herself to stop at six. She has enough energy to leave her room now. She'll do the right thing.

She can hear voices downstairs. There are always voices downstairs these days, but this isn't the smooth bland drone that pours tirelessly out from the living room television, endless documentary programmes about lives they don't live – in swamps, or the Arctic, or houses full of people all competing for the same job – interspersed with upbeat explanations of how random consumer goods are made. Tonight, she can hear actual human voices coming from the kitchen, voices that have the pauses and imperfect rhythms and moments when everyone speaks at once. Her parents, having a conversation. No, more than a conversation; an argument.

Her parents, who have not argued or even raised their voices to each other since the day it happened, are almost yelling at each other. How comforting. But what are they yelling about? And is she imagining it, or is there someone else in there too? She pads down the stairs and stops outside the kitchen door.

"Of course I came to the bloody funeral!" There's definitely someone else in the room. Another man. The sound of little movements; someone clattering in the cupboards, someone else pushing back a chair. "I didn't want to make a scene, that's all. So I parked outside and watched until after the cortege arrived – *just* me, mind, I didn't bring anyone else with me – and then I came in separately and sat at the back."

"You came in separately and sat at the back." Her mother's voice drips with contempt. Willow feels a curl of satisfaction lick around her heart. She hasn't sounded this alive since The Day. "Like a Victorian melodrama! Only you could find a way to make that day about yourself. Only you."

"Oh come on, Rose, be fair." The strange man again. "If I'd come in like a normal person and sat where you could see me, you'd have said I was showing up and showing off and making a fuss and looking for a fight. Or am I wrong?"

"Thank you for coming." Her father, using that special tone of voice adults only produce when what they really mean is to tell another adult, *This is what you're supposed to be saying*. It's strange to hear her father using it on her mother, who always knows the right thing to do. "It means a lot."

"It means absolutely fuck all," says her mother, with gloomy satisfaction. Willow clenches her fists to stop herself from gasping. She's never heard her mother swear. Before she can stop herself, she turns to where Laurel should be standing, so they can share the moment, and finds only empty space. Will she ever get used to knowing that from now on, everything new that happens will happen to her alone?

"Rose, come on." Her father again, sounding exasperated but also a little amused. Perhaps he likes hearing his wife swear too.

"What? What, exactly, does it mean that he turned up and sat at the back of the church and then cleared off without even saying hello?" A sound from the strange man that could have been *Rose*, muffled by emotion. "No, it's no good, Joe, you don't get points for trying. You weren't even bloody *there* for the last six years of her life, so why bother pretending you cared enough to say goodbye?"

Willow feels a tingle of excitement, because she suddenly knows who this is.

In her memories of Before, she finds a long bright afternoon a couple of years ago, when she and Laurel rummaged through the clots and clumps of paperwork that lived in the bureau. Tidying the bureau was a task her parents occasionally muttered about, but would clearly never attempt. Old bills and bank statements and fliers for double-glazing were crammed alongside family photographs and letters from long-dead relatives, no order or system other than the things that got dragged out and looked at tended to be closer to the top. Beginning with some vague idea of creating order from chaos and making their parents very happy, they'd grown distracted by the photos of their childhood. And among them...

(They'd spent long breathless minutes remembering. "He gave us that ostrich egg," Laurel said. "And he came for tea once and we asked him if we wanted jelly and he said he'd rather eat worms," Willow replied. "But then..." And they remembered the arguments, held in the evenings when Laurel and Willow weren't supposed to be awake to hear. An outbreak of muttered conversations, that stopped as soon as either Willow or Laurel went in. Their mother fizzing with tension; everyone walking softly around her. Their uncanny sense that she was desperately hoping they wouldn't ask questions. Their terror that there was some dreadful news coming (*maybe they're getting divorced? Or what if we have to move away?*), and the gradual easing of tension as the weeks and months went on, and nothing seemed to materialise. The slow realisation of who it was they weren't supposed to ask about; and then, the gradual shameful forgetting that he'd ever been part of their lives.

"Could you do that?" Laurel had asked her. "Could you forget about me and not see me for years?" And neither of them had been able to imagine it.)

"Oh Jesus, listen to me." Her mother again. "I'm sorry, I don't mean to be so horrible."

Behind the door, Willow wonders if her mother's apologising to her husband, or her older brother.

"Stephen, can you stick the kettle on for some coffee? And Joe, I didn't mean any of that. I know it was my fault as much as yours. I just... look, I'm glad you came. I am. It means a lot. And you'd have been welcome at the wake, you absolute prick. Give me a hug."

A pause. Laurel wishes she could see through the door and find out what's going on.

"So how was the journey?" That tone of voice again, that husband-to-wife instructional that she hasn't heard for so long.

"Oh. Um. Not too bad at all. No traffic really. Well, there was some, but it was all going the other way."

"That's good." Her father sounds as if he's not sure of his lines. "Grab a chair, why don't you? Dinner won't be long."

"God, no, honestly. It's fine, I don't expect you to cook for me, you weren't even expecting me. I'll get a takeaway."

"Don't you make me come over there and force you to sit down." How strange to hear her father teasing this man whose face she can barely remember, as if they've known each other for years and might even have liked each other once. "So, are you, I mean, did you, will there be anyone else joining us, or…"

A pause so awkward Willow can hear it through the door.

"No!" Joe sounds alarmed. "Rose, please, you know I wouldn't. I swear, it's only me."

"Keeping the bed warm back at home, then? You two are living together now, right?"

"Yes. No. Well, sort of. I mean, there's this business trip to get out the way first, and then… Look, Rose, I was on my own at the funeral as well, I swear. I know how you feel and I wouldn't—"

"For God's sake." Her mother sounds exhausted. "What does it matter now?"

"Tell you what." Her father's chair scrapes against the floor. "Do you want a beer?"

"That'd be great."

"Rose? Just this once?"

"No thanks." A pause. Will her father make the joke he always used to make, telling her mother that if she changes her mind she's not having any of his? "Actually, yes I will."

She can hear her father's footsteps as he goes to the fridge. Her parents used to drink quite often in the evenings, but now the same six beers and single bottle of Chardonnay have sat untouched in the fridge for months. Willow takes a deep breath and holds it, afraid her father will hear her through the door. Someone must have started cooking. She can smell ginger and garlic frying. Then there's the deeper sizzle of something being added to the pan, and finally the scent of mango and tomato and spices creeps around the edges of the door. She presses her hand to her stomach, afraid it will growl and give her away.

"Thanks, mate."

The click of bottle tops being popped off reminds her of the day when she and Laurel turned thirteen. To celebrate, they stole a bottle of beer each, and drank them in the bathroom. She can still remember seeing her own expression on her sister's face; their disappointment at the sourness, their determination to drink it anyway and plumb the depths of this mystery. She can feel the warmth in her belly, and the giddy feeling they both imagined was drunkenness. They'd laughed until they cried, and eaten a whole bag of mints to cleanse their breath afterwards.

"Rose, please talk to me. How are you really?"

"We're fine." Her mother's voice is a closed metal shutter. Nothing getting out; nothing getting in. Nothing to see here. *I'm fine.* The lie they've all been telling since it happened. How many times have they all said this, to teachers and counsellors and friends and colleagues and each other? Maybe it's the weight of this lie that's stopped the words in Willow's mouth.

"We're not fine." Her father, correcting her mother once more.

"We're fine," her mother repeats, and Willow can hear all the things her mother isn't saying, because they're the things Willow never says either. *I don't want to talk to you. This pain is mine, not yours. It's all I've got left of her. I don't want to share it. Not with anyone.* "What good does it do to talk about it? Especially not to *him*."

"Please don't say that. I'm your big brother, I'm supposed to look after you. And I know I'm not a parent so I can't begin to understand, but—"

"That's right. You can't understand. So don't try. And be glad you'll never have to."

"We're not fine." Her father's voice is low but penetrating, determined to be heard. "No, Rose, I'm not going to shut up, don't even bother trying. We're not fine and we're not coping and we don't know what to do. Well, I don't, anyway. We're falling apart. All of us. And none of us know how to make it better." The chair scrapes, and she hears the small sounds of her father standing at the cooker. "So that's how we're doing. Can you sort the rice out?"

"Yes, of course. Where is it?"

"He means me." Her mother, sounding weary. "Sit down and drink your beer."

"It's all right, I want to help."

"Well, guess what? *Helping* doesn't mean crashing around a strange kitchen looking for stuff you've got no chance of finding because you never come here."

"Rose, please." Nobody argues with her mother when she's in this mood. Is he doing it because he's her brother and he knows better? Or doesn't he know her well enough? "Tell me what I can do and I'll do it."

"Do you want another beer?" Her mother's voice is brittle, on the verge of cracking into something sharp and dangerous. "We must owe you quite a few drinks to make up for six years, don't you think?"

"Look, if you want to me to say it was all my fault, then I'll say that, okay? I shouldn't have tried to make you accept us as a couple, that was stupid and selfish of me. I should have come to see you on my own. I'll regret that for ever. But I want to—"

"Oh, it's always got to be about what you want!" The blaze of her mother's outburst is terrifying. "You think you've got anything to offer my family? *You?* It's my *job* to deal with situations like this, it is literally my *job* to help my poor girl get through this, and you know how I'm doing with that? Willow's a mess."

But I'll get better, Willow thinks desperately. *I will. I promise.*

"She doesn't speak, she can't go to college, she doesn't eat properly, she sleepwalks. She's broken every mirror in the house—"

No, I haven't, Willow thinks. *Have I?*

"She wets the bed, for God's sake. Seventeen years old and she sleepwalks into her dead sister's room and gets in her bed and wets it, and then she gets up again and puts the sheets in the wash because she thinks we won't notice."

Oh God, Willow thinks. *They know. All this time they've known.*

"And every night I think, *I won't take the sleeping pill tonight, this time I'll be awake when she starts wandering,* but every single night I give in and take it, we both do. Because we can't cope either. We take pills so we can get through the night and then we let our little girl deal with her own mess all by herself, because we can't bear lying awake in the dark. I can't even work out how to tell her that. No, I'm sorry. I'm sorry. I didn't mean to say any of that. No, Stephen, don't, I can't stand it."

"I only want to hug you."

"I don't want a hug. I want Laurel back."

"Do you think I don't?"

"Look," says Joe, sounding as desperate as Willow feels at her mother's sudden naked outburst, "why don't you let Willow stay with me for a bit?"

Willow feels the surprise hollow out her chest.

"What?"

"I mean, if she's not going to college anyway, why not? It might do her good. Give you all a break."

Tucked tight against the door, Willow lets the idea settle on her shoulders. She could go somewhere else. She could wake up in the morning and see a room and a house that Laurel has never been in. The mirrors that reflected her face wouldn't remember that there was once someone else who peered into them and looked exactly the same. Would that feel better, or worse?

"God, no." Her father this time. "We appreciate the offer, but there's no way we can—"

"Of course you can. Rose, look at you, you're a mess. Don't look at me like that, you know what I mean. You need to take care of yourself too. You can't carry on like this."

"Yes I can. I can do whatever Willow needs. I'm a mum."

"And how much good will you be to anyone if you go to pieces?"

Her mother's laugh sounds as if she's burning to death under the desert sun. "How can anyone, even you, *possibly* think that taking my daughter away would—"

"Stephen, what d'you reckon? Just think about it. I have to do something to help, I've got to. She won't have to meet anyone you don't want her to. I'm on my own for the next eight weeks."

"Eight weeks?" She can picture her dad shaking his head in respect. "Blimey."

"Tell me about it. Big investment project in Perth. It's not an imposition, you'd be doing me a favour, keeping me out of trouble while I'm on my own. And I'll look after her, I promise."

They're talking about me like I'm a dog that needs boarding. Is anyone going to even bother asking me what I want? Willow pushes open the door.

They're not quite in the positions she pictured them. Her father isn't standing over the stove but sitting at the table, and her mother's clutching the kettle like a weapon, ready to drown the still uncooked rice waiting in the saucepan. And there's her Uncle Joe, looking a little older but not so much that she doesn't recognise him, standing awkwardly by the back door.

Before she came in, she'd been determined to speak, ready to tell them all off for talking about her as if she has no desires or thoughts or opinions of her own. *I am actually a person, you know,* she wants to say. *I get a say in this too. You need to talk to me about what I think.*

But then her parents turn to look at her, faces gaping with guilty shock, and she feels the terrible weight of their gaze and their love, pressing down on her until she feels she might buckle beneath it. Speech is out of the question. She can hardly breathe.

I've got to get away from you, she thinks, *or I'm not going to survive.*

CHAPTER THREE

Willow leaves the house in a haze of tears that merge into the steady relentless rainfall, the battering of droplets against the windscreen counterpointed by the steady swoosh and thump of the windscreen wipers. She settles awkwardly into the passenger seat – a seat that's been positioned and adjusted for someone much taller than she is – and distracts herself from the discomfort by trying to make sense of how this has actually happened.

It took six days for everything to fall into place, and each of those days had been bursting at the seams, crammed with more discussions, more phone calls, more tears and more arguments than she'd known a house could hold. She'd watched as the three adults argued back and forth, whether Joe could or could not be trusted to take care of Willow, whether it would be helpful or damaging. The things they said (*It's too much to ask / She doesn't know you well enough / It's too far away / What if something happens*), and the things they didn't (*I know better than you do / Then how come she's not getting better / I hate you / I hate you too*) had echoed off the walls and the inside of her head. She'd watched, disbelieving, and waited for someone to remember they ought to find out what she wanted. When her father finally asked her if she thought some time away might help, she nodded, then doubled over with silent shuddering sobs that shocked her with their suddenness and intensity.

If there was a definite point when the mood shifted from *Joe that's really kind but there's no way you're taking Willow away with you* to *Okay now how do we actually make this happen*, she couldn't identify it. Perhaps it was like the tide turning. You looked at the waterline and suddenly realised it had retreated, and the change must have come some time ago, while you were staring at the seagulls or throwing stones at sandcastles.

But the turning of this tide had unlocked a whole new set of actions. Clothes were washed and sorted. Books were packed into boxes. Long lists of instructions, from her mother to her uncle, as if Willow was once again a baby with no voice or will of her own.

Yesterday, she'd sat at the top of the stairs and hugged her knees as she listened to her father on the phone to the college. *She needs some time off, she won't be in for the rest of this term*. She could fill in their questions from his responses. *No, we don't have a doctor's note. No, I appreciate that, but we've bought her some workbooks and found some tutors, so you don't need to worry about it*, and gradually, his irritation building, *Let's be honest, being in a familiar environment and keeping to a routine's not done much good so far, has it?* Then, in a magnificent crescendo, *I need you to understand, I'm not asking your permission here. I'm just letting you know. You do whatever you feel you need to, but Willow won't be in college until next term and I expect you to keep her place open for her and that's how it's going to be, are we clear? Yes, you do that. Indeed. Have a wonderful day.*

And then he slammed the phone down, and started laughing to himself, and her mother came in from the living room and put her arms around his waist and murmured to him, *You know, if you wanted to frighten them you could have gone down there with a gun*, and they held onto each other for a minute and then suddenly kissed, rough and sloppy and open-mouthed. She knew she shouldn't be watching, but she couldn't stop herself.

What are they doing now she's left them alone? Are they relieved or sorry that she's gone? She can still feel the tight press of her mother's goodbye hug, but she can't imagine what might come next. She's not at all sure this is really happening, that she's really leaving. She steals glances at Joe's profile as he peers into the rain and mutters about the traffic and curses occasionally at lorries, and wonders what on earth she's done. Apart from anything else, she suspects Joe may be the worst driver she's ever got into a car with.

"Shit and corruption," he mutters, and hauls the steering wheel over to the right so he can tear past a caravan. Behind them, a lorry honks a horn like a cruise ship and flashes its headlights. "Sorry about that. I hate hanging around. Can't stand drivers who dawdle."

(*And if you want to come home,* her mother began as she held Willow close, and her voice broke. *Oh Willow, what if you want to come home? How will you let us know?*

Say something, Willow told herself fiercely. *Come on. Speak to her. Say something. This is the last chance you'll have for weeks.*

But no matter how hard she willed it, the words wouldn't come.)

In the seat beside her, Joe takes a perilous moment to look away from the road.

"Are you okay there?" he asks. "Sorry, I know you can't... I mean, if you want to stop or anything, give me a sign somehow. Maybe grab the wheel or something. That's a joke, by the way, please don't actually grab the wheel." She smiles at him, not because she thinks it's funny but because he's trying, and she wants to try too. She needs him to like her. She needs them both to be right about this. She needs it to work.

(*We don't have to talk face-to-face,* her counsellor coaxed her at their last session. *You can make me a recording on your phone if you like, and email the file to me. Or you can write down what you're thinking and I'll read it. But you do need to start communicating if you want to get better.* A shrewd pause. *Willow, do you want to get better?*

Yes, she'd thought, *of course I bloody want to get better, how can you think I...* But no matter how hard she strained to get the words out, something stronger pushed back. Her fingers refused to grip the pencil or to touch the keyboard. When she started the recording on her phone, the sight of the face staring back at her from the screen, Laurel looking out from behind her eyes, was too much to bear. So now she's running away. What if this doesn't work either?)

"Do you want the radio on?" Joe suggests. "Pick a station, any station. Seriously, anything's fine. When we were kids – your mum and me, I mean – our parents always used to have Radio 4 on for long journeys. No music ever. So whatever you pick's got to be better than that."

(She's so fragile. She wasn't meant to overhear the conversation between her mother and Joe, but she had listened in anyway. *So we try not to put any pressure on her over things that don't matter.*

It's okay. I'm her wicked uncle, remember? She can sleep till noon every day and eat biscuits in bed. I won't mind.

To be honest, I don't know any more if the no-pressure strategy's right or not. Her mother's voice was wobbly. *I mean, that's what you're supposed to do. That's what I tell parents to do...*

We'll be all right, Joe said. *I promise.*

But, you know, if she wants to eat nothing but sandwiches for a few days or if she doesn't shower for a week, if you could just let her... Actually, forget it, whatever we're doing isn't working so do whatever feels right to you, it's got as much chance of helping as anything else.)

It takes her a minute to find her way around the touchscreen of her uncle's dashboard. What should she choose? She has no idea what Joe would like. How's she supposed to pick something that will satisfy them both? Is this some sort of test, a way of finding out more about her? Or does he want some background noise to fill the silence?

In a mild panic, she picks the local BBC radio station, just in time to catch the weather forecast. Rain, rain, rain, and traffic disruption at a junction on the motorway they're currently crawling down. Have they passed it already, or is it still in their future? She taps the screen to bring up the map, and pulls the focus out so she can see where they are.

"Thanks," says Joe in surprise. "God almighty, though, an accident at a junction, we could be here for hours. Why can't people drive more carefully?" He sighs. "Looks like this is going to be a long one, sweetheart. Sorry."

Her parents have always had a million pet names for her and Laurel, shared indiscriminately between them, but *sweetheart* has never been one of them. Another reminder that she's moving forward in time, whereas Laurel is forever frozen. She clenches her fists.

"Are you okay? Do you need to stop?" She shakes her head. "Don't worry, it's not a problem. There's a services coming up pretty soon, look. We'll stop there. Don't worry," he repeats, as if she might explode into panic at waiting another fifteen miles before she can get out of the car, and she's appalled by how little they know each other. The news bulletin ends and a woman's voice, sweetly processed and flawlessly tuned, pours out a song about a boy who wasn't worth it, and her plans for moving on.

In the days before, she and Laurel had had a system for car music. One of them synced their phone to the car, and then each person on the journey chose a song to stream, strict rotation, no complaining about anyone's choices. Now, she watches from the corner of her eye as her uncle whispers the words to the song to himself and curses at the other drivers.

(She sleepwalks, her mum said to Joe. *She usually goes to Laurel's room, but sometimes she goes downstairs. We make sure we take the keys out of the doors so she doesn't*

39

go outside. I don't know if she might stop wandering when she's with you, but just so you know. And sometimes she – she could hear the tears in her mother's voice, and felt herself flush with the shame of it – *it's not her fault, she can't help it, but sometimes she wets the bed. I wish she'd come and get me when it happens but she doesn't, she cleans up after herself. If you can't deal with any of this it's okay, say so.* And Joe's voice, bewildered but tender, *I'll manage, I promise. Let me do this for you. Please. You're dealing with the worst thing that's ever happened to either of us. I can cope with a bit of extra laundry.)*

The miles of road tear past the window, each marked out in a dozen ways, keeping track of where she is in the world. She can watch the red and white sticks in the hard shoulder, see the numbers on the lamp posts change, track the remorseless crawl of descending distances on the road signs as they grow nearer to strange towns and cities, then sweep past them, making room for new places at the bottom of the boards. Joe tailgates other cars in the fast lane, dives recklessly into implausible gaps, then takes a deep breath and forces himself to slow down again. She sees the same frozen food lorry over and over, the smiling ice-cube on the back doors leering towards her, then receding. She doesn't want to fall asleep, knowing she'll have to wake herself up again as soon as they reach the service station, but her eyelids are growing heavy. She used to keep herself awake by singing along to the songs and planning her next choice, but today the radio's making all her choices for her and her voice is trapped somewhere deep inside. She bites her lip and wills herself into alertness.

"Are you doing okay? Do you want me to pull onto the hard shoulder?" It's not only the sudden bursts of speed that make Joe such a terrifying driver; it's the way he pays attention to everything but the road. She shakes her head. "Nearly there now, sweetheart. Sit tight."

She doesn't want to stop. She doesn't need to stop. If anything she'd prefer *not* to stop, because she's still not sure she's doing the right thing and a stop is a chance for her to change her mind. But none of this is her uncle's fault. He's got no way of knowing what's happening inside her head. She wonders whether it would be nice or weird if she patted his arm.

The exit approaches and they take the sharp curve leading to the service station car park. Joe approaches it too fast and has to slam on the brakes.

"Bloody dangerous way to build a road," he mutters.

The curve in the road is there to force the drivers to slow from seventy miles an hour to twenty in the space of a few hundred feet. She knows this, so why doesn't he? Without thinking, she turns to look at Laurel so they can share this moment of superior knowledge, but finds only her own reflection in the window looking back at her.

The service station is loud and confusing, and she's spent too long cocooned in her own home and has forgotten how full-on the world can be. She takes a deep breath and tells herself she can do this. Joe hovers close to her, as if she's five years old and might suddenly bolt out in front of the traffic, and points her unnecessarily towards the Ladies.

"I'll meet you here by this…" he waves vaguely at a vending machine where an animatronic parrot guards a clutch of two-tone plastic eggs and squawks to attract passing custom. "This horrible thing. Okay? If I'm not here I won't be long, so don't wander off." She nods. "You're sure you'll be okay? I mean, I don't think they'll let me in there with you."

If she wasn't using all her energy to hold herself together against the noise and crowd and brightness, she might laugh. What does he think's going to happen to her? She's seventeen, the same height as her mother, almost an adult; he can't possibly think she needs his help.

The Ladies is warm and smells of floral disinfectant and

pink soap. Washing her hands at the basin, she sees there's an open back door at the end of the row of cubicles.

Let's do the Long Lost Twins, Laurel whispers to her from the mirror.

Willow keeps her eyes carefully down, concentrating on soaping between her fingers. She won't look. There's dirt under her nails. She wishes she had a nail brush.

I'll go out of that door. You go out the main entrance. We'll meet in the lobby. Long Lost Twins; their single twin-based party piece, the thing their friends begged them to do on every trip into town. How can it be that they'll never do it again? A flicker of movement in the back doorway grabs her throat and squeezes it tight with treacherous hope, and she can't stop herself from looking.

The crow stands strong and unafraid in the doorway, as if he has every right to be there. He turns his head to one side, then the other. His thick black beak, made for jabbing and tearing at dead flesh, transfixes her.

"Mum! Look!" A little girl standing at the washbasins, humming to herself as she diligently soaps her arms as high as her elbows, sprays water across the floor as she points. "A bird!"

"A crow," her mother says.

"He's friendly!" The girl laughs with pleasure. "Is he coming in?" She crouches low and makes an encouraging noise. "Come on in, little bird. Don't be scared."

He's not a little bird, Willow thinks frantically, *he's a great big bird, and he's not afraid of you or anyone, and he's here for me, he's come for me – no, that's stupid, it doesn't mean anything—*

The crow glances at the row of washbasins.

"He likes the taps," says the girl's mother. "Crows like shiny things."

"Do you like shiny things?" The little girl tilts her head and her voice grows squeaky, as if she's trying to entice an even littler child to be her friend. "Do you?" She fumbles in her pocket, produces a silver coin. "Would you like this shiny thing? Here, you can have it."

No, Willow thinks, *don't encourage it, please.*

She wants to run, but she doesn't dare look away in case it comes after her and tangles its feet in her hair. The crow takes three hops towards her. She wants to scream, but she can't force the sound past her lips. Then it spreads its wings and flaps clumsily upwards, up towards her face.

Crouched on the closed lid of the toilet seat with her feet drawn up, Willow's caught between shame and terror. *Stop being so stupid,* she tells herself fiercely. *You're pathetic. It was just a bird. Get up and open that door and walk out. Right now.*

But every time she tries, she thinks of the bird's outspread wings, the rush of air as it moved towards her, and she's paralysed.

This is ridiculous. Joe's waiting by the parrot. She's been in here too long already. If she doesn't make it out soon, he's surely going to decide she's too much like hard work, and take her straight home. She wants to get better, she does. She doesn't want to be the girl who can't open a door because she's afraid there might be a bird on the other side of it. A bird, for God's sake. People eat birds. She has to stop being so useless.

She manages to raise her hand to the lock, but she can't pull it open. A faint scratching sound outside sends her scurrying for safety.

Because even if she does manage to make it out, how will she ever explain what happened?

"Willow?" She doesn't recognise the voice of the woman who calls her name. "Sorry, I'm looking for a girl called Willow? Willow, are you in here? Are you okay or do you need some help?"

Call back to her.

She opens her mouth. Nothing.

"Willow? Sorry, everyone, I'm looking for a girl called Willow. I'm going to knock on the doors and if it's not you, could you say – no, sir, I'm sorry but you can't be in here."

"Willow?" Her Uncle Joe, sounding more panicked than she knew a grown man could. "Willow, are you all right? Where are you? Oh Jesus, there's a back door. Why the hell is there a back door?"

"Sir, you can't be in here, this is a Ladies toilet. Go outside and wait and I will come and tell you—"

"No, you don't understand, she won't answer you even if she's in here. Willow? Please be in here, please. Willow, are you all right? Are you shut in? It's all right, it's me, I promise everything's fine. Just make a noise, bang on the door or something."

This was a mistake. She ought to be back at home, where she's safe. She's not ready for this, not for any of it. This is more noise than she's used to and more people than she's used to, and she knows she can't stay in here for ever but she doesn't know if she can face going outside and seeing them all looking at her. They must be picturing a little girl, someone small enough to lock herself in by mistake. What will they think when they see she's a teenager? Will she be in trouble? She deserves to be. She's nearly an adult. She ought to be able to do better.

"Willow?" He's right outside the door.

Come on. Make an effort. You can do this.

She slides off the toilet seat and kneels on the floor of the cubicle. Closer to the ground, the smell of detergent is overpowering. She can feel it soaking into the knees of her leggings.

"Willow. Is that you?"

She slides her fingers out through the space beneath the door. After a minute, she feels his hand rest over hers. She takes a deep breath.

"What's going on with her? Is she too little to talk or

something?" The woman is sounding suspicious now. There is an interested hush as everyone pauses in their busy journeys to enjoy the drama.

"No, it's not that, but she finds it hard to speak sometimes."

Please, Willow thinks, *please don't tell everyone what happened. I don't want to come out and walk past all these people and have them knowing what happened to Laurel.*

"And she's your niece."

"Yes, my niece. She's staying with me for a bit."

Willow senses the change in mood, as a roomful of strange women begin to form their own judgements.

"Look, I tell you what." Joe sounds suddenly determined. "If you could get everyone out of here for a little while."

"This is a busy service station, we can't close the—"

"Just this bit then. Please. For a few minutes. Give me a few minutes to see if I can talk her into coming out. Then we'll be out of here."

"I'm not sure I can authorise that." The woman sounds as if she's beginning to suspect there is no niece at all, that this is some strange plot concocted by Joe as a means of getting access to the women's bathrooms.

"Please. Give us a few minutes. She has anxiety, she's been having treatment for it."

"Oh. So should we call a doctor? Look, I'll put the signs out but I can't leave you in here on your own. The cleaner will need to supervise you and see what's going on. This is a women's bathroom and you're not supposed—"

"I know, I know, I'm not supposed to be in here. Thanks for letting me. We'll be on our way as soon as we can, all right? Thanks, everyone, I really appreciate this."

She can hear the sound of retreating feet as the tide of girls and women recedes. There's a scrape of plastic against tiles that must be signs going out, declaring the area closed for cleaning. Then Joe's kneeling outside the door once more.

"Willow? Can you open the door? You don't have to come out or anything."

She wants to ask him if they're alone. She doesn't think she can stand the gaze of strangers.

"It's all right. There's no one here but me. Well, there's a bunch of people round the other side of the cones, but this bit's only us."

The lock's stiff, or maybe her hands are clumsy with guilt. It takes her several tries to slide it back. The door falls open.

"Yay." Joe gives her a cautious smile. "I mean, I've always wanted to know what the inside of the Ladies looks like, but I think I've pretty much seen what there is to see now."

You shouldn't make jokes like that, she thinks, remembering the woman who works here, who already suspects Joe of planning some unspecified crime.

"I tell you what, you get more mirrors than we do. And it smells nicer. The floors are still a bit gross, though. Shall we stand up? That's better." He pats her kindly on the shoulder. "You okay now? What happened?"

She's so ashamed she can hardly look at him. All she wants is for this moment to be over.

"Okay, so that was a stupid question. Right, let's do Yes or No… Were you being sick or something?" She shakes her head. "Did you get locked in and panic?" She shakes her head again. "Someone frightened you?"

Can we please stop this, she thinks desperately, and shakes her head again. Suddenly Joe's eyes gleam with mischief.

"You frightened someone else? You were summoning a demon? You're on the run from the FBI? You were overcome with a sudden urge to murder someone and you had to hide until the feeling went away? Work with me here. We need a good cover story or they'll get suspicious. Okay, you can tell me later. Let's get out of here. Are you ready?"

She glances towards the noise and bustle of the exit, and feels her insides squeeze tight.

"I know, I don't like the look of it either. They're not too happy with me to be honest, I think they think I'm some sort of pervert. And that animatronic thing in the lobby looks possessed. If they make us stay and explain we'll be here for hours. So shall we run out the back door instead, and drive off and pretend none of this ever happened?"

Like criminals, they creep towards the open back door and peer out.

"Coast looks clear," Joe says. "There's the car. See it? Good. Now, you ready? You sure? Okay, then go, go, go, go, go!"

Laughing and clumsy, falling over grass and kerbs and their own feet, they flee across the tarmac to the safety of the car.

"There," says Joe, and starts the engine. "And they say running away from your problems doesn't solve anything."

I'm not supposed to run away from my feelings, she thinks. *I'm supposed to stay with them and try and talk about them.*

Fuck that, she thinks, and smiles.

"Jesus," he says in surprise. "You look so much like your mum." They rejoin the motorway. The car behind them brakes and flashes its headlights. "So how long do you think they'll leave half of the Ladies toilets closed off before they realise we've legged it?"

Willow feels a small spark of happiness. It's the first time since The Day happened that she feels normal. Within ten minutes of setting off from the service station, she's asleep.

CHAPTER FOUR

She's on a train, and she knows she's dreaming because the seats are red velvet, and heavy gold-fringed curtains hang at the windows. When she tries to see out, everything's dark, and she's met only with her own reflection.

"I can't find the tickets." Laurel is beside her, pale and anxious. She's rummaging in an old-fashioned black doctor's bag by her feet. The sight makes Willow uneasy, partly because she doesn't recognise it, but mostly she's not sure if she's brought her own luggage with her. But surely her parents would have checked?

"They said we could come by ourselves," Laurel explains. "Don't you remember?"

She knows she's dreaming, because she can almost *feel* her brain busily working to fill in the blanks, making the scene believable and coherent. An image comes to her mind: she and Laurel, standing on the platform and waiting for the train, frantically trying to phone their mother. First they couldn't find their phones, and then they were almost out of battery. Then, mysteriously, Willow's phone burst into life and she was able to bring up her frequently dialled numbers and call her mother. "Is that you, Willow?" her mother had said. "What do you want?" And when Willow, longing to speak but unable to summon a word, had simply held the phone and stared at it, her mother had grown impatient and said, "You'll have to sort yourselves out, both of you. I don't have time to talk right now. Since you're both out of the house, I need to have sex with your father."

Oh God, Willow thinks. *Did she really say that to me? That's so gross.*

"Of course not," Laurel says. "She wouldn't say something like that to us."

Of course she didn't say that, Willow tells herself. *I'm dreaming. None of this is real.* But the cringy feeling in her stomach won't go away.

"We're not supposed to be here," Laurel says. "They're going to realise soon. Then we'll be in trouble."

Willow has no idea who *they* might be. Their carriage is empty apart from the two of them.

"No, not other passengers," Laurel says. "The other ones. The ones who are looking for us. They don't like that we're not together."

But we are together, Willow thinks. *We're right here.*

"This is a dream, remember? In real life I'm dead and you're still alive." Willow swallows hard. "Oh shit, Willow, where are the tickets? The inspector's coming down the train, I can hear him."

And now Willow can hear him too, and she knows who he's going to be. He rustles as he comes, as if he's shaking the feathers of his wings, and when he opens the connecting door between the two carriages, she knows he'll be tall and spindly, with a man's body but a crow's head. Laurel is still rummaging in the bag at her feet.

"Got it!" she shouts triumphantly. "I knew it was in here." In Laurel's hand is a gristly lump of something about the size of her fist, fat blood vessels large enough to put a finger in, its four chambers still contracting against Laurel's fingers, its surface streaked with white and dripping with red. "This is mine. But where's yours?"

This is a dream, Willow thinks, *so I can control what happens next. The train's stopping now. It's pulling in at a station. I'm going to get off and leave. He won't catch me.* She wills this with all the force she has in her, but if anything, the train gets faster, shuddering with speed as it tears through the darkness. The handle of the connecting door rattles.

"You can't get away from him by running." In Laurel's hands, her heart jumps and pulses as if it's trying to escape. "He always catches up with you in the end."

But I'm going to bloody well try, Willow thinks. She races to the end of the carriage and flings open the door.

Outside, the dark waits for her. She falls into its embrace.

CHAPTER FIVE

She comes back to consciousness with a stiff neck, a dry mouth, and the knowledge that she's escaped her dream relatively unscathed. She knows where she is and why; she's in her Uncle Joe's car, going somewhere she's never been before. She's waking in the same place she went to sleep, nothing broken, nothing missing; and thank God, thank *God,* she hasn't wet herself. A small victory. Her uncle's talking, but not to her. He must be on the phone.

"Willow's fine," he says into the air.

Willow peeks out through a crack between her eyelids. The rain has slowed and the road seems emptier.

"I'm sorry. I know I'm being daft." Her mother, her voice made strange by the car speakers. Willow keeps her breathing carefully even. She doesn't want them to know she's awake.

"No, you're not. You love her, of course you're worried. But we're fine."

"I miss her so much. Willow, sweetie, I love you and I miss you, okay?"

"She's actually asleep right now." She feels the car waver for a moment, as if her uncle has turned to look at her. "She looks about six."

I do not look six, Willow thinks to herself. She forces herself to keep her eyes closed and her face neutral.

"And you're sure you're going to be all right? I know it's

difficult when she can't tell you what's going on but she's quite good at letting you know in other ways, you just have to be alert—"

"We're getting on great, don't worry."

"She won't be able to tell you if she wants to stop or anything."

"It's all right, I thought of that so I stopped anyway, about half an hour ago." There's a slight chuckle in Joe's voice. "I'm on a strict schedule. A bit like having a new puppy."

"That's good. Was she… I mean, was she all right?"

"What, in the service station? She was great. Well, I mean, I ran into this mad security woman who thought I might be a kidnapper or a child trafficker or something, but Willow found a secret back door out and we ran away and escaped."

"You what?" Her mother's laughter is something she thought she'd forgotten the sound of. "No, you didn't, you're making that up. Aren't you?"

"I tell you what… What would you prefer the answer to be? And then we'll both agree it's that one."

"You're an idiot. I've missed you." A pause. "So she's not… I mean, she hasn't said anything?"

"Not yet." Joe sounds as unconcerned as if he's reporting on a parcel that hasn't arrived.

"She might be absolutely fine in some places, and not in others." There's some deep emotion in her mother's voice, but she can't quite decide what it is. "Some kids are complete chatterboxes at home, but they can't talk at school or in shops or whatever. She was like that at first. She'd talk at home to us sometimes, but not anywhere else, and not when people came round…" Her mother's voice is shaky. "Then she got worse and worse. The horrible thing is I can't even remember exactly when she stopped talking – I wasn't really paying attention, I just thought she was a bit quiet – and when I realised it must have already been a couple of days."

"It's not your fault," Joe says, very gently. "She's like

you, that's all. You never want to talk about things that are upsetting you either."

"But it's not the same thing, this is… I'm sorry, I'm being stupid, ringing you up and crying like this."

"It's not stupid. But you don't need to worry. I'll look after her and she'll get better and you'll get better and you'll find a way to have a good life again. Different, but good. I promise."

"I'll settle for Willow having a good life. I don't mind about me and Stephen. Just Willow. That's all that matters."

"No it's not. You all matter. That's the whole point of this, remember? You and Stephen having some space to grieve without having to worry about Willow."

"It's such a relief." Her mother's voice is suddenly very low and soft. Willow has to strain to hear her. "Being able to cry without worrying that I'm upsetting her. Not having to worry she's going to notice. Not having to see Laurel's face when I… Oh, shit, I'm sorry, I'm sorry."

"Good God, will you stop apologising for yourself?"

Willow keeps her eyes carefully closed. Breathes in and out. In and out. This isn't news. She realised it weeks ago. She knows she's making it worse for her parents, because how can she do anything else? How could anyone move on if, every day, they were forced to look at the living face of the child they laid in the ground, made strange by its presence on someone else's body?

"Sorry again for calling. You haven't been gone three hours yet and I'm already hounding you. I promise not to ring again until tonight."

"Rose. This is me you're talking to. Once a day was your idea, not mine. Call whenever you want to."

"No, I'll wait until tonight." A hesitation. "But, will you ring me, though? When you get there? So I know you're there safely?"

"No problem at all."

"I know it's silly but I worry."

"Of course you do. But I'll get us both home all right."

"Love to you both."

"And to you both. Bye for now."

A moment of stillness, and then the music begins playing again. To the sound of soft rock, Willow considers what she's overheard. Every word her uncle said was true, but somehow he's taken the near-disaster of the incident at the service station and turned it into a story her mother would want to hear. How strange. She breathes in, breathes out, then stirs and opens her eyes.

"Hey." Joe, concentrating fiercely on the road, nonetheless notices her return to consciousness. "Your mum called."

Willow tries to make her face look like someone who's just woken up, and hasn't at all been listening in while pretending to be asleep.

"She sends her love," Joe says, and pulls out to overtake a well-stuffed Renault Scenic where two children sit in the back like prisoners, staring straight ahead at screens hanging over the backs of the seats. For several moments, she's beside the child in the car next to her. He turns his head towards her and gives her a tiny wave, as if they're secret conspirators. She waves infinitesimally back.

"Sleep all right?"

Willow nods.

"Want to stop again?"

Seriously? It's barely been an hour. She shakes her head. *And you're annoying that driver by passing him so slowly. He can't get past the lorry until you're out of the way.*

"Okay, well, let me know if you want to."

Concentrate on the road, she thinks. Joe tears along the centre lane for a while, then suddenly pulls back in behind a lorry. The man in the Renault roars past, giving their car the finger. She wonders if the children in the back can see him doing it.

"I told your mum we're fine," Joe continues. Another gap opens up to his right and he swings the wheel so that the car leaps into it. It's a constant surprise to her, how adults can be such dreadful drivers.

"I didn't say anything about earlier," Joe continues. "I hope that's okay. Only I had this very strong feeling she probably didn't need to know about me being a Service Station Ladies Toilets Pervert."

As if that was the most embarrassing part, Willow thinks. Her knees still smell faintly of disinfectant. She can smell it when she moves.

"I mean, I'm not asking you to lie to your mother or anything," Joe adds. "I wouldn't do that. But, you know… she'd only worry…"

Joe's attention is completely focused on her; they're drifting between the middle and the inside lanes, way above the speed limit. That wouldn't be her fault at all, not the way it would be if she were to cut herself or fill her mouth with pills, and she could go to join Laurel with a clear conscience, and she wouldn't have to go to this strange house, or go to sleep in a strange room, and wake up tomorrow in the strangeness of another day with her sister…

She pats Joe on the arm and points imperiously towards the road.

"Shit! Sorry. Sorry." A moment of floundering, and they're safely in the inside lane and everyone who has watched them struggle flies past, turning to look in through the windows with accusing faces.

"If you don't mind," Joe says carefully, "if you don't mind… maybe let's not tell your mum what a crappy driver I am either? Normally my other half does the motorway driving. Bloody business trips, eh? Still, if it wasn't for that I don't think your mum would have let me have you. I mean, she thinks *I'm* all right and everything, but…"

Now his steering's all right, but he's pressing hard against the accelerator so the car leaps forward like a fish, taking them close enough to the lorry in front of them for her to read the lettering on the transit stickers. Bereft of words, she's forced to improvise. In her bag is an outsized bag of Haribo sweets, put there by her mother when she thought Willow wasn't looking. She opens the bag and offers one to her uncle.

"Thanks," he says. "We'll be okay. I'll look after you."

Just try not to crash before we get there, Willow thinks, then offers him another sweet in case he can read her thoughts and see what she thinks of his driving.

When she next wakes, the rain's slowed to a fine mizzle, and they've paused at a spaghetti tangle of roads she can't begin to make sense of. To her surprise, Joe seems completely at ease, humming to himself as he turns into a thin single carriageway surrounded by trees.

"You missed the bit where I cut up a man in a Lambo and I thought he was going to take me out," he says, and she catches her breath in surprise and wonders if he really can read her thoughts. "But I'm all right now, I know these roads. Home in half an hour. We might see wild ponies if we're lucky, they cross the road sometimes."

She's too old and too urban to be excited about seeing a horse, wild or tame, but the thought of one of them lurching out from the trees and dashing into the road gives her something to focus on. She spends the rest of the journey watching the speedometer and wondering how it would feel to crash into the horse's body, see it smash through the windscreen to crush them to death. *Beware horses in road. Beware cattle in road. Beware pedestrians in road. Beware cyclists in road.* Thanks to the trees, the visibility is poor. *Slow, Slow, Slow, Slow, Slow.*

Then they're approaching a cluster of houses (rumble strips, a giant-sized '30' sign and the plaintive request, *Please Drive Carefully Through Our Village*) and a sudden left turn that feels like driving into a wall. Finally, they're pulling into a space like a small farmyard without any animals, with an unkempt garden beyond it.

Her Uncle Joe's house is small and low and built of long,

flat, ancient-looking stones that make her think of dry-stone walls. Against the wall, a thick worn flight of steps comes down from a door in the first floor, hugging the outside of the house and melting into the ground. Is that the way in? And why is it upstairs? She can't even tell if this is the front of the house or the back. While she's staring, Joe opens a door that hides in the shadows at the foot of the staircase.

"Hey!" he calls cheerfully as he opens the door into a tiny slate floored lobby where a washing machine and tumble dryer sit crammed tight against the wall. "Just me, nothing to worry about..." And in the silence as they wait for an answer, Willow feels the hairs on the back of her neck rise up. It was supposed to be the two of them. What if someone replies?

Then Joe sees her face, and laughs.

"It's all right," he says. "I like to do that in case someone's come in while I've been away." He takes a note from the table, crumples it in his hand. "I leave a note for the burglars as well, so they don't make a mess looking for the valuable stuff. Sorry, I didn't mean to scare you. Come on in properly."

The kitchen should be the warm and cosy heart of the house – there's a huge stove, a sturdy table and chairs, a green gingham sofa nestled beneath a window – but the air's almost as chilly as it is outside. She'd thought she was sick of being in the car, but suddenly the stale comfort of engine-heated air seems quite appealing. She tries not to shiver.

"It gets cold stupidly quickly if there's no one in the house," Joe says, and once again she's struck by how observant he is, and how naked it makes her feel that even in the depths of her silence, she can still be read and interpreted. "It'll warm up once the stove gets going. Okay, so through here's the living room."

Another room that looks as if it should be cosy, a room made for twilight and cold evenings and stormy nights. The windows are set into the thickest walls she has ever seen, walls so deep you could climb into the windowsill and close the curtains and be perfectly comfortable there, as long as you were wearing at least fifteen layers of clothing, to keep out the chill that radiates off the rough creamy walls. Someone's laid a soft black sheepskin rug into the window to the left of the front door, as if Joe likes to sit there sometimes to read. Or perhaps he prefers the wing chair next to the black wood burner. Everything is relentlessly, scrupulously, intimidatingly clean.

"Through here to the stairs," Joe says, opening another door at the other side of the living room (*So many doors!* she thinks. *It must have been built before they invented corridors*). The stairs are narrow and creaky and lined with pictures, ending with a thin chilly landing.

"That's the bathroom. It gets cold at night but there's a heater if you need it, and there'll be plenty of hot water once the Aga gets going."

But it's freezing right now, Willow thinks despairingly. *How can you live in a house this cold?* She's read books where characters find frost on the inside of their windows in the mornings, or wake to find ice on the surface of their water jug. But she's never appreciated before what that says about the temperature of the rooms they were waking up in. She peeks into the bathroom, registers the ornate silver mirror that hangs on the wall. Flinches back from it before it can trap her. Makes a mental note to keep her gaze carefully downwards when she's going in or out. Back on the landing, Joe opens another door.

"This is my room."

A cream carpet, a double bed, one tidy bedside table with a lamp and a photograph frame, and – the first sign she's seen that anyone truly lives here – one extremely untidy one, with a wild litter of books sprawled across the floor. She's unsure how closely she's supposed to look, how much interest she's expected to take in the bedroom of an almost-stranger. She's relieved when Joe pulls the latch closed again.

"And this is your room."

Her room is deep-walled and low-ceilinged, enclosing her as tenderly as a nest holds an egg. The floor is varnished wood, slightly uneven, and covered with bright woollen rugs to shut out the faint draught of air from below. The bed's weighed down with blankets and topped with a patchwork quilt so intricate she thinks at first it must be a printed duvet cover, but when she touches it she can feel the tiny seams, the intricate lines of quilting. The windows are too small to sit in, but there's another full-length curtain, drawn closed even though it's daytime, and behind it she finds the wooden door that leads to the stone staircase, and outside.

"The curtain's to stop the draughts," Joe says. "When we did the room up…" He pauses, and glances shyly at her. "Well, we were thinking more of weekend visitors, and they tend to come in the summer when the cold's not as much of a problem. But if you keep the curtain shut you should be okay."

She has her own front door. Her own private entrance and exit. When the dreams get bad, she could creep out and spend all night walking around, and no one would know. She grabs the thick iron ring of the handle.

"You need to unlock it first." Joe reaches over her shoulder and turns the key. It's smooth and brown, fat and heavy-looking, the kind of key that belongs in a child's book. "But you know, if you want to sneak out and meet a boyfriend or something… right, turn the handle again, and…"

The door opens outwards, smooth and easy, and there are the steps leading down into the yard. The air is clean and sharp, laden with a scent that makes her think of fairy tales and witches and old, dusty places long forgotten. She supposes it must be the scent of the forest.

"I'll bring your suitcase in." Joe is across the room in three big strides. She can hear his feet clattering on the staircase.

Well, that's silly, she thinks. She hops down the stone steps instead, and is waiting for Joe when he comes out through the kitchen.

"Oh." His smile is definitely one of the nicest things about him, warm and endearing and transformative. "Why didn't I think of that? No, don't tell me, I don't want to know how exactly big an idiot I am."

She's spent so long with everyone waiting breathlessly for her to speak that she's forgotten what it's like to be told to keep quiet. She wants to tell him what this means to her, but has to settle for taking the suitcase from his hands and dragging it up the staircase by herself, enjoying the scrape-bump rhythm of it, and the warmth that comes with the movement.

"Well, okay, then," says Joe with a shrug, and lifts his own suitcase from the boot. She wonders if he'll follow her up the steps, but he goes to the kitchen door, and she's left alone to explore her room.

She ought to unpack her things into the chest of drawers that sits under the window, to choose where to put her underwear, her t-shirts, her hoodies, her leggings, her jeans. She ought to line up her boots and shoes in a neat row along the wall. This is clearly a home where housekeeping standards are high. But she's grown used to being pampered as some kind of holy freak, freed from the chores and expectations of everyday life. So instead she closes the door to the outside, takes the key from the lock, pushes her shoes off so they fall with two muddy thumps onto the blue-and-beige-squared rug, wraps the beautiful patchwork quilt around her shoulders and sits on the bed to let the atmosphere of the room settle into her, turning the key over and over between her fingers, feeling it grow warmer with the stolen heat of her skin. She can hear the faint sounds of someone moving around in the room below. Joe must be lighting the stove. How long will it take this place to warm up? The quilt is surprisingly cosy. She draws it closer around her shoulders.

She's looking around the room once more – feeling proprietorial already and planning where she will put her books, her phone, her hair brush – when she realises what makes this room so welcoming; there's no mirror. And as if this realisation has somehow unlocked another, it occurs to her that in the same way that Joe had both told, and not told, her mother the truth about what happened at the service station, he also carefully edited his conversation with her mother. If she'd only listened to what he told her, she'd think her mother only phoned to say hello. Her uncle seems honest, maybe even childish, but he's rather good at keeping secrets.

Or did he know she was listening all along?

She doesn't want to think about this. It's much more comfortable to believe Joe is as simple and goodhearted as she wants him to be. She lies back on the bed, closes her eyes, and hears the faint *clink* of the key as it falls from her fingers and lands on the wooden boards below. She's waiting for something, but she's not sure what. She has the feeling that the house is waiting too.

CHAPTER SIX

"Hey, Willow. We miss you already."

On the phone, her mother's voice sounds both oddly unlike her, and oddly familiar. She sounds like Willow's grandmother, who used to phone every Thursday night to talk to her granddaughters. Each week without fail, the phone had rung at six forty-five precisely – never earlier, never later – until the day the phone rang on a Monday at five fifteen, to disclose a stranger calling from her grandmother's number with news of a trip to the hospital. Now, that faint old-lady hoarseness has taken root in someone else's throat. Do the dead ever truly leave this world? Or are they continually resurrected in these unexpected hauntings? This is a glimpse into how it feels for her mother, constantly confronted with her lost daughter's mirror image.

"How was the journey? Joe said it rained most of the way."

Her mother's voice is a warm lick of comfort, flowing over the top of Willow's head and down the length of her back. She would like to crawl inside it.

"D'you know, I hate driving in the rain." Her mother sounds unsure, as if she's feeling her way into this one-sided conversation. Willow wants her to talk and talk and talk, so she can lose herself in her mother's voice. There are too many gaps between her words. "I don't mind snow, I don't mind ice, but I can't stand driving when it's raining. I mean, I know it was perfectly safe, Joe's a good driver or I wouldn't have let him take you."

Uncle Joe's a terrible driver. She knows something that her mother doesn't know, about her own brother. If Laurel was here, they would have shared the pleasure of this secret, successfully kept from the adults in their lives.

"This is so weird. I don't really know what to say." Her mother's voice wobbles. "I want to talk to you, I want to keep you on the phone, but I don't know what to say. Are you still there?"

Talk to her. Talk to her. Tell her you miss her. Tell her you love her. Bereft of words, Willow makes her breathing as slow and as loud as she can, so that on the other end of the line, her mother will hear her and keep talking. *On the other end of the line,* as if they're connected physically. As if Willow's a fish her mother has caught.

"I can hear you breathing. It's nice to hear you breathing." Willow's mother laughs. "Okay, that makes me sound like a—" She stops suddenly.

Finish her sentence for her. Say 'dirty phone caller'. Say 'serial killer'. Make a joke about dick pics. In the last months before, their parents had begun to open up new sides of themselves, making jokes that were funny and dark and rude and cynical, jokes they wouldn't have dreamed making even half a year ago. It felt as if they were trying on the possibility that their daughters were becoming adults. She and Laurel had first been appalled – *I never knew they'd seen that film! Can you believe Mum said that? I didn't know Dad even knew what that meant* – and then been hungry for more, keen to find their way into this new aspect of their family lives. But Laurel's death closed the door again, and now Willow's stuck in the room labelled *troubled daughter*, while her parents, frantic to find a solution, debate on the other side. *Say it. Say serial killer. Dirty phone caller. Sex line worker.* If she could force the words out of her throat…

"Oh, sweetie." Her mother sighs. "I wish I could give you

63

a hug." She takes a deep breath of her own, making herself strong and resilient. "Right. So, college work. Obviously don't worry about it tonight. And don't worry about it tomorrow either, I know how tiring travelling is. You wouldn't think it would be, would you? Sitting in the car and watching the world go by. But it is. So have a day off tomorrow."

She has a new email address, and tutors who'll send her modules of work to complete, and are available to talk to her by email if she needs any guidance. There's a box in her suitcase containing a glossy stack of textbooks and revision guides. These things took time and ingenuity to organise, and have cost money. Can she honestly picture herself sitting down on her bed with her back against the wall and her laptop open? Or perhaps she'll work at the kitchen table by the stove? None of this seems remotely likely.

"But the day after tomorrow, you probably need to make a start. I know it'll be strange doing it all by yourself, but give it a go, all right? Just give it a go and see how you get on."

Before The Day, her parents had been bright and hopeful for both of their futures. She and Laurel had compared notes on the bus, discussed scores and differences, argued over who was doing better (or sometimes, when they were feeling nihilistic and wanted to wallow, who was doing worse). Before The Day, they'd grumbled about the pressure they were under, how their parents had no idea what it was like to be the guinea pigs for an endlessly changing curriculum, how it wasn't fair that they'd been born into a time when you were expected to start your career with a fifty grand debt hanging around your neck, and if Mum would *stop asking*, if Dad would *chill out*…

"You're breathing really loudly again." Her mother's voice is tender. "Is that so I know you're still there? If you've had enough you can blow me a kiss and hang up. I won't be offended."

Has she had enough? She checks the clock. They've been talking for six minutes and already she's exhausted.

"Oh, do you want to talk to your dad for a bit?"

This is a question she's not expected to answer. If it was completely up to her, she'd keep her mother on the line for a while longer. But perhaps her mother's tired too.

"Stephen?" She can hear the slight distance as her mother turns the phone away from her. "Do you want to talk to Willow?"

He hates talking on the phone. Don't make him. Another thing she couldn't possibly say out loud even if she could speak, any more than her father could say *No thanks, I love Willow but I'd rather eat my own head than talk on the phone…* Does he know that she knows how he feels? Is this another thing Willow knows that her mother doesn't? She hears the phone being passed from one to the other.

"Hello." Her father sounds upbeat and cheerful. "How was the drive? I had a look on Google, the traffic looked rough."

You're saying you stalked me? The words are there in her mind but she can't bring them out. And even if she said it, would it sound like a joke or would he think she was being serious? If it goes wrong, she might not be able to explain. She settles for a deep, noisy breath, so he'll know he's not jabbering into empty space.

"I had a look at the house on Google Maps as well. It looks nice."

Her father's right. The house is nice, even nicer now that Joe has lit the stove and the wood burner by now, and the house is beginning to warm through. Soon, even the bathroom might feel warm and welcoming. Is it just the slowly vanishing cold that makes her feel as if they're still waiting for something so they can begin? Is it only the relentless tidiness that makes it feel like a house on pause?

"So, your mum's spoken to you about a schedule for your college work, but obviously don't worry about that tonight. There's no pressure. No pressure at all. Do what you can, that's enough for us."

She won't cry. These are the words they both used to declare they'd love their parents to say, while also secretly enjoying the knowledge that their parents were proud, and paid attention. But she won't cry. She won't. It's not going to happen.

"Willow? Are you still there?" Her father sighs. "Sorry, I know you're still there, I don't mean to… Look, I love you, all right? I'm going to give you back to your mother now. Unless there's anything else you, um, no, sorry, ignore me, I'm talking rubbish."

Unless there's anything else you want to say. Willow can fill in the pauses in her father's conversation as easily as her mother's. She takes a deep breath

(Dad I love you I love you both I miss you I miss you so much I'm so sorry)

and lets it go again, realising too late that this sounds like a sigh of dissatisfaction.

"I know. Dad-speak nonsense. Love you."

I didn't mean that. I like hearing you talk. I miss you.

"Hey, Willow, it's me again… so, um. Was the journey okay?"

You already asked that. How can she ever end this conversation when she has no voice to do it with?

"Hey." Her Uncle Joe appears from the kitchen. He's wearing a stripy blue and white apron, worn-looking but spotless, and he's holding his hand out for the phone. "Do you mind if I have a quick chat? I'll give it back to you afterwards."

Liberated, she passes the phone over and goes to inspect the kitchen. The Aga sends out waves of soporific heat, and now the sofa makes perfect sense as a place to sit. She circles the cupboards, wondering if she can find some biscuits to hide away for emergencies. The drive for order continues even here: the tins and jars have their labels turned out towards the front, the mugs are lined up in rows with their handles turned to identical angles, and the plates are perfectly stacked. Instead of biscuits, her guilty investigation leads her to an unlikely treasure: a pack of long thin wafery cylinders stuffed with nutty chocolate paste, that make her think of Paris. She crams her mouth and lets the sugar soak into her stomach.

She can hear Joe, at this moment her saviour, telling his sister his carefully edited version of their journey. *Traffic wasn't too bad. We made really good time. Much better than the Sat Nav said.* No mention of the times he nearly crashed, the mad pounces between lanes, the glares and honks of the other drivers. Or maybe Joe's such a dreadful driver that he didn't even notice. Maybe he thinks that's what driving is supposed to be like.

Back in the kitchen, something bubbles gently on the black stovetop. She lifts the lid and sniffs at the fragrant steam.

CHAPTER SEVEN

She's aware, as she always is, that she's dreaming, because Laurel's here with her, and these days, she never forgets that Laurel is dead. When it first happened, falling asleep was terrifying because she knew that when she woke, she'd have to live through that moment of forgetful ignorance before memory crashed back into her like a tidal wave. These days, it's sleep itself she fears. Not just the frightening dreams, but the ones like this, that brim with treacherous sweetness.

She's in her room at Joe's house. Her belly's full, not aching with famine, not gorged with stolen junk, but comfortably full. The delicious scent in the pot translated to a chicken curry, served with rice and naan bread and poppadoms and sweet chutney. The room's cool, but no longer cold. Her bed is warm and the covers are comfortingly heavy. All of this she knows.

She also knows that somewhere in the darkness, the Congregation are waiting, beaks clattering, eyes bright and eager, and at the end, the Death Bird, his face white beneath the white skull. But tonight, she's not going to church. She's not going anywhere. She's going to stay here in her bed. There's no mirror for her to glance into and see Laurel looking back at her. She's completely safe.

The door opens, and Laurel comes in, walking softly.

"I was in the bathroom," she explains, as if she made the same journey Willow did, and has taken a little longer getting ready for bed. Her feet and hands are bluish, but that could be from the cold that haunts the bathroom like a wraith. Her crow-black hair is brushed. Her face is clean. She's smiling.

You're dead, Willow thinks, and – another reminder that she's dreaming – she knows that Laurel can hear her thoughts. *Sorry,* she adds, seeing the look on Laurel's face. *But you are*.

"We've got an extra door," Laurel says, and pulls back the curtain.

It's locked.

Laurel's eyes are bright and mischievous.

"But we've got the key."

She thought she'd left the key in the lock. But when she reaches beneath her pillow, her fingers close on sturdy iron.

"See?" Laurel's sitting on the end of the bed now. The mattress shifts beneath her weight. "Now we can go outside."

She's still asleep, still warm beneath the covers. Her breathing's deep and steady. Her eyelids flutter as she dreams. She knows this because she can see it all happening; she's watching herself from the end of her bed. She wonders if this is what it felt like for Laurel after she died.

"I'm not allowed to tell you about that," says Laurel, and plucks the key from Willow's fingers. "Let's go."

The key turns, the door swings open, the night rushes in. The moon's high and fat. Standing on the top step, Willow feels the whole world underneath her feet.

We can't do this, Willow thinks.

"Of course we can," Laurel says. "We can do anything. Well, I can. You've still got shit to deal with. But no one's watching. And if you come with me, I'll take you to someone who can help you."

Willow's body is calling her back, a magnetic tug that she has to fight to resist. Does she want to go with Laurel?

"Come on." Laurel's tugging at her arm now. "I'll be with you, it'll be fine. And you won't feel the cold once we get moving. You're not cold now, are you?"

She can't tell. She's not even sure who *she* really is. Is she the self who lies beneath the covers, breathing slow and even, warm and well-fed, essentially safe and protected, despite her dreams? Or is she the self who stands barefoot at the top of a flight of stone steps, her dead sister tugging at her arm?

"Come *on*." Laurel is surprisingly strong, much stronger than Willow remembers. In life, they were equally matched. But Laurel drags her down the steps, one by one, until they stand together on the ground. Willow stands obediently and waits for Laurel to tell her what to do.

"And now you can come and be with me," Laurel says. Her eyes are bright and eager. "You will, won't you? I miss you so bloody much. It's awful without you. We've never been apart until now. Do you remember what it was like at the beginning? It was so warm and dark, and we were all squashed?"

And for a minute, Willow *does* remember. The water swooshing in her ears; the warmth. The tightness. The sense of peace.

No, she thinks. *I'm making it up. Nobody remembers before they were born.*

Laurel's smile is beautiful and terrible.

"That's not your memory, that's mine. You can't remember properly until you die. But then it comes back to you. It's like a book, and you can look at any bit of it you want. It's really lovely. Come on, I'll show you. Out in the woods, there's someone who can help us. He's waiting for you. That's why you came here. Didn't you know?"

Laurel's tugging at her arm with that surprising strength, trying to lead her towards the woods. But now, the memory of her warm body resting beneath the sheets tugs her in the other direction. The result is a stretching, tearing feeling that drags at her chest and her pelvis, a feeling that begins as mild discomfort but rapidly becomes almost unbearable. If it doesn't stop soon, she'll be torn in two.

"Stop fighting," Laurel whispers. "Trust me, if you stay, you'll be sorry. There's something going to happen soon, something you won't like. But if you leave now, you can get away from it."

Please, Willow thinks, *please stop hurting me like this.*

"I know I'm hurting you," Laurel says, sounding as if she's carrying out an unpleasant job that she's only persisting with for Willow's own good. "But if you come with me then I won't have to do it, will I? Oh come on, Willow, *please*, I hate having to do this to you. Stop messing me about and come on."

I want to go back, Willow thinks. *I want to be back in bed, right now. If I close my eyes and open them again, that's where I'll be, and it won't hurt any more. This is my dream, so I can control it.*

She closes her eyes. Opens them again. The tearing feeling still drags at her centre. Laurel watches calmly.

"So are you ready now?" she asks, and increases the pressure on Willow's arm until Willow, desperate, almost believes for a moment she might be able to scream. "Trust me, little one, I know exactly how much this hurts. Transitions are always painful. But I'm doing this for you. I'm only here because you called for me. Once you're where you belong, everything will feel better."

And, with a shock that shakes her heart and turns her knees to water, Willow realises this person beside her, this person wearing Laurel's skin and looking out at her through Laurel's eyes, is not Laurel at all.

"Well, of course I'm not," the creature in Laurel's body says. "She can't come back for you. It's a one-way journey, I'm afraid. Whatever it is you're seeing is a product of your imagination." And then it laughs through Laurel's mouth, spreads Laurel's arms out wide, except the laugh is not a laugh, it's the hoarse shriek of a crow, and Laurel's arms are enormous and covered in black feathers while her body is suddenly small, small and light, and her face has contracted into almost nothing around the fierce thick jab of her beak, and she flies at Willow's face, and Willow is falling, falling, falling as the crow tries to tear out her eyes.

CHAPTER EIGHT

She wakes then, as the living always must. She's left her bedroom, and she's standing at the bottom of the steps, in the place where Laurel led her. For a moment she thinks she's still dreaming. But then she comes fully into her own body and feels the penetrating cold that creeps and presses against the soles of her feet, the stirring in the air that moves her hair, and the ache in her bladder that tells her she cannot wait a second longer. Beyond embarrassment, she pushes her pyjama bottoms down, squats and pees, glancing around for the accusing gaze of the neighbours she knows aren't there, for the windows she knows aren't looking out at her, all the while thinking defiantly, *At least I didn't do this in the bed*. A rat, sleek and glossy, rustles out across a flat patch of dandelions, glances in her direction with bright intelligent eyes, then dives between two clumps of grass and is gone again.

She stands up, impressed and disgusted at the volume of liquid she's produced, and the steam that drifts upwards. For once, her sleepwalking's paid off, but she can't rely on this happening every night. First thing tomorrow, she needs to find the washing machine, and then go through the cupboards until she finds where her uncle keeps the spare sheets, so she'll be ready when the inevitable happens. But what if the sound of the washing machine disturbs him? And where will she hang the sheets afterwards? Joe told her mother he didn't mind, but how will he feel when he's confronted with the reality? Why can't she be normal, the way she used to be?

Her feet ache with cold, but still she waits, fascinated by the darkness. Has she ever been outside, on her own, at night, before? Although she feels in a general way this must have happened at some point, when she tries to recall the specific circumstances, she can't find anything that fits. Her parents have never been the camping type. They're glorious comfort-seeking technophiles who take pleasure in hot sunshine, nicely furnished villas, and soft beds. As Brownies, she and Laurel slept in church annexes and sports halls. They never even camped out on their own lawn. Perhaps this is the first time, after all.

At the bottom of the garden is a fence, and on the other side of the fence, the trees wait with their arms spread. Is Laurel dancing somewhere beneath them, waiting for Willow to join her? She feels loose and dreamy, as if she might be still asleep, and her body's growing oblivious to the cold. Without letting herself stop to think, she climbs over the fence – it's easy to do, as if it was built for climbing – and then she's alone in the woods, and the world stretches out in front of her like an ocean, split by a dusty line of pathway that winds between the trees.

That's it, croons Laurel. *Come and find him. He's waiting.*

Within a few paces, the darkness becomes alarming. She'd assumed there would be light coming from somewhere or other, perhaps the moonlight, perhaps some sort of leftover from the day, turning her skin blue and her clothes white but nonetheless, enough to see by. Now she realises she's simply imagining the way the world looks on screen when actors roam through a filtered day-for-night landscape, pretending to be lost in the dark. She takes three more steps, stumbles over something that could be a tree root or a dead body or just a bump in the earth, and comes to a stop. Then a flat heavy weight bumps against her thigh, and she realises she has her phone stuffed in her pyjama trouser pocket.

You're bloody glued to those phones, her mother and father used to say on a regular basis, and sometimes, *For God's sake don't take them into the toilet with you, it's disgusting.* But even alone and even in her sleep, she's a child of the twenty-first century, and she'd no more leave her room without her phone than without her clothes. Now, she holds it out in front of her and lets the bright circle of light guide her way.

I'm lost in the woods and nobody else even knows I've gone, she thinks, with savage gladness.

The woods might go on for ever for all she knows, but she keeps walking anyway. Not all the brief rustles and disturbed twigs seem to come from her footsteps, and she imagines small creatures scattering as she passes clumsily through the space that's usually just for them. What do they think of her? Are they frightened? Or only curious? She'd like to see a rabbit, but there's nothing much for them to eat in the woods. The soil beneath the trees is dusty and parched, and the occasional clearings are filled with tangly, spiny shapes that make her think of fairy tales. The pathway reaches a fork. One broader branch that leads downwards, and a thin little line, barely wide enough for both of her feet, that seems to lead nowhere in particular.

Which way should she go? The narrower path is more alluring. On the other hand, this adventure is already bordering on the stupidly dangerous. She's not sure she wants to tempt the universe any more than she already has, by ignoring the clear signal left by all the people who have passed this way before her. She's turning away from the narrow path, about to take the broader fork, when the light of her phone snags on something bright and glossy high up in the trees, a flash of white that she instantly knows must be man-made, because nothing natural would advertise its presence so boldly, and before she can stop herself, she's off to investigate.

This is how horror movies start, she thinks as she picks her way delicately along the thin rivulet of earth. *This is literally the start of a horror movie. You're out at night, in your pyjamas, and you're about to do something you've already decided is stupid and dangerous.*

The white splash is beginning to take on shape and form, growing square and solid. It's a notice board, nailed to a tree. The nails have leached iron oxide in long rivulets down the bark; or perhaps it's the tree's wounds, bleeding. She can see the shapes of letters, almost ready to form up into a message. Another few steps, and she has it.

PRIVATE PROPERTY
NO TRESPASSING

The lettering is meticulously neat, as if it's been printed by machine rather than painted by hand. Nonetheless, she can see the lines left by the brushstrokes, the faint indentation where someone has marked out the shapes of the letters with a ruler and pencil, the tiny imperfections at the edges where the damp has begun to steal the first vulnerable flakes of paint. There's something eerie in the competence of the unknown sign maker. The effort they've put in seems far too great for the task. When she tries to get closer, to see if she can reach up and touch it and make sure it's real, something thick and sharp presses against her stomach, and something else grabs at her ankles, almost sending her over. Someone has strung two long taut reaches of barbed wire around the trees, cordoning off a patch of land.

There are other signs on other trees, all proclaiming the same message. PRIVATE. KEEP OUT. VISITORS NOT WELCOME AT ANY TIME. NO PUBLIC RIGHT OF WAY. POSSIBLE ARMED RESPONSE. And, most alarmingly, IF YOU TRESPASS ON MY LAND I WILL NOT BE RESPONSIBLE FOR MY ACTIONS.

But it's the middle of the night, Willow thinks. It's not as if she's doing this in broad daylight, in a bright crowded place where everyone watches everyone else for signs of deviation. In this whole cold world, she's surely the only human being awake. No one's going to be patrolling the woods at this hour. And for all she knows, the patch of wood they've claimed goes on for miles and miles and miles. The chances of them both being in the same spot at the same moment must be miniscule.

Besides, look at how far she's come already. She's left her room, climbed a fence, followed the path and she's still here, still alive and intact and perfectly fine. What difference can it make if she goes a little further? Just a little bit further. Just to prove she can.

Moving carefully, she lifts the barbed wire and ducks beneath it, feeling it take a few strands of hair in painful tribute. The woods on the forbidden side of the wire are exactly the same as before, until the path dissolves beneath her feet and the ground becomes scuffed and bare and she has a sudden sense of change.

The wavering circle of light from her phone exposes patches of shapes and textures with merciless detail and clarity, but it takes her a while to put it all together. It's only after she's scanned the puzzlingly large and regular shape in front of her for the fourth time that she finally understands she's looking, not at a huge and confusing group of trees, but a wooden house.

I've found an old deserted house, she thinks, forgetting all the clues that tell her otherwise – the path she followed, the signs she studied, the barbed wire fence she climbed through – *Maybe nobody but me even knows it's here. How long has it been here? Maybe there's even furniture.*

But then she looks again, and sees that the house is robust and solid and well kept, a building in the prime of its life rather than an empty shell. A wall of split logs huddles under the eaves. Cords of fat black electrical cable sag from the veranda roof. The door fits neatly and cleanly in its frame and the three steps leading up to it look solid and strong. Running beside the steps, the railing looks as if it was repurposed from stolen scaffolding; it's ugly, but it stands straight and true and bare of rust.

VISITORS NOT WELCOME AT ANY TIME. The competent construction of the house, its craftsmanship and its ugliness, makes her nervous. IF YOU TRESPASS ON MY LAND I WILL NOT BE RESPONSIBLE FOR MY ACTIONS. She ought to stop, she ought to go back, but she can't tear herself away. As she takes in the details, running the light of her phone methodically up and down over pitch-coated boards and steel-drum furniture with the logos half worn off, a square of yellow light appears in the wall.

It's a light going on; nothing more. She tells herself this even as her knees clench and her palms turn sweaty. It's a light going on, nothing more, but still, before she's aware of making a conscious decision, she's turned off the torch on her phone, and crouched down in the shadow that pools at the base of the nearest tree.

She's waiting for someone to call out, to open a window and shout *Who's there? Is there anybody there?* She tells herself that she must have frightened whoever's inside. The white glare of her torch must be as visible to them as the yellow glow inside the house is to her. At night, in the heart of the forest, the only possible source of light is another human being, and whoever lives in this house is someone who doesn't want to be visited. They're frightened, that's all. She doesn't need to worry. In a minute they'll assume they imagined it and settle down again, and she'll be free to leave in her own time. She sits in the darkness. Waits for her eyes to adjust. Waits for the person in the house to speak. Waits and waits and waits, listening hard over the sound of her own breath. She's aware once more of how cold and sore her feet are.

There's still no sound from inside the house. Only the square of light, that stares out at her as if the house has opened a never-blinking eye. Maybe the house's inhabitant is too terrified to investigate. Or maybe they've woken up on their own, nothing to do with Willow lurking in the darkness, and now they've decided to read for a while before going back to sleep. The person in the house can't possibly be watching her. They'd never see her, looking out from a room filled with light to the darkness of the trees. Maybe they've gone back to sleep with the light on. Whatever they're doing in there, Willow doesn't need to see any more. She should leave and go back to her bedroom. She tenses her muscles to stand up.

Then, with startling suddenness, a figure appears in the window. It's tall and spindly, so tall that the top of the head is above the top of the frame, and because the light's behind it she can't make out any features. It waits by the window for a moment, then the house turns dark and blank once more as the lamp flicks off.

Has it seen her? Has she been seen? Her skin prickles with fear. PRIVATE PROPERTY. NO TRESPASSING. She's alone in the woods, without even shoes on her feet, and she's trespassing. What's going to happen if she gets caught? POSSIBLE ARMED RESPONSE. They can't actually mean they'd come after her with a gun, can they? She hears the creak and scrape of a door opening, and then another light blooms out into the night and she can see a man, standing in the shelter of the gable over the door.

He's not quite as elongated as he looked in the window, but he's high and thin and narrow, and his arms hang loosely at his sides. She thinks at first he's leaning on a stick, and feels a thump of relief. If he needs a stick to walk there's no chance he'll be faster than she is. Then she looks again and realises he's holding a rifle. He's not aiming it or even preparing to, just letting it rest at his side. His head's shaved so close to the skin that she can see the shape of his skull. If he makes eye contact with her, what will happen to them both next?

Don't look at me, she thinks frantically. Even the small rustlings of the woodland creatures have stopped. Maybe they can smell her fear. Or maybe they know better than to get so close to this man who stands in his doorway, his face turned towards the dark.

Just as Willow reminds herself that this man, however sinister he looks, can't possibly see her – that he'll be blinded by the porchlight, and besides, he doesn't even know if there's anybody *there,* he doesn't even know she's still *there* – he reaches up one gangly arm and turns out the light.

Now they're both blind in the darkness, waiting for their sight to return, waiting to see who will crack first. Does he know where she is? Is he coming towards her? Could he move quietly enough to get closer without her realising? If she moves, will he hear and come after her? She waits and waits and waits. Is he going to say something? Her pulse is thundering in her ears, and she's breathing very fast and very shallow, keeping the movements of her chest as small as possible. She has no idea how long she's been here. She blinks, blinks again and then suddenly she can make out his shape, still standing on the porch. He's scanning the forest, turning his head slowly from one side to another, his eyes like searchlights sweeping the darkness.

He knows she's there. Of course he knows. She's trespassed on his property. She's the unwelcome visitor. Now he will not be responsible for his actions.

And as if he's heard her thought, he turns his face towards the place where she cowers, and – can she really be seeing this, or is she making it up? – he smiles, a slow understanding smile, as if she and he are sharing a secret, as if he's someone she knows and loves, and they're playing a game they both adore. Then, with the unhurried precision of someone who knows he has all the time in the world, he leans the rifle carefully against the porch.

Still smiling towards the spot where Willow waits, he slowly raises his arms, an unmistakeable mime of a man taking aim at a target. An invisible barrel rests in his cupped palms. An invisible stock nestles against his thin cheek. She wills herself to stillness, so fiercely that for a moment she imagines she's managed to stop her own pulse. In the utter silence of the night, she hears the click of his tongue as he fires.

Then, still smiling, he picks up his rifle, breaks it open and shucks something onto the veranda. His body is so long and twig-like that the supple bend of his waist looks almost unnatural, as if he might snap in two with the pressure of folding himself forward. He holds something up between his fingers, and she realises he's showing her the cartridge from his gun, telling her that it was loaded and ready for action, and if he'd wanted to, he could have shot her for real.

Then he steps backwards into his house and closes the door.

For a moment she's unsure if he may have somehow killed some essential part of her, his imaginary bullet flying straight and true to the place where her heart bangs and yammers. She crawls stealthily backwards, watching the door in case he comes after her. She keeps this up until she tumbles backwards over a tree root, and lands flat and painfully on her back and realises that if she tries to get back through the woods, in the dark, not looking where she's going and without even her phone light to guide her, she'll never make it.

She gathers her courage. Is the man in the house watching? Will he come after her? No, there's no point worrying about that; whether he can see her or not, she has to put the torch back on. There's no other way. *If he wanted to kill me he'd have done it already,* Willow thinks, trying to find comfort in the thought. *He was trying to scare me. That's all. Stop being such a baby. Put the torch back on and go home.* She holds her breath, presses her thumb to the screen and cups her hand around the light as if she's trying to stop it from spilling. She will keep it as hidden as she possibly can.

Nothing around her looks familiar, and for a dreadful moment she thinks she may be completely lost, but then she sees the cluster of signs nailed to the trees like sacrifices, and the world turns and settles around her as she regains her bearings. Once she's on the other side of those signs, surely she must be safe. She stumbles gladly towards them.

As she crawls back underneath the barbed wire and into what feels like safety, she feels something smooth and slippery beneath her knees, something that threatens to spill her off her course and into... into what? Is this a trap? Has he set a trap? Is she going to fall into a pit and starve to death? They'd look for her, her Uncle Joe would look for her, but how would he ever find her when she can't call out to let anyone know she's there? Her fingers scrabble for purchase in the ground, coil around the edges of something they can grasp. She regains her balance, forces herself to be calm. She's not about to fall through space; she's not balanced over a pit. She's kneeling on a board.

To prove she's still sane and in control, she makes herself climb off the board and brush away the leaf litter that's half-submerged it. It's another sign, one that doesn't match the others. They're solid and neat-edged, thick planks joined firmly together, but this is a flimsy sheet of plywood with torn edges. The lettering of the other signs is precise and accurate, black as fresh newsprint, but this is written in exuberant splashes of dripping scarlet. The corners are missing, as if someone has torn it down and buried it.

She scans her torch slowly over the surface, and forces herself to read the words.

THE SLAUGHTER MAN

PART TWO

OCTOBER

CHAPTER NINE

Willow wakes the next morning late and reluctantly, anxious about facing the world and all its consequences. She'd got back to find her bedroom as empty as she'd left it, no sign that Joe had woken and wondered where his niece had gone; but what if the Slaughter Man had somehow known who she was? What if he'd followed her back to Joe's house? What if he complained to Joe about what she'd done? What then?

Her phone tells her that it's 11:27, that she has no new Snapchat messages, no new emails, no new likes on Instagram, and (a possible comforting explanation for all the rest) no WiFi signal. She'd like to think that the absence of notifications is only because her phone can't find the router through the thick walls, but she's grown used to online silence. When she stands up, her feet feel pulpy and tender. What was she thinking last night?

Gritting her teeth, she braves the bathroom, avoiding any possible glimpse of her reflection in the mirror. She's starving, but she makes herself get dressed first. Maybe Joe might believe she's been up since the dawn, silently studying in her bedroom. Then, trying not to limp, she makes her way downstairs. Will she be in trouble for sleeping so late? She should have thought to set an alarm. But then, how would she know what time her uncle gets up?

The house has that special sense of silence that comes when only one person is in it, but there's a note on the kitchen table:

I haven't been a teenager for a while but
I remember being able to sleep for England
so I thought I'd leave you to it. There's bacon
in the fridge, eggs in the bowl on the side,
bread in the bread bin, jam in the cupboard,
cereal in the pantry, milk in the fridge…
you get the idea.
Back by one. J x

The easy choice would be cereal, or ideally biscuits, but she's committed to getting better, and *better* means not taking the easiest route. The bacon in the fridge is the kind that comes in a black packet, and has a slightly pornographic description of the extra ingredients that mean it's twice the price of ordinary bacon. She isn't sure how much she wants to eat something seasoned with juniper and hickory smoke and hand cured with sea salt, but this seems to be the only kind there is, and she wants some to go with the eggs.

After some rummaging, she finds a frying pan, nestled tenderly in its own thin drawer. Its weight takes her by surprise and she almost drops it, catching it just before it crashes into the slate tiles. The thought of letting it fall and smashing her uncle's beautifully kept floor makes her toes curl up inside her socks, and she lifts it onto the stove top with exaggerated care. The shells of the eggs seem thicker than usual, and the yolks are a deep rich orange.

The food is delicious – even the poncey bacon, which she had her doubts about – and because there's no one watching she can shovel it into her mouth without any fear of being looked at, and judged for taking such pleasure in her meal when her sister is dead. Even the slick of fat on the plate looks tempting. If she licks it off, who's going to know? No, that's disgusting. If she starts behaving like a pig because nobody's looking, where will it end? Maybe this is why Joe's house is so clean and neat even though he's alone in it. Once you let yourself go, who knows how far you might fall?

He isn't always alone, though. There's someone else who usually lives here, and there's clearly something her mother doesn't like about her, because nobody's even bothered to tell Willow her name. Maybe she's much younger than Joe? Or much older? She remembers the photograph she glimpsed by Joe's bed. If she's going to do some snooping, now is her opportunity, but the dirty frying pan in the sink, the splatters of grease on the stovetop, drag her back into the room.

She has to at least make an effort.

She scrubs the frying pan, washes her plate, rinses her glass, cleans her cutlery, stacks them all neatly on the draining board. The clock on the cooker says 12:15, so she definitely has time. She stubbornly refuses to listen to her conscience, which tells her that *time* isn't the reason she ought to be hesitating. She climbs the stairs.

The door to her uncle's room is ajar. Almost, she tells herself, as if he's inviting her in. Maybe that's why he's gone out, so she can get used to the place by herself and in her own time. Maybe he wants her to look. The bed's neatly made, three cushions lined up in a row against plump smooth pillows, giving it the look of an unused hotel room. Her own bed is a mess, the beautiful patchwork quilt crumpled in a heap at the end. She ought to be in there, cleaning up after herself and doing some of the worksheets her parents have spent money on so they can spring her out of school. But the house is still quiet and this will only take a minute and besides, what's so dreadful about looking at a photograph? She takes the last few steps with a deliberate heavy tread, a show of innocent defiance for whatever spirit might be watching, and picks up the photo frame with a firm grasp.

The frame holds two pictures. There's her Uncle Joe, looking younger and fresher, standing on a black pebbled beach. Standing beside him, another man, a little taller, a little chunkier, a lot greyer. They're wearing matching jumpers, creamy white with a complex geometric design knitted into the neck and shoulders. In the first photograph, they're laughing towards the camera, the older man with his arm around Joe's shoulders. In the second, they're kissing.

Oh, she thinks. *Oh.*

Is this why her parents stopped speaking to Joe? Surely that can't be it. But what if it is? She's always assumed they think the same way she thinks, the way she's assumed everyone thinks these days. But what if she's wrong? Have they talked about this? They must have, but she can't remember. She doesn't think her parents actually know any gay couples. Is that a coincidence? Or a conscious choice? She tilts the photograph towards her again, wondering if she'll catch a glimpse of a wedding ring, but both men are wearing gloves.

And Joe, she realises now, has been playing the pronoun game, carefully not mentioning names. Does he really think he needs to keep this a secret? Does he think she'll be shocked? How can she tell him she's on his side?

She wants, very much, to be able to call her parents and ask them about this, and then to raise her voice and drown out theirs. She wants to tell them that she's right and they're wrong and love is love, and they need to buck up their ideas right now or she won't be able to respect them any more. How good would that feel, to reclaim her voice on behalf of someone else, who needs her help? She takes her phone from her back pocket and holds it to her ear. *Hey, Mum. Did you really not speak to your brother for years because he's gay, because I think that's awful and you ought to be ashamed of yourself? I mean, what if I told you I'm a lesbian? Would you disown me too?* She can feel the pressure of the words in her chest. This is important. This is something that needs to be said. She'll find a way to say it.

She opens her mouth wide, then wider. But even alone in this strange house, with her parents far away and no possibility of them hearing her, she can't speak. She leans forward, pressing at her stomach as if she can force the words out that way, but only makes herself retch.

She puts the photograph carefully down again, studying the possessions that surround it. Two combs; two hairbrushes; two cans of deodorant. She wonders which belongs to which man. Do they share the pot of hair gunge between them? No, that must be for Joe. The other man has his hair clipped short. He'd have no interest in a messed-up shape that will last all day. Curious, she unscrews the pot and sticks in a finger, withdraws a glob of something that smells waxy and faintly masculine. She rubs it between her palms. Now her hands are sticky and the smell of the wax makes her feel as if her uncle's in the room with her. She wipes them on her jeans. As she replaces the little pot, she finds a long wooden box. Opening it up, she finds forbidden treasure: her uncle's razor.

Why is he keeping this in here? Because of her; he can't leave it in the bathroom in case she finds it and steals it. *Doesn't he trust me?* Of course he doesn't trust her. Except that he does. He's taken his razor into his bedroom, but he hasn't thought to lock it away. He's completely misunderstood the ways she'll break the rules. She might have come into his bedroom without permission, but she's not going to do anything stupid.

Except that her fingers are already folded around the stalk of the razor, creeping up towards the head with its little cage of blades. She could have it apart in a few minutes, set the blades free to do whatever they want. How good would that feel?

No, she thinks. *I don't want to die. I want to get better.*

But maybe this might be part of getting better? She's wondered before if she might reawaken her voice through pain. Imagine if Joe came back from wherever it is he's gone and found she could speak again. How incredible would that be? And all it would take would be a few little cuts…

Of course, it might take more than a few little cuts to do the job properly. She might have to cut quite deep and dangerously. And perhaps while she was doing that, she might get carried away and find herself going further than she meant to, walking the path that will lead her back to Laurel.

Caught between fear and longing, she glances up towards the mirror.

Oh, she thinks. *There you are.*

And then in a sudden flurry of movement, she flings the razor back into its box, drops the box onto the dresser and runs. She's hurrying so much that she can hardly put on her trainers, and her hoodie becomes a mystery of tangled sleeves and strings that catch around her waist and wrist, but she doesn't slow down. Another fierce minute and she's ready, and she throws open the door and runs out into the yard, across the little garden where a plastic henhouse stands empty and barren, past the concrete animal pen where nothing lives, through the tangle of plants, over the fence and out into the woods that wait beyond.

In the daylight, everything seems smaller and simpler, the expanse of the forest more manageable, the trees shrunk down to their usual size. She'd thought there might be birdsong now the sun's come up, but she can't hear anything. Maybe they're afraid of the noise she's making. She thinks about sitting down, but then she sees a long thin orangey centipede writhing across the leaves, and she shudders and leans against the trunk of a tree instead. (Did she really come through here in bare feet last night? What if a centipede had run across her foot? What if it had *bitten* her?) She's reached the fork in the path, that last night led her to the Slaughter Man, and that strange communion as he fired his imaginary gun into her heart. Did that truly happen? Or was it a dream within a dream?

Last night she was half-awake and terrified, stumbling through the dark. Today she's in control, standing in the sunlight that slants between the trees. It's not terror that makes her tread softly as she makes her way down the path. She's simply being cautious. The barbed wire fence is dull and hard to spot, but she's ready for it this time. She's not going to fall over it or tear her skin against its points. She ducks beneath it without stopping to look at the signs, and slows her pace so she can move more stealthily.

She hears him before she sees him. He's singing to himself, not a continuous musical flow, but little chunks of song that seem designed to provide a rhythm to work to. The beats of the song coincide with the *crack* of whatever he's doing. She remembers the split logs, stacked tight against the wall of the house. It sounds as if he's chopping something. After a minute, the song smooths out and the chopping sound stops.

The Slaughter Man is in the clearing in front of his house. He's lit a small fire in the yard, and over it, he's suspended a cooking pot on fat chains that hang from a metal tripod. She wonders for a minute why he's cooking outside. Then the smell slithers into her nostrils and she has to force herself not to choke.

How can he stand it? Is he going to eat it? The Slaughter Man takes a pair of gloves from his back pocket and puts them on, then reaches into the pot with a pair of long barbecue tongs and lifts something up for inspection. The thing he lifts up is brownish, whitish, steaming; little clots of something fall away from it into the water. She can barely move for nausea, but he seems oblivious to the stink, turning it around so he can inspect it.

"Get you to my lady's chamber," he says. "And tell her, let her paint an inch thick…"

Oh God, she thinks. *It's bones. He's boiling animal skulls.*

"He was a wise man, that Mr Shakespeare," the Slaughter Man continues. "He knew a thing or two." He touches his gloves cautiously to the surface of the bone, then discards the tongs and takes it into his hands, cupping the jaw with its long fangs to keep it in place. Then he turns towards the trees and bares his teeth in Willow's direction. "I wonder if the audience agrees?"

I'm not here. There's no one here. You can't see me. She's frozen to the spot, even more still than the trees. Perhaps that's how he can see her there; because she's keeping too still. Or maybe it's the treacherous red of her hoodie, shrieking against the green and brown of the forest.

"Alone in the woods, talking to a boiled pig skull. No wonder people think there's something wrong with me." When he strokes the surface of the skull, a thin slick of cooked meat comes off against his gloves. Willow feels her breakfast rising in her throat. "They all tell their children not to come here. They're worried that I might… do things to them." He holds the skull up towards his face so its eye sockets are level with his own. "Maybe they're right. Do you know what you call human flesh that's been prepared for cooking?"

She wants to run. She wants to walk out into the clearing and go closer. She can't move.

The Slaughter Man takes hold of the loose jawbone, and moves it up and down.

"Long pig," he says, and for a moment she imagines the skull itself is speaking to her.

When she comes back into her head, she's not even sure which way she's going. She's simply stumbling along a path, trusting that it must eventually take her to safety. The armpits of her t-shirt feel swampy and her knees are trembling.

It wasn't a human skull. The jaw was elongated, the teeth sharp and fang-like. It was a pig. He said it was a pig. It's all right to kill a pig, that's what they're for, they're bred for eating. (Then she remembers the clots of cooked flesh falling from the skull, and wonders if she'll ever eat pig again.) It's all right. It's all right. He's not following her and she doesn't have to go back there ever again. She doesn't have to go back there ever again. She doesn't have to…

Then she reaches the end of the path and finds herself looking into a field with a clump of indeterminate farm creatures in it. Her legs are aching, and she's glad of the chance to stop and lean on the heavy wooden fence that separates her from what she presumes must be someone's farm.

The fence is solid and comforting. She takes a few deep breaths, then drags her hair into a rough plait, fastening it with a hairband she finds in her pocket. If this was a film she'd look glamorous and ready for action. This isn't a film, so she probably just looks plain and sweaty, her hair in an unflattering scrape, but there's no one here to see her. She can relax and get her breath back and watch what's going on.

The creatures sound like sheep, but they're too rangy, too leggy, and not woolly enough. It takes her longer than it probably ought to before she realises they're goats. There's a small open animal shed where they presumably sleep (*Do animals go to bed at night like people?* Willow wonders. *Do they choose their own bedtime?*), but as far as she can tell, there's no one in it at the moment. Whatever's going on at the other side of the field, the goats seem very pleased about it. They jostle and toss their heads and barge into each other, and she can hear them calling. Then, with a sudden burst of movement, the herd breaks up and scatters, and the gate swings open to let someone through.

That's the farmer. Maybe he's brought them treats. She has vivid memories of long-ago walks with Laurel, of stopping by a paddock where a giant chestnut horse bent his curious head down to whiffle at their hair, then fumbled polos from their splayed palms with velvet lips. When the figure in the field turns to shut the gate, Willow sees that the farmer is a woman, with a thick bundle of hair gathered against the base of her neck. She shoos the goats away, upends the sack she's carrying, and pours out a thin stream of pellets into a low metal trough. The goats eat as if this is their first meal in weeks. They come in an implausible range of sizes, some no bigger than spaniels, others more like small ponies.

Will I be in trouble for standing here? Maybe leaning on the fence is the same as looking into someone's garden. The woman's utilitarian plainness contains its own beauty, the beauty of something shorn of all frivolity and shaped to fit perfectly into a specific kind of life. There's something slung over her shoulder. Willow stares hard at it, trying to make it into anything other than what it looks like, which is a gun.

What if she points it at me? Is she allowed to shoot me? It's the second time in twenty-four hours she's had to ask this question. She shrinks away from the fence, wondering if she should run, but the woman's already walking off in another direction, towards the side of the field. Another minute and she's over the fence, climbing with quick economical movements that make it look as simple as opening a door and walking through.

Then, someone else; a boy about her own age. He's wearing skinny jeans, Converse trainers and a beanie hat that slouches down the back of his head. His hair's long enough to get in his eyes. He struggles with the catch of the gate, and when the goats leave their trough and swarm around him in a hopeful, jostling crowd, he looks alarmed. Are they going to attack him? She's used to thinking of animals as something humans eat, milk, and generally exploit for their own benefit, but these goats seem to have figured out a way to level the playing field. The biggest goat, a huge hairy creature with strong horns and hair so thick it looks like a mane, chases the others away and puts itself between the boy and the rest of the herd, watching him carefully. The boy waves his arms, then yells. She can hear the uncertainty in his voice; he doesn't expect the goat to obey. Nonetheless she envies him his freedom, to open his mouth and call out to the empty sky.

Eventually he reaches a truce with the goats, or else they simply accept he has nothing to offer them. The boss goat turns away; the rest scatter; the boy's been set free. He looks around and shrugs, as if to tell the universe that he wasn't bothered at all. His gaze turns in her direction. When their eyes meet, they both feel the jolt of their connection.

Now what happens? She ought to say something, because

she's the one who doesn't belong here. She gives him a small wave, so he knows she's not laughing at him.

She's a girl and he's a boy, so of course he's not going to come over straight away, any more than she's going to leap the fence and walk up to him like an over-eager lunatic. They have to approach gradually, guided by the million interesting distractions in the space between them. He wanders diagonally left and picks up a long stick, then meanders around a series of molehills. She climbs the fence and sits on the top rail, balancing fiercely and praying she doesn't fall off. As he gets closer, she slips her feet onto the ground, and he leans against the fence a few yards down from her.

"All right?" He's trying to sound casual, but she can hear the tension in his voice. It cost him a lot to come over here. Now what? She smiles, hoping this will be enough.

"You live near here?" His accent makes her think of London, a rich Estuary sound. It would make a great contrast to her own flat Northern vowels, if only she could speak.

She nods.

"I'm staying for a bit." He waves his hand vaguely towards the other side of the field. "Been here a few months. It's all right. Bit boring sometimes."

This is when she's supposed to speak, but she can't, and this is why she doesn't have any friends any more. There's only so much you can do with body language, and even the kindest (or most self-absorbed) listener eventually gets freaked out by her lack of words. In a minute he'll realise there's something wrong with her and walk away. She risks another smile and a slight shrug, trying to draw out this moment of belonging, of feeling normal. It's her turn to speak, but she can't. What's going to happen next?

Struggling against her own body, battling her own will, she's suddenly saved; a shattering *bang* that tears through the air and sends up a flock of clattering wingbeats into the sky. The shock of the gunshot takes her breath away. A second

95

shot, and then something small and black and folded-in tumbles from the cloud of wings.

"It's all right." The boy is watching her. "That's Katherine. She's clearing the crows out. Says they make a mess of everything. Peck holes in tarpaulins and that. She knows what she's doing. She won't shoot you by mistake."

Willow thinks about the woman's plain clean face, the bundle of hair at the base of the neck, the confident strides measured out in green wellingtons. A woman with a gun, who shoots crows. She might just be Willow's personal heroine.

"She puts out food in the field and then picks them off when they come down for it," the boys adds. Willow can't tell if he's saying this with disgust or admiration. The shotgun rings out again, one round and a pause as the birds circle and soar, then the second round and a second black clump tumbles like a falling star. She wonders how it would feel to hold the bird's body, feel the heat dissipate and the flesh stiffen between her fingers.

"You don't say much, do you?" The boy's glance makes her feel guilty. He's worried that he's making a fool of himself, that she's laughing at him, that he's made himself open and vulnerable, and now she's going to dive in and tear out his guts.

"There summat wrong with you?"

No, there bloody isn't. Her tenderness dissipates. *Why should I have to talk just so you'll feel comfortable?*

He's waiting for her to speak and prove him wrong. What happens now? Will he walk away, or turn on her? She wonders if he can tell what she's feeling, if she's as open to him as he is to her.

"You got, like, no tongue or something?" He looms closer, not touching her exactly, but right in her personal space so she feels as if he is. She can smell the hair wax that keeps his elaborate quiff from tumbling into his eyes, and the body spray he's doused himself in. His eyes are large and blue. She lifts her chin and tries not to look intimidated.

"Or are you, like, *special*?"

How fucking dare he? Of course she's not *special*. She needs time, that's all, time and for everyone to leave her alone.

"How about if I, like, flick your nose? Will you talk to me then?" She can see the endless possibilities of minor torture flaring in his mind. He raises his hand and she flinches. "God, you daft cow, I'm not actually going to do it." He laughs. "But if I did, would you tell anyone? Or would you let me do it?"

Get the fuck away from me. The words are there, she can feel the shape of them, but the pressure won't yield. *Get the fuck away from me*. If she told him to back off, would he obey? From across the field, he'd looked vulnerable. Now he's someone else, excited by the thought of hurting a stranger and getting away with it. She can hear his breathing, faster and deeper than she'd like. *Get the fuck away*. If she thinks it hard enough, perhaps he'll be able to read it in her eyes.

"Bloody hell, Willow." A voice from behind her; her Uncle Joe, out of breath. She turns towards him thankfully, even though she knows she's probably about to be told off for disappearing without telling him where she was going, because although it will be humiliating, at least it will get her away from this boy.

"It's okay," he says as soon as he sees her face. "I got back and you weren't there, but you left me some clues to follow so I found you. Shoes gone, back door open, footprints in the grass. I didn't think you'd get so far, though. A mile and a half through a strange forest." He takes a deep breath, and then, to her surprise, laughs. "I keep forgetting you're seventeen and not ten. Sorry about that. Oh, hi, you must be Luca. Nice to meet you."

"How do you know who I am?" The boy sounds about ten himself. To compensate, he shuffles down inside his hoodie and glowers out from underneath his beanie hat.

"Don't worry, mate, I'm not the police. Katherine mentioned she'd got a young lad called Luca staying with her."

"So who are you then?" Luca is trying to sound tough and cocky, but it's coming off as uncouth.

"I'm Joe, I live over the other side of the woods. Is Kath around?"

"She's shooting crows." Luca is still refusing to make eye contact with Joe, but Joe doesn't seem to mind.

"Okay, I'll catch up with her later. Willow, d'you want to come home for lunch?"

Willow nods, glad for a reason to turn her back on Luca. But before they can leave, they're going to have to say hello to the woman with the gun – Katherine – who's appeared over the fence and is now striding towards them, sturdy and sure, belonging to the land in a way Willow knows she could never achieve if she lived here from now until she turned ninety.

"Joe! Nice to see you." Katherine aims a friendly smile in Joe's direction, keeping her gun pointed carefully downwards. "How are you?"

"You know me. Doing great. As always."

"Not too lonely by yourself?"

Joe laughs. "It's only for a few weeks. Do us both good to get some space, I expect. And anyway, I'm not on my own, my sister lent me my niece for a while. Willow, this is Katherine, she has a farm."

"Smallholding," Katherine corrects him.

"Smallholding, but I'm too thick to know the difference, so I keep saying *farm*. Kath, this is Willow."

"Hello, Willow." Katherine has a way of looking that Willow finds comforting, as if she's been evaluated not for her looks or her stylishness but simply as a specimen of human animal, catalogued without judgement and then left to continue being herself. "Come over here whenever you like. There's always plenty to do. Just come through this field and there's a path through the garden." She lays the shotgun across her knee and breaks it open, takes out the two spent cartridges and replaces them with two more from her pocket.

Willow watches Luca from the corner of her eye. He's

watching her, too, the pair of them carrying on a silent dialogue as Joe and Katherine discuss a gate on a footpath, and a meeting of the parish council.

"Right." Katherine shoves hard at a goat that has crept up on her and stuck its nose in her pocket. "Get off, there's nothing for you in there. Joe, are you and Willow staying for some lunch? About an hour from now. You can hang around the house and play with the cats while you're waiting."

"That's really nice of you, but we'd better get back."

"You're sure? It's no trouble."

"Honestly. But thanks."

"Is he looking after you properly?" Katherine's sudden shrewd gaze sweeps on Willow like a searchlight. Willow nods, and tries to look like someone who didn't leave the house without permission in the middle of the night and almost get herself killed by a strange man whose land she was trespassing on.

"Well, make sure you keep an eye on him," Katherine says. "He's a nice man, your uncle, but he's as daft as a brush. He's not fit to be left on his own."

"It's true." Joe doesn't sound at all insulted. "That's why I have Willow staying with me. Otherwise I might forget to get dressed or leave the house ever again. But she'll see me right."

"He's a funny one, though, isn't he," Joe says suddenly, as if he and Willow have been talking the whole way back through the woods, rather than tramping along in rhythmic and companionable silence.

Willow looks at him blankly.

"Luca, I mean. Nice enough kid, until he remembers he's decided not to be. I had a boyfriend like that at uni. He was lovely, but only long as no one was watching."

His voice is light and casual, but she can't miss the slight overemphasis on the word *boyfriend*, the sideways glance to make sure she's listening. She's always thought of *coming out* as a singular act, a grand declaration instantly disseminated, because that's what it's been like for the two or three students who've done it. Her college is a closed system; all news is shared with everyone. It hasn't occurred to her before that the real world requires an endless repetition of this same small act of courage. She hooks her arm through Joe's, and hopes he'll understand this as the gesture of solidarity it's meant to be.

"By the way," Joe adds, "there's something I need to tell you."

She can see the turning coming up that would take her to where the Slaughter Man waits with his pot full of bones. She already knows what Joe is going to say.

"If you want to go and visit Katherine, that's absolutely fine, she's lovely. But you see that path there? Don't go down that way. It's not safe."

Willow nods.

"Seriously though, I really mean it. Willow, are you listening to me?"

He's stopped walking, and now he takes hold of her shoulders and turns her towards him

"There's someone who lives at the end of it and it's best not to disturb him. He's… well, he's a strange man. It's best to leave him alone."

Willow nods again.

"He won't bother you unless you bother him. But if you do bother him… well, just don't, all right? Promise? Good girl. Okay, lecture over. Let's go home and get lunch."

Willow hooks her arm back through Joe's. In her head, she can still hear the click of the Slaughter Man's tongue, still feel that strange sensation in her chest, as if the bullet he fired was not imaginary, but only invisible, and had torn its way through her flesh and burrowed its way into her heart.

CHAPTER TEN

The phone pressed to her ear, Willow curls herself into the corner crease of the chair that sits by the living room fireplace. When she scoots herself down like this, folding her legs into her belly and tucking her neck against her chest, her mother talking quietly nearby, she feels a sense of safety that is somehow, faintly, known and familiar.

"I was thinking the other day about when you were little," her mother says. "About reading to you both at bedtime. Do you remember the chairs in your rooms?"

It's as if her mother can see through the space that separates them. Of course this is what she's thinking of, of course this is why it feels so good to fold herself into this tiny space. She can almost smell the warm milk they used to slurp from their Sippy cups, long past the age where they actually needed them, can almost feel the twirl and twine of her mother's hair between her fingers.

"Your dad and I used to take it in turns to read to you," her mother continues. "Both of you together but one story each, and alternating rooms each night."

Yes. Yes. She remembers all of this, the strange doubleness of their lives as children, the way their parents fought so tirelessly to keep everything equal, everything balanced. Their bedrooms, the same size but with different decoration, her own painted in shades of yellow and Laurel's in shades of green. Neutral colours. And in the corner of each room, a chair big enough to just about hold one squashed parent and two squashed toddlers. As long as the two squashed toddlers sat still and didn't fidget too much. The nightly litany, *We're in Laurel's room so Willow chooses the first story*, and then the next night the other room and the other twin choosing first, two nights with their father and two nights with their mother, a rota they all came to know deep in their bones. The times when the beautiful order would break down in a fierce pointless squabble – *but I wanted to choose* The Cat In The Hat*, that's not fair* – both of them ignoring their harassed parent, explaining they'd both get to hear the story whoever chose it, so what did it matter?

"That was always the best part of the day. Even when we'd been stressed and shouty, we loved reading to you. We used to wonder if we should try doing it differently, so you got some alone time with us both. Only when we suggested it, you were both so horrified, you'd think we'd tried to change your names or something. But we never wanted you to feel like you were a sort of matching set. We wanted you to know we'd have been just as thrilled if we'd got you one at a time, instead of together."

She and Laurel had always liked their twinship. It felt like a lazy kind of superpower, a way of being special and admired without even trying. As babies, they'd slept best when crammed in the same cot, so their parents had switched them between rooms, to ensure both places were equally familiar. When they graduated to toddler beds, they'd begin the night separated, but more often than not, they'd end up crammed in together, one of them creeping out to join the other. It was only as they grew older that they appreciated the effort their parents had made to shield them from the endless, endless comparisons, to give them the space to be the way they wanted to be. *Are you going to dress them alike or differently? What if they have the same favourite colour? Which is the princessy one? Which is the tomboy? Who's bossiest? Which one is in charge?*

"And do you remember," her mother continues, "you used to get hold of my hair and twiddle it? You both did it, and I couldn't stop you because I was holding the book. The first thing I had to do when I'd finished reading was brush all the tangles out. In the end I cut my hair short so you'd both stop. Then you started on your own instead..."

They'd both begged her not to cut her hair. They loved the long rich fall of brown, loved the secret female mystery of the way she twined it up into a bun at the back of her skull. Until she came home with a shorn head and a satisfied look, they'd refused to believe she'd go through with it. It was one of the reasons they'd insisted on growing their own hair long and flowing. Even as teenagers, they'd still occasionally wondered why their mother had chosen to cut her hair. Now she has the answer, but Laurel does not. Another station on the journey that takes her away from her sister.

But you can stop it, Laurel whispers. *You can come back to me.* Willow can feel her, right there in the chair, conjured by the voice of her mother.

"And we'd have to leave you all tangled up," her mother continues, "because you both hated having your hair brushed and you were all sleepy. You used to end up with these little clots of hair, like dreadlocks. Yours were on the left side, and Laurel's were on the right. That's how we first knew you were left-handed. Because of those little dreadlocks you used to make."

But I'm not left-handed, Willow thinks. *That was Laurel. You're thinking of Laurel. Or is it me who's got confused?* For a moment she can't remember. She raises her hand to her hair, letting muscle memory guide her.

CHAPTER ELEVEN

It takes about a week for Willow and Joe to find a rhythm to their lives. She'd imagined she would be alone a lot, but Joe seems oddly unoccupied – or rather, whatever it is that occupies him doesn't often require him to leave the building – and his life is both routine and mysterious. He wakes early, and cleans the house with the kind of meticulous care that makes Willow anxious about taking mugs upstairs or leaving her socks lying around. At nine o'clock, he sits at the desk in the living room and begins what she presumes is his job, although he never mentions to her what he's busy with. After watching cautiously over his shoulder as he types up and issues an invoice, she works out that he's a website designer, although not a particularly busy one. Up in her room, she does some calculations to try and work out if this can possibly be all the money he makes, and decides that it probably isn't. Maybe he has a second life she doesn't know about. Or maybe her parents are paying him to look after her. Or maybe he's already got rich.

At half-past ten, he leaves the room to make a regular phone call that she thinks must be to his partner, out in Perth. At eleven, he leaves the house and goes shopping, coming back around an hour later with paper-wrapped meat and fiddly cheese and fancy bread and vegetables in paper bags. He fusses around Willow, making her meals and bringing her snacks at regular intervals, comes to check on her when she's up in her room, talks to her about what they might have for lunch or dinner, but without expecting any sort of answer. When she tries to imagine what his days would be like if she wasn't there, all she can conjure is the image of Joe cleaning his already spotless house, or perhaps sitting in the living room window and staring out at the road like a cat waiting for its owner. The kind of food he likes to eat is beginning to grow on her.

Because he has a routine, it's easy for her to get into one too. She applies herself to the assignments her tutors send her, surprising herself with the amount of progress she can make without the distractions of lesson changeovers, teachers, and other people in general.

Each night, she dreams.

Since coming to the cottage, her dreams have changed. The Death Bird has a human face now and occasionally she glimpses it, looking out at her from beneath the crow-skull. Sometimes, he holds a pig's head; sometimes carries a gun. Sometimes, she wakes outside, standing at the base of the stone steps and looking out towards the woods, as if the Slaughter Man is calling to her as she sleeps.

It's a whole week before the inevitable happens. She wakes up gasping and retching, sweating with the horror of a nightmare – she was tied to a metal table, the Slaughter Man standing over her with a sharp metal beak strapped to his face – to find her pyjamas and bedsheets are soaked. For the last few nights she's managed to wake in time. She'd hoped she might be getting over it, that this humiliating phase of her life might have finally passed.

You're pathetic, she thinks, as she peels off her pyjamas. *Absolutely vile*. The skin of her thighs and buttocks is damp and itchy. Furious and ashamed, she claws recklessly at herself, gouging at the soft flesh until she's marked with raggedy lines of bloody dots that make her look as if she's been pecked by a crow.

Her penance paid, she strips her bed and finds clean pyjamas. She doesn't dare venture out of her room to look for fresh linen. She'll have to manage without sheets tonight. Can she risk going downstairs to put on the washing machine? No, she can't, she might wake her uncle, but if she doesn't, her room is going to stink. How can she hide the evidence?

Of course, she thinks, and opens the door to the outside staircase. The air smells fresh and sweet, and strong enough that within a few minutes, her room feels clean again.

It'll be all right, she tells herself. *You can sort it out in the morning. He'll never know.*

She shuts the door on the heap of soiled linen, and crawls back into bed.

"Anyway, I thought we might have a stir-fry tonight." Joe has a habit of starting conversations as if they've been talking for a long time already, and have accidentally strayed from the main point. "Maybe something with beef strips, marinated. Five-spice powder, maybe. Some soy, a bit of honey."

She's sitting at the table, eating her breakfast and wondering what to do with her day. Around her, Joe is cleaning the kitchen. The second day she was here, she tried to join in, and he laughed and shooed her away.

"Not sure whether we should have rice or noodles though. What do you think?" He squints up at her over the top of the dishwasher. "Rice? Or noodles? Okay, you're right. Noodles it is."

She's getting used to being treated as if she's a pet rather than a person. Who would Joe talk to if she wasn't here? The cottage with only him in it must be almost unbearable. Joe empties the dishwasher, closes the cupboard on the meticulously stacked plates, and goes into the utility room.

She bites at her toast, feeling the crunch echo in her head. Yesterday she'd been rereading *Rebecca* and thinking about the heroine's strange relationship with food, the time she stole dull plain biscuits and ate them in the woods because she didn't like to go to her own kitchen, in her own home, and ask for something nicer. *I used to do that,* she thinks, *but now I eat meals at normal times like a normal person. Does that mean I'm getting better?* And because she's thinking about feeling better and about the texture of the toast against her tongue, she forgets to keep a watch on what Joe's doing, and when he comes back in again and says, "So I'll grab the laundry baskets and we can blitz through the washing. Do you mind me sorting through your stuff or would you rather do it yourself?" it takes her a moment to remember that she has her own secrets to keep from last night.

She leaps from her chair, but it's too late, he's already up the stairs and in her room, looking at the naked mattress and the crumpled quilt and the outside door slightly ajar and the sheets lying dead on the steps outside, and then he turns towards her and the look of compassion on his face makes her skin crawl with shame.

"Oh, look," he says, and holds out his arms to her. "Hey, it's okay, you know. And you didn't have to sleep without sheets. Why didn't you come and get me and I could have helped?"

Because, she thinks, *because I don't want you to help me, I don't want anyone to help me. I want to be left alone to sort everything out by myself.*

"You don't have to deal with stuff like this on your own," Joe continues, kind and courageous, and she feels as if she might burst with the pressure of all the words that she can't speak. "I mean, seriously, Willow, this is my specialist subject. I'm astonishing at laundry. I'm the God Emperor of Clean Washing. I'm the Persistent Stain Ninja. Next time, bang on the bedroom door and give me a shout. I won't mind, I swear. I quite like being awake in the middle of the night anyway, we can come downstairs and eat cake in the kitchen while we're at it…"

And what good would you have been anyway? Because

guess what, Joe, you put a sleepwalker in a room with a door that goes straight to the outside, and I've been going out there without you knowing anything about it. I went right into the woods and I went up that path you said I shouldn't go up, and I saw him, I saw the Slaughter Man, and he shot me in my heart.

"Don't look at me like that, I mean it. You can come and get me, any time. I want to help you. But you have to talk to me, okay? Tell me what you need and—"

He realises his mistake and puts his hand to his mouth, but it's too late. He's said the words, he's done the one thing he promised her mother he'd never do. And even though she knows he didn't mean it, even though her mother did the same thing multiple times a day without realising it, even though she doesn't even really mind, she knows she's got the upper hand. Now she's allowed to flounce off, because putting pressure on her to speak is the one absolute taboo everyone around her is supposed to observe.

She feels a twinge of mean triumph as she storms off through the back door, leaving him to deal with her horrible sheets. She's glad she's already wearing her shoes.

To start with she's worried Joe might come after her, but within a couple of minutes she realises he's not going to. She wants to be alone, of course she does, but does she want him to give in to her? Sometimes what she wants isn't good for her. She slows down and looks back through the trees, wondering if he might simply be struggling to catch up.

Hey, croons Laurel, from inside her skull. *We don't need him anyway. It's nice out here on our own.*

Willow closes her eyes. Why can't ears come with some sort of shutdown device too? She can hear a bird singing, loud and shrill, the sort of sound that you're supposed to love but that probably means *this is my tree, you bastards, all mine and none of you are coming in it.* In the pocket of her hoodie is a long curved metal stalk with a thick rubber grip. Her fingers trace the length and hesitate over the top, where the stack of five little blades sits innocuously behind the thin cover of plastic.

When did she steal this? She remembers going into Joe's room, looking at the photograph, finding the razor, putting it back. Has she been back since and forgotten? Or is she remembering wrong? The bird's stopped singing and stands effortlessly balanced on a curve of bramble, watching her with oil-drop eyes.

Whatever I do with this is Joe's fault, not mine. It's his job to keep me safe. He's not supposed to leave stuff like this lying around. But I'm not going to do anything stupid. It's just something to play with.

She takes the razor out and pops the head off the body. She can't do much with it yet, it's built to cut hair while protecting delicate skin, but if she takes it apart she can get at the true prize, which is the little stack of cutting edges. She snaps off the top and picks diligently at the sides. They're not made to withstand a determined attack. If she works away at it for long enough, then eventually…

The razor head comes apart with a satisfying click. The blades spread out across her palm.

This is what her parents are terrified of, but they don't need to be. She's only curious. She's not really interested in tablets or razors or bleach. It's only that they've hidden everything dangerous away from her so successfully, they've started to acquire a charm all of their own.

She won't cut herself, she won't. She just wants to *see*. All teenagers experiment with danger, and now she's doing it too. This is a healthy sign, a normal thing. She presses a blade gingerly against the vein in the crook of her elbow, trying not to let herself flinch. They take blood from here. How much can it possibly hurt?

Remember when we saw that stupid movie about those two boys? Laurel says. *And they cut their thumbs and swapped blood? And we did it ourselves later on?*

She remembers it perfectly. The two of them, seven years old and crouched in their parents' wardrobe, clutching the kitchen knife they were forbidden to touch. The moment when she dropped the knife and had to fumble for it, and Laurel squeaked, *Be careful, don't cut yourself!* And they'd laughed as quietly as they could at their own absurdity, because what was the difference between a cut by accident and a cut on purpose? Then, the breathless tension as Willow pressed the point of the knife hard against the pad of her thumb, and the bright startling pain as it slipped beneath the surface of the skin and the blood began to flow.

You took ages, Willow thinks. *I was afraid mine was going to stop bleeding before you were ready. But then you did it. And we mashed our thumbs together and said,* Now you're my blood sister. *As if that was going to make us any closer than we already were. What was wrong with us? We were so fucking weird.*

She can see her pulse throbbing in the little fat blue worm of vein. It's surprisingly tough, like trying to cut into a rose-stem. Or is she not being brave enough? She bites her lip and presses harder, sawing a little, and then the pain of remembering is blotted out by a different pain, and she's rewarded with a thick dark trickle of blood.

The flow is steady and satisfying. It gathers to a rich point on her elbow, then frees itself in little droplets that patter onto the leaves under her feet. The bird – what sort of bird is it, anyway? A small brown one, like a million other small brown birds in the world – hops off its bramble. She closes her eyes, then opens them again. The bird is almost at her feet. It dips its head into the leaves. When it raises its beak, the end is wet with blood.

She wants to scream, but even this relief is forbidden to her. Instead she gasps silently, like a fish, her arms wheeling. The bird flutters upwards, and she thinks that if its wings brush against her skin, she will die.

It takes her a moment to coordinate her limbs, but then she

finds her way back into her body again and she's running, one fist clenched tight inside her pocket to keep hold of the blades, and it's not until she gets to the other side of the woods and throws herself over the fence, charging among the goats that toss their heads and scatter to the corners of the field, that she realises where she's going.

She comes towards the farmhouse through a thin muddy path that leads past vegetable beds filled with cabbages and salad leaves and a long stand of neglected-looking vines, with curling leaves and long browning bean-pods and withered tendrils coiling around sticks. The beds look untidy, but the smell of earth and greenery is comforting. On the other side of the vegetables, there's a hedge and a fence and then a field, where two pigs lie blissfully in a mud-wallow and bask in the sun. At the top of the garden, a worn wooden gate seals off the garden from the farmyard.

Is she really allowed in here? Katherine told her to visit whenever she wanted, but saying it isn't the same as meaning it. A couple of chickens are squabbling over scrummaging rights in a patch of ground that looks exactly the same as all the rest of the yard, but that must be better in some way only chickens know about. A flock of fat geese stalk around with tall necks, pecking bad-temperedly at each other. When she opens the gate, the geese turn towards her as if their heads are tied to the latch. She waits for them to lose interest in her before slipping inside.

What happens now? If she knocks at the door, what will she do when Katherine answers it? She can't just stand there, she'll look insane. Perhaps she can look around for a bit and creep away again and no one will know she's been here. The geese stretch their necks and hiss warningly, but don't come near. She wonders if a goose can actually hurt a person. When she takes her hand out of her pocket, she finds she's cut her fingers on the blades. Perhaps the geese can smell the damage. Perhaps that's why they're staying away.

Halfway down its length, the farmhouse gives way to

a series of stables. She wonders what goes on inside them. Milking, possibly? Feeding? Sleeping? Do goats come in at night, or do they live in their field all the time? Through a door that's closed at the bottom but open at the top, she hears a scuffling sound as if something's jumping about, and a quiet continuous stream of swearing.

The stable's divided by a chest-high panel of chicken wire with a gate in it. On one side of the panel stands the boy, Luca. On the other – guarding the gate with a menace that's surprising in a herbivore – is a plump white goat with a long, intelligent face and a duo of miniature replicas skittering nervously beside her. Luca is holding a pitchfork, and the mother goat's clearly decided this makes him a threat, because the expression in her big yellow eyes is clear and eloquent. *Don't you mess with me, mister, or I will destroy you.*

"You stupid fucking animal," Luca says in exasperation. "I'm not trying to *hurt* you, I'm trying to change your bastard bed. See?" He holds the fork out towards the goat. She lowers her head and scrapes at the straw with her foot. The smell of goat is overpowering.

"Look, get out of the fucking way, will you? Get in the corner and eat your food and let me get the place cleaned up." He gestures to a limp clump of leaves tossed in the corner. "I've got to get this done, all right. Stop fucking about and let me get on with it. Get in the bastard corner, you freak."

The goat jumps forward and tosses her head. The kids cower at their mother's ankles. One ducks its head beneath her stomach and takes a long, pointed nipple into its little mouth. The other jumps on the spot, straight up and straight back down again like a burst popcorn kernel. Willow wonders how the goat feels to touch, if its hair will be soft or coarse, and how warm the skin would be beneath.

"Jesus Christ," says Luca wearily. He leans the fork against the wall and pushes the gate open.

The goat squares her shoulders. Her head goes down. There's a firm little thump. Then Luca is leaning against the wall and gasping for breath, and the goat is back in her pen with a satisfied look on her face.

"You fucking bitch," Luca wheezes. "You utter fucking bitch." He grabs the pitchfork and shakes it towards her. "I ought to stab you though the fucking belly with this fork."

The goat looks at him smugly and rotates her jaw.

"For God's sake, will you please... let me... fucking... clean!" Luca lunges forward again, and the goat bleats in alarm. The pitchfork gleams bright and menacing. Willow imagines the sound it will make as it stabs into the goat's belly, the thick wet thud and the slow sucking squelch as he pulls it out again, and the high scream of the babies as they see their mother fall.

She wants to call out to him. She wants to shriek, *No! Don't! Don't hurt her! She's trying to protect her babies!* She charges into the stable and makes a wild grab for the pitchfork.

Without hesitating, Luca turns on her, his fist raised. Waiting for his blow to connect, knowing there's nothing she can do to stop it, she thinks of the phrase *a mask of rage*, and wonders if the intent, focused, desperate look he wears is truly a mask, or his real face, suddenly exposed. She looks at him, his pretty-boy features destroyed by anger, and thinks, *Shit. And I really thought I might like you. I'm such an idiot.*

And the next moment, the rage is replaced by a wide, cocky grin.

"Oh come on, you didn't think I was going to hit you, did I? Don't be such a loser. I don't hit girls." He shakes the pitchfork towards the goat. "I might still stab that bastard thing though. She's a fucking psycho. I think all goats must be."

Willow's pretty sure the goat isn't the potential psycho here. She holds her hand out for the pitchfork.

"Don't bother asking or nothing," Luca says, but passes it to her willingly enough. "Am I not worth talking to or something?"

She ought to find a way to explain, but she quite likes his belief that her silence is somehow under her control, so she shrugs dismissively, as if he's not worth her words. The goat and her kids huddle in one corner of the enclosure, watching her with bright, knowing eyes.

It's all right, she thinks, and opens the chicken wire gate.

"If you go in there she'll have you," Luca warns.

I'm not going to hurt you, Willow thinks. She forces herself to look away from the goats, watching them only from the corners of her eyes. *See? You're fine. I'm not with him. I'm not even like him. We can work this out. Why don't you come out here and wait while we clean up?*

And, as Luca watches incredulously, the goat shakes her head, looks around her, then walks out of the enclosure, closely followed by the two little kids.

So there, thinks Willow, with a hint of smugness.

"It's cos she knows I could kill her if I wanted," Luca says. "They get, like, grudges against people they know are stronger than they are."

It's crowded in the little area between the enclosure and the stable door. Willow can feel the warmth radiating from the goat's body. She isn't sure if she likes this or not. Maybe the goats feel the same, because one of kids lets out a mighty bleat, popcorns straight up in the air, hooks its front legs over the top of the stable door, scrabbles wildly, and disappears into the farmyard.

"Perfect." Luca shakes his head. "That's why you're supposed to keep them in the… Oh, no, don't you go as well!" Another leap, and the second kid follows the first over the top of the door. The mother goat looks mockingly over at Luca, stands up on her hind legs, drapes herself over the door and leaves them too.

"Well, that's brilliant," says Luca. "Good work there. Thanks for your help."

Yeah, that was totally my fault, Willow thinks. *You were doing fine without me. It's not like you couldn't get in to clean them because they thought you were going to stab them with the pitchfork or anything.* Bereft of sarcasm, she settles for going into the enclosure and jabbing at the straw with the pitchfork.

"Oh, come here." Luca takes the pitchfork from her. "We've got to rake it all out and put it in the barrow outside and take it to the muckheap, and then put down new straw." He sighs. "And then get the fucking goats back in."

We don't have to do anything, Willow thinks. *That's your job.* Nonetheless, she goes out to the yard for the wheelbarrow, surprised by how hard it is to steer. As she jams it into the doorway, she wonders how Luca was ever going to get it into the stable without letting the goats out.

"You're supposed to pull the gate right round and pen them in the corner," Luca says, demonstrating. "I think it's a bit cruel to be honest. You're doing some of this too, by the way. There'll be a spade or something in the shed next door."

Willow folds her arms and looks at him.

"You let the bastard things out," he says. "So you can help get them back in and all. And we can't get them in until we've cleaned them out. So you're helping. All right? Don't even bother arguing cos you ain't going nowhere until we're done."

The knowledge that she could ignore him and walk away from the whole mess makes her feel more warmly towards joining in. In the tool shed next door, she helps herself to a shovel. One of the kids appears briefly in the door and stares at her, skittering away when it sees her looking. Outside, she finds it balancing on a bale of straw with its head held high. *You're the King of the Castle,* she thinks, and reaches out to pet its head. It lets her tickle briefly at the bony patch of hair between its tiny nubby horns.

Cleaning out the shed takes a long time because Luca is as squeamish about the dirty straw as she is, holding the pitchfork at arm's length and shuddering in disgust when a few brown-black pebbles tumble against his hand. A true-bred farm boy would either touch the goat shit without flinching, or have a pair of gloves tucked in his back pocket. He's an outsider, like her.

"Fucking disgusting creatures," Luca says as he wheels the barrow inexpertly into the yard. "Can't believe the amount they shit. Ought to send them all for slaughter. Katherine says the herd's getting too big." Nonetheless he spreads the straw with care, testing it for softness with one hand and adding an extra layer, and lays down a heap of cabbage leaves like an offering. Willow thinks about the look on his face as he turned on her, the heft and lift of his fist.

"Right," Luca says, leaning casually on the pitchfork. It slips against the concrete and he staggers a little. "How are we supposed to catch the little fuckers?"

In the yard, the kids are playing with an upturned bucket, taking it in turns to push each other off. The mama goat stands watchfully by, chewing a mouthful of bramble leaves.

"If we get the babies, d'you reckon she'll follow?" Luca grabs for the kid on the bucket. It skips out of his reach, tossing its head as it bounces joyfully away.

"Little shit," says Luca. "We've got no chance."

Of course we've got a chance, Willow thinks scornfully. If goats were that hard to catch, how would they ever have been domesticated in the first place? Two humans can catch three goats easily.

Except that every time they get close to one of the kids, it slithers out between their knees, or bounces through an impossibly small gap, or leaps in an unexpected direction, or – when Luca finally grabs a triumphant handful of flesh and hair – lets out such an impassioned wail of despair that he lets it go again. The mama goat watches, but does nothing to either help or hinder. Perhaps she's enjoying the show.

"I can't believe you fucking let them out," Luca pants, gasping for breath. He's just chased both kids three times around the yard, trying to panic them into returning to their stable. "What were you thinking?"

Willow is so angry with this characterisation that for a glorious, treacherous minute, she thinks she might manage to say something in reply. Her mouth opens, she takes a deep breath, the words hover on her tongue.

At least I fixed it so we could clean them out.

And the disappointment when she can't speak is so huge that she feels tears prickle at the corners of her eyes.

"God's sake, I'm *kidding*! Don't be so sensitive. We'll get them back in. No one's going to shout at you or nothing. Katherine'll be fine, she always is. I let the geese into the lane once. She wasn't too mad about that either."

What's the connection between Luca and Katherine? Katherine belongs here and Luca doesn't, so she can't be his mum. Is she his aunt, maybe? And if he is, why does he call her by her first name? The mama goat has finished eating bramble and moved on to the single dandelion that pokes out, thin and spindly, from the rich mucky loam around the base of the hen house. One of the hens stretches its long neck to peck at the stalk, but the goat turns her head and the hen backs away again.

"Tell you what. If you get them in by yourself, I'll give you a fiver." He looks her up and down. "And if you can't, you've got to give me a flash of your tits."

The way he's looking at her makes her tingle. She's not sure if it's excitement or rage. How dare he? But then again…

The kids are prancing around together, bleating and butting heads, but when they see her coming, they scatter in alarm. She hesitates, then chooses her target. The little goat runs and runs, but she has a plan, and she's pretty sure plans beat agility in the end.

Instead of chasing it around the yard, she puts her arms out and herds it towards the wall. The goat leaps and dashes left and right, but she persists until she has it penned in a corner. Then she grabs, slipping one hand under its chest and one around its warm little middle. The goat gives a piteous bleat and she has to force herself not to let it go.

"Mate!" Luca frowns. "Be a bit gentle, will you?"

She holds the goat against her, feeling its heart beating

against her hand. She's not sure if it's frightened, or if this is how it always is. The mama goat watches her with a meaningful expression.

Right, then. I've got what you want. Now you're going to do what I want. Moving slowly, the mama goat right at her heels, Willow carries the kid into the stable and lays it reverently on the clean straw. The second kid bounds in behind its mother, and ducks beneath her belly for a celebratory suckle. Luca slams the gate shut. The mama goat sniffs briefly at the straw, then dips her head to the cabbage leaves.

"Well done." Luca sounds as if he really means it. "I mean, it was your fault they were out in the first place and that, but still. And I was looking forward to you flashing me and all. Hey, you're covered in hair." He reaches out and brushes at her shoulder in a rough, brotherly fashion. She tries not to flinch at the unexpected contact.

"Fucking chill out, will you?" His voice is so gentle that it takes her a moment to hear the harshness of the words. "Don't be such a pleb. I'm not trying to, fucking, grope you or nothing… You've got goat hair on you, that's all."

Her breath is suddenly short. She's not sure if she likes him touching her or not. Can he see that he's making her uncomfortable? Is that why he's doing it?

"I mean, it's not like you haven't got nice tits or nothing. Cos you have."

The tender crease of her elbow stings where she sawed at it earlier. Has it started bleeding again? If it has, she hopes the blood won't soak through her sleeve.

"Anyway." His fingers have come to rest above her collarbone. Is he going to touch her breast? And if he did, would she like it?

"Can I ask you something?" His face is very serious, as if he's trying to solve a complex problem in his head. She nods.

"This not talking thing… when you go to McDonald's, how do you place an order?"

Her cheeks burn.

CHAPTER TWELVE

"Oh, come on." Luca touches one finger to her cheek. "Don't be like that. I was only messing about."

She's not crying. Why would she be crying? He's nothing to her, just some boy. It's time for her to go home anyway.

"Look, I'm sorry, all right? I was only messing with you, I wasn't being serious. You've got to learn to take a joke."

I don't have to do anything you say, she thinks, and turns away.

"I know I'm a bit of a knobhead sometimes. Don't go off in a huff with me, Willow. Please."

It's the word *please* that makes her hesitate, the way he sounds as if he really is sorry, as if he really does know he's been a bit (or more than a bit) of a knobhead. And as she hesitates, Katherine appears, striding across the yard in thick green wellies coated with streaks of mud, and they can both relax because now there's someone else here who will take charge and determine what happens next.

"Luca, are you done with mucking out? Hello, Willow, nice to see you. Come and get cleaned up, the pair of you. Lunch on the table in ten minutes."

So she's going to see inside the farmhouse after all, without even having to knock on the door. She follows Luca in through the little porch and into a dark, welcoming room where a single chair sits by a huge enamel stove, several cats lie stretched out on the rug, and a thin Grandfather clock ticks sedately in the corner. The warmth of the stove is instantly seductive, a soft invitation to laziness. If she was here on her own, Willow would be lying down among the cats, letting her belly grow warm and toasty in the heat.

"Shoes off," says Katherine. Willow sees the strands of straw she's already left on the floor and cringes, but Katherine doesn't seem to mind. "That's it. Now you can get washed up. Bathroom's upstairs on the left if you want it. Or you can wash in the kitchen."

The window of the bathroom is set so low in the wall that the frame is level with the floor. Willow washes her hands at the basin, astounded by the grime that comes off in the suds, and wonders if all the upstairs windows are the same. Maybe it's a sign that it used to be a barn. Does every house around here have this slight air of improvisation, of having been repurposed from something else? Nevertheless, this house is welcoming in a way that Joe's house, no matter how clean and how full of food, somehow lacks. She can feel the life pulsing in the walls. Coming down from the bathroom, she pauses by the stove to stroke the cats, and to listen in on Luca and Katherine talking in the kitchen.

"She is *really* strange," says Luca, with some feeling, and Willow feels her shoulders clench up tight. "Does she talk, like, fucking, *ever*?"

"Language."

"But is there something wrong with her?"

Katherine just laughs.

"I mean, obviously there's *something* wrong, cos she doesn't ever talk, but—"

"I'm sure she's got her reasons," says Katherine. "She'll tell you if she wants you to know."

"So you do know, then? Why she doesn't talk?"

"And do you know what? She doesn't know a damn thing about you either." Willow can't see into the kitchen, but she imagines that Katherine might have reached out to ruffle Luca's hair. "Check your sleeves for goat shit, okay? Oh, hello, Willow. No, it's all right, don't worry about taking stuff through, this is the last of it."

Katherine picks up a slab of wood where a fat loaf of bread rests, and carries it away. At the sink, Luca has his sleeves rolled his elbows and is soaping his arms as carefully as if he's about to operate. When he sees Willow, he rolls them down hastily.

"Otherwise you end up with goat shit in your dinner," he says, pulling his cuffs over his hands as if thoroughly washing is somehow shameful. "Or chicken shit. Or goose shit. Or pig shit. Farming is basically just every type of shit you can imagine."

She's already washed upstairs, but now she feels as if she needs to do it again. There's a distinct tideline at her wrists. Luca passes her the bar of soap, hovers critically as she uses it, then passes her the towel. *I can do this myself,* she thinks, but lets him supervise anyway, so he can re-establish his expertise at farm living. The cats raise their heads to watch as they walk back through the entrance room and into a cosy dining room with a low ceiling, deep-set windows, cupboards built into the fireplace alcoves, and a huge table that fills half the floor space.

Lunch is fresh bread, wedges cut from a huge ham, a bowl of tomatoes, a yellowy brick of butter, a bowl of salad, a jar of pickled onions floating in their vinegar bath like miniature aliens, a jug of iced water, and a huge teapot. There are crumbs on the tablecloth and a pile of papers in the window. The rag rug by the fireplace has a dusting of cat hair, and something smooth and slinky coils and purrs around her feet. It's the most relaxed Willow has felt in weeks. She tries not to eat too greedily, forcing herself to slow down and take small bites.

"Those new little kids are coming on nicely." The sight of Katherine pouring tea from the pot reminds Willow of her grandmother. "They can go out later."

"Okay."

"Take them down this afternoon. It's fun seeing the little ones out for the first time." Luca and Willow exchange a secret guilty glance. "Willow, if you've got time you can give him a hand if you like."

Time. Has she got time? And what time is it anyway? She's been out for ages, she left without saying where she was going, and Joe has no idea where she is. What if he's looking for her? She fumbles frantically in her pocket for her phone.

"It's a bit after one," Katherine says. "It's all right. I was on the phone to him earlier. He knows you're here. Have you both got room for cake?" She's already on her way out of the room, as if wanting cake is a foregone conclusion. Willow thinks about Katherine calling Joe to tell him Willow's all right, and cringes.

"It wasn't because of you," Luca says while Katherine is out of earshot. "They call each other every morning. Like he's her teenage kid or something. I thought he *was* her kid for a while. It's fucking weird. I don't know why she does it. I mean, if she was a bit younger I'd think maybe he was like her toy boy or something."

Well, that's definitely not it, Willow thinks, with some smugness. She puts her phone back in her pocket. Luca watches her curiously.

"So can you make phone calls?"

She tears a careful mouthful from the crust of her bread.

"How about text messages? Can you send text messages and that? I mean, I could give you my number and you can send texts instead of talking."

He's trying to find a way to talk to her. Why can't she do something to meet him halfway? She can feel the blood rising in her cheeks again. Luca's fingers scrabble over the tablecloth and fold around the elaborate bone-handled pickle-fork that lies beside the jar of pickled onions, ancient and fiddly looking. He jabs it experimentally into the tablecloth, and smiles.

"How *does* it work, then?" Without warning, his free hand

grabs her around the wrist, pulling her arm across the table towards him. He touches the tines of the fork gently to her skin, and she tries not to shiver. "If I jabbed this into the back of your hand, would you scream?"

Would she? She truly doesn't know. She didn't scream earlier, when the thick rope of her vein yielded to the edge of the razor. Was that because she knew what was coming? Luca is staring into her face now, intent and predatory. Is he genuinely going to stab her with the fork? Is she quick enough to stop him?

You don't frighten me, she thinks. She takes the fork from his hand and reaches for the pickled onions.

"Mate." Luca looks disgusted. "You are *not* going to eat one of those things."

Without pausing, she unscrews the lid. A blast of spicy vinegar claws at the back of her throat.

"Seriously. Don't do it." Luca is watching in fascination. "They're not, like, normal ones. She makes them herself. She says they're enough to wake the dead."

For a moment, she imagines the onions as eyeballs, and the end of the fork becomes the stabbing beak of a bird.

"Hey, don't make yourself sick to impress me," says Luca. "I can't fucking stand puke, it makes me puke too."

It's not the onions, she thinks, *it's you joking about waking the…* But no, it's better that he doesn't know. She's sick of people watching what they say around her. She stabs at the biggest onion in the jar, lifts it dripping into the air, and shoves it into her mouth.

The crunch echoes through her skull. Vinegar floods out and burns her tongue. Her eyes water and she feel as if she might choke. She chews and swallows, chews and swallows, wondering if she'll die from the burn, if she'll ever reach the end of her mouthful, if she'll be able to keep it down once she's swallowed, and what she was thinking in the first place. Then, blessedly, her mouth's empty and her stomach resigns itself to what she's done, and she wipes the tears from her cheeks and finds Luca is staring at her in awe.

"I literally cannot believe you did that," he says.

"Did what?" Katherine reappears with a cake slick with buttercream and topped with walnuts.

"She ate an onion," said Luca, and Katherine smiles.

"Really? And I always thought they were uneatable. Good work there." She puts the cake down and hands Willow a napkin. "Mop yourself up and have some cake."

Luca is watching Willow as if he's not quite sure what she might do next. She dabs at her eyes, and thinks how peaceful it is to be with someone who doesn't ask *why* she felt compelled to eat the pickled onion in the first place. Katherine is transferring a large wedge of cake into a small tin with roses on the lid.

"Take this back for Joe," she says.

She's not sure how Luca ends up walking her home.

He gives her a casual half-wave when she leaves, the kind that tells her he's not really interested in her going and certainly isn't bothered about her coming back, and disappears upstairs before she's even out of the door. Then, as she lingers by the vegetable beds, stealing a long dangling brown pod so she can break it open and examine the row of half-dried beans nestled inside, he's suddenly there again, carrying an empty bucket that bounces irritatingly between them on the way down to the goat field. In the field, he wanders into the straw stack enclosure where the goats seem to be having a meeting, and she hovers for a moment, not sure if she's supposed to wait for him. When he doesn't come back, she sets off alone, hoping he hasn't seen her hanging around. Then somehow he's ahead of her at the fence – without his bucket this time – offering his hand for balance as she climbs over, letting go again as soon as they're in the woods.

Then they're wandering side by side along the path,

scuffling at the leaves to hide their shyness. Even if she could speak, Willow can't think of a thing she'd want to say.

"I saw a deer in here once," Luca offers suddenly. "I thought it was one of the goats got out into the woods. It was massive. Not hidden away or anything. Just crashing around in the bushes like an idiot."

She glances around the woods. Is this likely? Could an animal the size of a deer really be hiding in these widely spaced trees?

"It was sort of spotty," he goes on. "Fur spots, I mean, not diseased spots. Big eyes. Legs like sticks. You all right, mate?"

In the summer before their last summer, she and Laurel had leaned from the window of their car and fed deer at a safari park, murmuring in amazement at the touch of their nibbling lips, the wetness of their noses, their strong gamey scent. Afterwards Laurel had found a tick burrowing against her wrist, and her mother had pulled it off with tweezers and thrown it away. Will she ever get to the end of these memories that lurch out of the darkness? Will there ever be a day when she can remember without feeling like she's being stabbed in the chest?

"It wasn't dangerous or nothing. Only had these little stumpy antlers, crappy little things they were. Wouldn't be able to take out a mouse with them. And it was on its own as well. Maybe it was lonely. It didn't run when it saw me looking."

She keeps her focus on the placement of her feet on the uneven ground, breathes slowly and carefully. Her grief is for her and no one else. She will not show it to Luca, a boy she barely knows.

"They kick the young males out of the herd so they don't shag their mothers and sisters and that. Shame I didn't have a gun with me." He grabs at a long twig and pulls it off from the tree, leaving a greenish-white wound in the bark, and takes aim. "One shot. Straight to the heart. Drop it on the spot."

Shut up, she thinks. *Shut up, shut up, shut up.*

"Then after that, it's just butchery." Luca flings his stick away, cracks his knuckles with elaborate casualness. "Cut its throat and bleed it out... open up its stomach... take its guts out so they don't, like, taint the meat on the way home... leave them for the foxes and that... what? You ate that ham at lunchtime. Where d'you think meat comes from, you pleb?"

She swallows hard and forces herself to look at him.

"Oh my God, mate. You are so fucking easy to upset! I didn't actually do it, you know. Just stared it down until it got scared and legged it off into the woods. Left it for that survivalist nutter that lives out here. He'd take it down in a minute. No fucking question. Someone did warn you about him, yeah?"

She nods, but she can tell Luca is going to tell her anyway.

"What it is, he's this local legend, right. Lives in this, like, log cabin job he built himself. They don't normally let people build stuff in the woods but he's got some sort of agreement with the authorities and that. He used all local materials, like logs and twigs and stuff he found lying around the place."

If Luca had seen the house, there's no way he could believe it was built from logs and twigs and stuff he found lying around the place. For all his talk of stabbing goats and shooting deer, Luca has never been up the path to spy on the Slaughter Man. He's not as tough as she is. She keeps her face carefully neutral.

"He's completely off-grid. Harvests rainwater, has a generator for electricity that runs off, I don't know, diesel or solar or hamsters in wheels or something. And he's got loads of guns and that, and he absolutely hates anyone disturbing him, so nobody ever does. I mean, he probably belongs behind fucking bars to be honest, but for now he's, like, out there." Luca pauses dramatically, then plays his best card. "See that path there? You follow that path for about half a mile and it comes out right by his house. Only, don't. Seriously. Don't ever go there. Cos what he's known for, right, is that he kills his own meat." Luca's eyes gleam as he looks Willow up and down. "And you'd be, like, prey."

In her ears is a ringing, a sound like the ringing of a bone-saw, which she's never heard in life, but that haunts her dreams. She can see it glinting beneath harsh blue lights, feel the chill in the air that keeps the meat fresh, as the saw descends and takes its first greedy bite out of the ribcage. She can hear the rustle and squeak of the blue plastic gloves as the hands slither in, reaching for the red-black glossy slickness of the heart...

"Fuck." She's leaning against something warm and yielding, something that staggers a little under her weight. "Willow, I swear I was messing with you, all right? We're having a laugh, I'm not serious. Come on, sit down here for a minute. I've got you. It's okay."

She's all right. She's all right. She's just out of breath. It's been weeks since she did this much exercise. She's going to be fine. She's very conscious of Luca's arm, the shy pressure of it against her waist, the warmth of his splayed fingers. She sits down on the log. Her legs are trembling with exertion, not with fear. She's absolutely fine. Luca hovers and stares like a visitor in a zoo.

"You want to stop taking everything so literally. I don't mean nothing by all that stuff." He sits down beside her on the log. "I mean, if you're not going to speak then it's all on me, right? You can't complain if I don't pick something you want to talk about."

I didn't even ask you to come with me, she thinks. *You invited yourself along.*

"I didn't mean to make you pass out, though," he says. "I mean, it was kind of funny seeing you go that colour, but I'm not trying to... I mean... You need to be a bit tougher, you know? And start fucking talking! Or you're going to be stuck with me going on about serial killers and that."

One of her trainers is coming unfastened. She reties her

lace, making a careful double bow, and wonders what he would think if he knew.

"I mean, I know you've got your reasons for not talking. Katherine hasn't said nothing. I know she knows why, but she won't tell me. She never explains nothing about anyone." He raises his finger to his mouth and bites at a shred of loose skin by the nail. "It's the best thing about living here to be honest. No one explaining stuff. I bet you don't even... I mean, you know Katherine's not my mum, yeah?"

She nods.

"Well, she's not like my auntie or nothing. We're not related at all. She's my foster mum." He's trying to look at her as he says this, but he can't quite meet her gaze. Instead he's looking intently at a point past her left ear. "I mean, I'm in care." He says this very loudly and aggressively, as if daring her to be sorry for him.

He's trying to trade secrets, fishing for the explanation that will make sense of her silence. If she could tell him what happened to make her like this, would she want to?

"She doesn't do it for free or nothing," Luca continues. "She gets paid and that. It's like a job really. I've been here about six months now."

It's costing him something to tell her this. What can she give him in return when she can't speak? Their eyes flick over each other's faces, then away.

"Anyway. So what, right? Not like it matters or nothing." She's not sure what to make of his expression. Is he disappointed that she hasn't shared something in return? Even if she could speak, how on earth could she say it? *I was an identical twin. I am an identical twin. I'm not an identical twin any more.* She reaches into her pocket and takes out her phone.

"What?" Luca takes the phone from her. "You want my number or something? So you can text me? Only the signal's a bit crap around here so don't be all funny with me if I don't text back." He turns it over, presses with his thumb, holds it out to her.

"You need to unlock it."

No, she thinks. *For God's sake, can you shut up for a minute and look at what I'm showing you? Look at the lock-screen photograph.*

"Hello? Anyone in there?" He waves his hand in front of her face. "I can't unlock your phone." He presses again. "Look. Locked. My thumb won't work."

Why is she trying to show him something so personal? This is a mistake. She's about to take her phone back, let him put in his number so he can wait for the text she'll never be able to send, when she sees him suddenly get it, sees him realise what he's looking at, and her stomach sinks because now there's no going back.

"Hey," he says. "Is that you with your sister? Shit. She looks just like you." His face is radiant with delighted astonishment. "Oh my God. Are you an identical twin? Have I met both of you and you've been, I don't know, running some fucking number on me?"

She shakes her head and wills her eyes not to fill with tears. He's not looking, he's not listening, he's lost in the sound of his own voice.

"This is so fucking cool. I've never met identical twins before. Where is she? Which one are you? Was it you both times? I mean, I'd like to think I'd know, but—"

She takes her phone back from him. He doesn't even notice.

"Is that why you don't speak? Because I might guess which one I'm talking to? Do you both sound different or something? How would that even work, though? I mean, aren't you supposed to be, like, exactly the same?"

Yes. Yes. We are. But now we're not. I'm alive and Laurel's... She presses her hand hard against the throb of her heart. Her perfect, treacherous heart.

"Are you going to fill me in, or have I got to guess?" He looks exasperated now, as if she's doing this solely to get on his nerves. Maybe he'll get bored and walk away. "Is she here with you? Yes? No? No. Okay. So did you have, I don't know, a big fight with her or something? And you had to be separated, like, for your own good?" She shakes her head. "Did one of you commit a murder? And now they don't know which one of you to put on trial? Well, Jesus, I don't know, do I? Or is one of you—"

He stops as abruptly as if he's been shot. The weight of his guess hangs in the air between them.

"Fuck," he whispers. "Sorry. I don't mean to… Oh, shit. Is that it? Is your sister… is she… is she ill? Is she going to… Or has she, is she already… Oh my God, is your sister…"

Say it, Willow thinks furiously. *Say that word. Say 'Dead'. I dare you. Go on.*

His face turns white with shock, then crimson with shame. Behind his eyes, she can see their conversations spooling out across his memory, a grinning parade of all the things he should never have said. Hurting. Stabbing. Killing. Butchery. The Slaughter Man who lives at the end of the path. Pickled onions that could wake the dead.

"I mean, how was I supposed to know?" She can't tell if he's talking to her or to himself. "How the fuck was I supposed to—"

Maybe I didn't want you to know, she thinks. *Maybe I liked you not knowing.*

"Well, fuck this for a laugh," he says. "See you around, mate."

And then he's gone, not running, not hurrying, simply swaggering off the way he came, leaving her alone in the woods.

Fuck you too, she thinks, and strides away in the opposite direction.

She's half-expecting to meet Joe coming through the woods to meet her, and then half-expecting he'll be hovering by the back door, frowny-faced and anxious, ready to pounce the moment she arrives back. Instead, when she pushes the kitchen door open, she sees Joe sitting slumped at the kitchen table, his back to the door, the phone pressed to his ear.

"I know you're busy." Joe's voice is low and hesitant. "Or are you? I don't really know what you do when you're not with me. Not in detail, anyway. Are you at work?"

A pause. She can hear the tinny alien chitter that tells her the other person is replying.

"I know, I know, I know what we said. I'm sorry. It's just you've been gone so long. I miss you. So, so much. It's so lonely without you."

Another pause. He must be talking to his partner. Is he pleased to hear from Joe, or annoyed that his working day's been broken into? Or is it night-time, in the place where he is now?

"You know I do." Joe's voice is low and urgent. "I miss everything about you. I miss your smile. I miss your smell. I miss kissing you. I miss holding you. I miss your mouth. I miss your hands."

She knows she shouldn't be listening. She should go back outside and then come in more noisily so he'll know she's there. But it's so strange to hear someone in real life, someone she knows, sounding so tender, so open. It's like something out of a romantic movie.

"I miss your cock."

The embarrassment is total, as if someone's poured scalding water over her head. Without hesitation, without worrying whether she can be heard, she flees outside. Then, horrified by the thought that Joe might hear her, she races up the outside stairs to her bedroom. Thank God the door's unlocked. She can pretend she's been in here for ages, come downstairs and surprise him. She wishes she could take her brain out and scrub it.

I miss your cock. That's not sweet, that's disgusting. No, it's not, she's being a child. If anyone's disgusting, it's her, for listening in. They're adults. Of course they do more than hold hands and kiss. But still, did he have to say… She shies away from the words. *Stop being such a child. It's not gross. It's not gross. It's not.* But she somehow hadn't thought of her uncle as…

Are they still on the phone to each other? What would she have heard if she'd stayed there longer? *I miss your cock.* Was that the start of them having phone sex? Is her uncle in the kitchen right now, his belt unbuckled, his jeans unfastened, one hand on his phone and the other on his… She squeezes her eyes tight and wills herself not to think about it.

Her bed has been remade, the sheets crisp and fragrant, the quilt smoothed perfectly into place. She'll concentrate on that, not on the awful thing she overheard and definitely not on what Luca said, but on the nice thing Joe's done for her. She'll lie here on the quilt, maybe even have a little sleep, and then by the time she goes downstairs, she'll be able to forget all about it.

On the edge of sleep, her mind wanders to her parents. What might they be doing, in the secret darkness of their home with no need to worry about waking their daughters?

CHAPTER THIRTEEN

"It's so quiet here without you."

Hearing her mother talk is like a caress of her hair, like a kiss on her forehead. Willow closes her eyes and lets the words flow over her.

"Your dad and I have had to start having proper conversations." Her mother's laugh sounds easy and natural, as if she's been doing more of it recently. "Just the two of us, all by ourselves. I thought we might have forgotten how. We talked about politics last night. Can you believe it?"

In the time before, there were sometimes family Sunday lunches where – instead of brief exchanges about what film they might watch later and whose job it was to clear the table – they would have proper conversations. A *proper conversation* involved the exchange of real and serious views, about life and death and healthcare and euthanasia and US politics and the gender pay gap. In a *proper conversation*, everyone's opinions were valued, and the phrases *because I'm the adult here* or *that's just you being old* were never spoken. A *proper conversation* meant a chance to discover that, as well as loving each other as family, they also liked each other as people. A *proper conversation* couldn't be engineered or planned for; it could only happen spontaneously, thanks to some strange confluence of time and inclination and the right question being asked at the right time. There had been no *proper conversations* since The Day.

"It made me realise," her mother said, as if she's following the same path as Willow. "We haven't really talked properly since… since Laurel died. I've missed that so much."

And then I stopped talking all together. Willow aches with longing.

"Do you remember the time Laurel asked your dad if he got paid twenty per cent more than his female colleagues? And you said he ought to tell them what he earned, so they could compare and see if they were being underpaid?"

The memory swims upwards like a fish. She remembers sunlight pouring through the window, and the scent of the jug of daffodils on the table, the blooms going over and pungent with pollen. She remembers she and Laurel simultaneously realising they had their father on the ropes. *Yeah, Dad, you should do that. It'd be brilliant. I mean, you don't think we should get twenty per cent less just because we have vaginas, do you? So stand up for your colleagues! Be an ally. You'll be our hero.* And the look on their father's face. Boxed into a corner by experts, or maybe just a man who knew he was outnumbered. His quick glance towards their mother, wondering if he was allowed to call them out for saying *vagina*.

"She was so fierce," her mother says. "You both were." She catches herself. "I mean… I mean—"

But what does her mother mean? Willow closes her eyes. She doesn't want to talk about Laurel. She only wants to hear her mother speaking to her.

"Anyway. Joe says you've made friends with a local boy who lives on a farm, is that right?"

She's been trying not to give Luca any headspace at all. *A local boy who lives on a farm. Made friends.* It sounds so healthy, so wholesome. Nothing at all like the sick-sweet feeling in her chest and stomach when she was near him. It's probably for the best that she hasn't seen him since he walked away from her that day.

"I couldn't work out if he meant friend or, you know, *friend*," her mother continues. "I mean, I know you probably wouldn't want to tell us anyway."

Identical twins in their teens. In the days before, she and Laurel were uneasily conscious of the seedy half-formed fantasies their doubled nature provoked, growing and swelling like an underground tuber. The questions, from strangers sharing the same train journey or standing behind them in a queue or even selling them popcorn at the cinema: *Do you ever pretend to be each other? Do you wear each other's clothes? If one of you showed up to the other one's date, would your boyfriend know the difference?* It had made them both wary of the boys who asked them out; they were never quite sure if it was their singular, different selves, or their doubled nature, that had pricked the boys' interest. She remembers Luca in the woods, the astonished joy when he first saw the photograph.

"It's all right to be happy, you know."

The unexpected words jolt Willow's gut so that she lets out a little gasp of surprise.

"Willow? Sweetie? Did you—?"

If she could speak, what would she say?

"Happiness is so precious," her mother continues at last. "I know nothing's the same without Laurel. We'll all miss her every day of our lives, and that's never going to stop. But we have to learn to carry that, find ways to be happy alongside all that grief. Because there's so much life still left to live, and I want – *we* want – you to have it all, all the lovely things you can still have."

But we're not going out, Willow thinks. *I'm not even going to see him again. He's a complete dickhead. If you knew…*

"And I know Laurel would want you to be happy," her mother continues.

Would she, though? If she'd died and Laurel had lived,

would she have been okay about Laurel going on without her? Each day takes Willow further away, as if they were taking a train journey and Laurel got off at an earlier station. One thing she's sure of: Laurel would have hated Luca.

The sky outside's growing dusky, but the curtains aren't closed yet. If Willow opens her eyes, Laurel will look back at her from the windowpane.

CHAPTER FOURTEEN

"Right." Joe straightens the corner of the tablecloth and minutely arranges a fork. "The table's laid. The salad's ready for dressing. The cheese is out of the fridge. We're good." He catches Willow watching him and gives her a wink. "Never ask a gay man to host lunch. We're a nightmare."

But at least you know where to get all the best deli meats, she thinks. Would this be too rude to say out loud? Maybe it's a good thing she can't speak. Joe's smile is bright and innocent. She'd never have guessed at that other side of him, the man who hunched urgently over the phone and murmured his longing across the distance between the two of them.

No, she thinks. *Think about something else.* She neatens the cheeses on their flat slate platter, and turns the jars filled with three different kinds of chutney so the labels are aligned.

What's the matter with her? She's started to adopt Joe's habits: tidying things that are already tidy enough, assigning places for objects she's previously left lying wherever she last finished using them, wiping every surface she sees then washing her hands afterwards. Her bedroom looks almost as unused as the day she first came. Cleaning and tidying has begun to feel like a ritual, and the farmhouse has begun to feel like another world, somewhere she visited once but will not go back to again; the pigs in their mudbath, the hens and geese roaming the yard, the clever suspicious faces of the goats.

Every part of Katherine's home teemed with life, leaving you smeared in it, coated in it, grimy with it. Did she really chase goats round the farmyard and hold one of the kids in her arms? Has she imagined the sprawl of cats by the huge enamel stove, reaching their arms out and stretching their long bellies for her to stroke?

Did Luca wrap his fingers around her wrist and rest the sharp points of the pickle fork against her skin, whispering threats that sounded like promises?

No, she thinks. *Think about something else*. Her mind serves up an image of a goose flinging itself across the yard, hissing and flapping its wings, and Katherine grabbing it effortlessly by the neck and saying firmly, "No, you don't. Go on with you." And after a minute the goose calmed down again and retreated to a corner, where it consoled itself by pecking viciously at another goose that happened to be walking past. Did that really happen? Or did she make it up? She won't go back again – Luca has seen to that – but there's a special pleasure in turning over her memories like a stone in her pocket. Her room here is beautiful, her Uncle Joe is kind and loving, but there's still something missing.

(*Of course there's something bloody missing*. Laurel is here, and she's not pleased. *Are you forgetting me?*

For God's sake, not everything's about you! Willow's shocked by her own anger; she forces herself to breathe through it and let it go. *I'm sorry, I'm sorry, I didn't mean that. I only meant this place is so... so...*)

What is the word she's looking for? She almost had it, but now it's gone again. Staring at Joe, humming to himself as he arranges crackers on a plate and absent-mindedly rubbing a water stain off the edge of the sink with one finger, she has the sense that despite his cheerful little song, he's not relaxed at all. He's coiled up tight inside his own skin, making preparations, holding himself ready and alert. *Waiting*.

Well, of course he's waiting. They've got visitors due any minute. But then, why is he like this all the time?

And then Katherine and Luca arrive, with the suddenness that comes when there's no crunch of car wheels to announce you. Katherine wears a pretty pink tea dress with roses printed on it, incongruously teamed with tall green wellies. Luca trails reluctantly behind her in the masculine version of Willow's own outfit. Skinny jeans and Converse trainers. A band t-shirt. A hoodie that he'll defiantly describe as 'my new one' if anyone tells him he's not dressed smartly enough. Does anyone tell him this? She can't imagine Katherine fussing about someone else's clothes.

"Hey, lovely lady. Sorry it's been so long." Joe holds his arms out to Katherine for an embrace.

"How are you?" Katherine hugs Joe tightly for a minute, then looks carefully into his face. "Not too lonely?"

"I'm fine." Joe's smile is sweet and confident. "It's not for ever, you know. And I've got Willow keeping me company."

Luca glances awkwardly at Willow, then looks away again. The quick word he mutters in her direction could be 'hi', but it's over so fast it's hard to be sure. She gives him a grudging nod, but she's not sure he's even looking. Instead he's messing about with the positioning of his beanie hat, which he took off as soon as he came in and is now trying to put back on again without anyone noticing. Katherine takes off her wellies and replaces them with black silky-looking ballet pumps with fat ribbony roses on the toes, produced from her dress pocket like a magic trick. Her long grey-black hair fans out around her face. She looks surprisingly pretty.

"The pigs are coming on well," she tells Joe. "Be ready to go soon."

"They're doing all right, then?"

"Happy as anything. Big fat porkers they are now. They'll do you proud. I've got some kids about ready to go too. I'll give Francis a call in a couple of weeks, so have a think about how you want them dressing."

Joe laughs. "What would I know about dressing a pig? You pick, and I'll go along with it and pay the bill."

Joe and Katherine are easy and relaxed with each other, which makes up for the stubborn silence between Willow and Luca. Thank God no one's suggested they go off and leave the adults to talk; thank God all they have to do is sit at the table and not look at each other. Joe pours tea for himself and Katherine. She hasn't seen anyone use a teapot that she can remember in her entire life, and now she knows two people who seem to think it's perfectly normal behaviour.

"There's Coke and Diet Coke and various other awful fizzy things in the fridge," Joe says to Luca. "Help yourself to whatever you want. Willow, do you want to show him what there is?"

She's sure Luca is more than capable of opening the fridge door and looking inside, but she stands up anyway, and offers him a silent tour of the contents of the bottom drawers. The cans stand two-by-two, four each of everything. Luca chooses a can of Pepsi Max. Willow resists the urge to re-arrange the remaining cans to fill the space.

"What about you? Are you having one too?" He's trying to catch her eye. Tough luck; she's not interested. She takes a can of Fanta without looking at him, and sits back down at the table.

Despite the presence of two silent teenagers, the lunch is surprisingly not awkward. Joe and Katherine keep up an effortless flow of quiet conversation, talking about nothing in particular that Willow can put her finger on, just filling the air with a pleasant hum of words that make her faintly sleepy. She eats more cheese than she really wants, enjoying the salty crumble against her tongue, and takes an ambitious chunk from a white wax-paper-wrapped cylinder that sends up a pungent and faintly recognisable aroma.

"That's goat's cheese," Joe says. "Made with the milk from Katherine's herd."

Willow hesitates over the crackers. She knows intellectually that all milk comes from lactating mammals, but this seems uncomfortably close to home.

"It's all right," Joe says. "You don't have to eat it if you don't want it."

"Only cheese in the world that smells like the animal it comes from," says Katherine. "That girl ate one of my pickled onions. She'll manage a bit of goat's cheese if she wants to."

She isn't sure she wants to, but she doesn't want to let Katherine down, so she spreads a sliver of cheese onto a cracker and forces herself to eat it. Luca breaks into semi-sarcastic applause, blushes violently, and hides his head in the fridge in a quest for another can of Pepsi Max. *Roll up, roll up*, Willow thinks, *and see the amazing Twinless Twin! She never speaks! She eats anything! Ladies and gentlemen, for your viewing pleasure…*

"Are you both done?" Joe smiles at Luca and then at Willow in a kind but unmistakeable dismissal. "You don't have to hang around if you don't want to."

Willow wants nothing more than to stay at the table and carry on ignoring Luca. She pushes her chair back and wonders whether she can possibly get away with going to her room, leaving Luca to fend for himself. It would be rude, but so what? He started it.

But Luca is standing by the back door and looking at her with such unguarded hope that she can't make herself do it. *This is such bullshit,* she thinks. *Why do I have to be nice to him when I don't even like him?*

"You know," Luca says, as soon as they're decently outside, "no offence, but your uncle's very strange. Why's he got a henhouse but no hens?"

Willow shrugs. She's wondered the same thing, but she doesn't want to hear Luca picking over it.

"And you know those two pigs, right? The ones in Katherine's field? They're his. But he gave them to Katherine."

This time Willow doesn't even bother shrugging.

"Look," Luca says. "I wanted to say…"

How good would it feel to tell him to forget it?

"I'm sorry if I was a bit of a twat the other day."

Her stomach burns. If she had her voice she could shout him down.

"I mean, all right, I definitely was. And not a bit of a twat, a lot of a twat. I wouldn't have made all those jokes about, like, killing the goats with a pitchfork and that. If I'd known, I mean." His eyes snag on hers, then slide away again. "Not that I think that's what happened to—"

She ought to be grateful for the effort he's making, since this is clearly the worst conversation he's had all year, but she only wants him to stop.

"And I wouldn't have asked about you not talking. And I wouldn't have made jokes about it – I mean, I shouldn't have done anyway cos it's not funny, but – and I shouldn't have stormed off like that, but it was such a fucking shock. I mean, I'm not trying to make out like it's all about me or nothing, and I appreciate you telling me—" He laughs. "You know what? I am so fucking lame at this."

She could tell him to shut the fuck up.

"I mean," he continues, and then stops.

She could smooth over this moment for both of them by saying something quick and meaningless.

"I mean," he repeats.

But then, why should she save him from awkwardness, when he's made her feel so naked? She won't reach out and touch him, she won't. She isn't curious about the way his hand would feel in hers. She isn't watching the shape of his mouth. His lower lip looks plump and vulnerable. How would it feel if she took it between her teeth? When his eyes meet hers and then flicker away, she realises she's holding her breath.

"This is going to sound well dodgy," he says, and she has to harden herself against his smile. "But do you want to come back to my place and see some kittens?"

It takes them a while to find a walking rhythm that works for both of them. He's trying to slow down to match her pace, without bothering to find out if she can keep up with him. She takes long swift strides to throw him off, irritated by his assumption that she's weaker than he is.

"You're a bloody fast walker, you are," he says after a while.

I have to get from one end of college to the other in five minutes and our site's massive. She and Laurel used to tease their parents: *You're so slow, keep up, we can't walk as slowly as you do!*

"For a girl," Luca adds, watching to see if she's going to rise to it.

Willow climbs carefully over a tree root.

"I can't tell if you're not answering me cos you can't talk, or if you're not answering me cos I'm boring you," he says. "Hey, watch out." He takes her elbow to help her over a gully. She shakes it off. "God, you're touchy. I'm only trying to help."

Even though she's wearing long sleeves, her elbow feels warm where his hand briefly rested. Has she hurt his feelings? And why would she care if she has? Luca is in her head a lot, she'll admit that, but then what else is there around here to think about? She doesn't fancy him. She doesn't. He's the only game in town, that's all. At the edge of the wood, the goats are clustered eagerly around the fence.

"Fuck's sake," Luca mutters. "What do they want?" He reaches out a hand towards the bearded muzzle of the nearest goat, flinches a little when it tosses its head. "What do you actually want?"

Willow wonders if goats have an idea of the future, if they make plans and have dreams and imagine growing old in a field in the sunshine somewhere. Do goats tell stories? Do they have nightmares? Best friends? Do they love each other?

"Fuck off, the lot of you." Luca flaps his arms. The goats hesitate, then move away a little. Willow feels the itch of their gaze between her shoulder blades as they cross the field.

"Nosey twats," Luca observes, and flicks at a heap of goat

pellets with a stick he picked up in the woods. "Too many of them at the minute. That's why they're all a bit weird and pushy. They're not following us, are they?"

Willow looks over her shoulder. The goats are standing in a clump, staring. Their gaze is mild and innocent, but multiplied across a couple of dozen faces, it becomes sinister. She feels as if they're playing Grandmother's Footsteps.

"Sometimes they come right up behind you and shove you in the back," Luca explains. "And the beardy ones get all slime and dribble in their beards and they wipe it on you and it's so unbelievably gross." He puts a protective hand around her shoulders and steers her out of the way of another pile of pellets. "Watch it. And again. And again. Fucking hell, are you doing this on purpose?"

His arm stays across her shoulders for the rest of walk across the field, pressing her into the earth so she has to walk more slowly. When they reach the gate, he climbs over, then holds out a hand to help her do the same.

"Quicker than opening it," he explains; and even though it's clearly not quicker, and him holding her hand makes it harder to climb over rather than easier, she lets it happen. As she swings over, her hair falls forward into his face, and he tuts and catches it in his free hand and then holds it still, as if she's so fragile that even her hair needs protection.

"It's all right," he says, and his fingers caress her wrist, a small slight delicate movement that she could almost tell herself she's imagining. "I've got you."

She doesn't need his help. She's safely on the ground, so close to him she can smell the warm spicy scent of his deodorant. His grip tightens.

"You need to be careful, going off with strange men like this," he says, and although it has to be a joke, it sounds like a genuine warning. "I mean, I could do anything to you right now."

Is he going to kiss her? Does she want him to? She doesn't like Luca, not really, but she likes the shake and tumble of her heartbeat, reminding her that she's alive and young and there's a boy who likes her.

I don't feel very well, Laurel whispers.

She shakes her hand free, snatches her hair back as if he was trying to tear it out of her head. An instant later and she's ashamed of herself – he was helping her over a gate, not tearing her clothes off – but when she looks at him apprehensively, he looks… relieved.

"Come on, then." There's no mistaking it, he looks *happy*, as if her hand was a burden he didn't want to carry. If she had her voice she could destroy him, but instead she has to follow him through the vegetable beds. He's not even watching as she wipes her palm ostentatiously on her hip. In the yard, the chickens have found a dandelion, and are now pecking viciously at each other's heads as they fight for the last few shreds.

"We'll have to climb," Luca explains at the foot of the stack in the hay barn. No reach this time for her hand; no exaggerated care for her welfare. He scrambles onto the first tall dusty greeny-yellow step without looking back at her.

She's never climbed a haystack before. She's surprised by how unwelcoming it is, filled with dust that gathers at the back of her throat, crammed with prickly twigs that catch at her palms. The stack shifts and rocks as they climb, and there are deceptively deep gaps in between the bales that could easily swallow an arm or a leg or maybe even a whole person. Suddenly they're seven bales high and underneath the roof, and the distance to the ground is dizzying. Are they allowed to do this? Is it safe?

"They're round here somewhere," Luca says, and makes a shushing gesture. "Listen a minute and we'll hear."

In the silence of their held breath, Willow hears an urgent squeaking sound, too high and unformed to be called a mew.

"That's them." Luca clambers across the bales. Willow follows him gingerly. "Thought it was rats at first. I was all ready to smash them, but when I looked—"

There's a tunnel in the hay, a little burrow where two bales aren't quite butted up together, and at the end of the tunnel a soft round place holds a heap of furry things, squirming and squealing and clambering over each other until it looks as if they're all one creature.

"Come on then." Luca scratches at the tunnel entrance. "Come on out. That's it. Come on."

A single stripy scrap detaches itself from the heap and walks out towards Luca's hand, skinny tail pencil-straight and vertical. Its stride is proud and purposeful, its feet slightly splayed, as if it's marching in a parade and keeping time with the music.

"There's five," Luca says, his gaze fixed on the approaching kitten. "They'll all come in the end, but this one's the bravest."

More kittens detach from the knot, joining the procession and marching out to meet them. Two more stripy, and two coal-black. Their faces are tiny beneath outsized ears, their eyes round and innocent. Willow clenches her fingers in longing as the first kitten reaches Luca's knee, stretches out a tiny paw, and swarms up the small hill of his leg to reach his lap.

"Ow ow ow ow ow." Luca winces. "You spiney little fucker. Do that again and I'll throw you off the haystack." But he's already petting the eager little head, his fingers rubbing at the spot behind the soaring sails of the ears. He strokes it for a minute, then scoops one hand beneath its belly and holds it out towards Willow. "Here. You have this one."

Willow takes the offered kitten, afraid she might break it, not sure if she's holding it properly. The kitten squeaks its displeasure. When she drops it hastily on her lap, it puts out four pawfuls of tiny spikes and hooks itself into her flesh.

Spiney fucker, she thinks to herself. *That's exactly what you are. Spiney, spiney, spiney little fucker.* She strokes the little back with her fingertips. She thinks of baby creatures as fat and luscious, but there's barely anything to this one; she can feel the tender bones beneath the skin.

"If he sticks his claws in, pick up his feet and he'll let go." Ignoring the three other kittens who swarm eagerly around him to sniff at his fingers, Luca is trying to attract the last one, who sits at the entrance to the tunnel, watching him with wide eyes. "He's an idiot but he'll get the idea if you keep telling him. And if he doesn't you can lob him over here and get another one."

The kitten is purring now, kneading enthusiastically at her leg. Afraid she might break him, she reaches two fingers around each miniature paw and unhooks his claws. He wobbles, then finds his balance. She strokes him over and over, from the place between his ears where his stripes form a tiny 'm' to the tip of his ridiculous stringy tail. His proportions are all wrong, his ears and feet too big, his tail too thin. In the place where she unhooked his front right foot, a thin dot of blood spreads out across the leg of her jeans.

"Want another?" Luca passes over a black kitten with dusty-looking fur and the roundest eyes Willow has ever seen. "Sometimes they fight. That's quite funny. Ouch, you little bastard." He snatches his hand away. "Yes. You. Learn your manners or I'll fucking drown you." The kitten bats at his outstretched finger, trying to catch it and bring it to its mouth. "You're hopeless, mate. No point trying to train you at all."

The black kitten has rolled itself into a tiny circlet and apparently gone to sleep on her knee. The tabby kitten has swarmed up her t-shirt and made a den between her shoulder and her hair. Nobody is biting her, not even a little bit. She allows herself a moment of smugness at her superior kitten wrangling skills. There's a small red-and-white tear in Luca's brown hand.

"You've got to handle them a lot when they're little or they grow up feral," Luca explains. He licks blood from his skin, then scoops his hand around the belly of the littlest kitten, who is taking long stripy steps towards the precarious edge of the bale and considering the leap downwards. He's studying Willow in quick little sweeping passes, as if his gaze might burn her if it rests on her skin for too long. "That's what Katherine says, anyway. I mean, maybe she thinks it's good therapy for me to go up in the hayloft and play with kittens."

Willow thinks this is what he says, but she can't hear him properly over the excited snuffly purr in her left ear. Maybe Luca's strange, spikey behaviour is because he wasn't handled enough when he was little. The kitten is making a nest out of her hair. How will she ever get the knots out? Perhaps she'll have to cut it off. Another step away from Laurel.

The kitten on her shoulder squeaks as her hands grab too tightly. The kitten on her lap tumbles off onto the bale. She makes her hands relax, makes herself soothe their ruffled fur and ruffled feelings.

"D'you miss her?" Luca asks. His voice is too loud and his words are too quick, as if he needs the momentum to get them past his teeth.

She could pretend she hasn't heard him. She could climb back down the haystack and leave.

Keeping her eyes firmly fixed on the kittens, she nods.

"It wasn't long ago, was it?" He picks up the tabby kitten and returns it to her lap. "I mean, in that photo you look the age you are now."

Of course he's still talking; he's got no way of knowing she wants him to stop. But she could make her feelings clear in other ways. She could push the kittens off and climb back down the haystack, leave him here alone, to play with them until his hands are torn to shreds. She risks one quick look at him, their eyes meeting and then darting away again. She hopes he can't sense how she feels.

"I mean," Luca says. "I'm not trying to upset you. And I wouldn't ask out of, fucking, like, nosiness or whatever. It's horrible when people look at you like you're some sort of freak just cos some shit happened to you once. It's… I mean… I mean—"

If only there was a way for her to shut him up. They could sit together in the hayloft with two lapfuls of kittens and all the things they can't say to each other, and enjoy the peace. Perhaps she should kiss him to make him stop talking.

"I mean," he continues, "I know what it's like."

She looks at him in disbelief.

"No, I don't mean like that. I mean, you know, sort of. Well, not really. I haven't got a… I don't have any brothers or sisters, but—" His hands stroke frantically at the kittens clustered on his lap, tugging at the scruffs of their necks, pulling their eyes long and almond shaped.

Stop talking, she thinks. She pushes her fingers into the centre of the rolled-up kitten on her knee, feeling the vibration of its answering purr. When she tickles its belly, the kitten's purr deepens.

"What it is," Luca says, "I'm in this court case. I mean, not the family courts and that. Not about where I live or who I live with or anything. Proper court. Crown court. I mean, I'll be on trial and that. For what I did."

What? What did you do? Are you a robber? A rapist? A murderer?

"I mean, he deserved it," Luca says hastily. "It wasn't some random defenceless bloke. He had it coming. I was defending someone else."

Violence, then. Some sort of fight, someone who got hurt. But it was all right, because he was defending someone else.

Well, she thinks, *you would say that, wouldn't you?*

"So, yeah." Luca shrugs. "That's why I'm here. Because I had to be away from where it happened. What it is, right, they're worried about what might happen. They think I might… you know. Do something bad. Something else bad. To him, I mean. He's afraid I might do it again before the trial. I mean, I wouldn't, at least I don't *think* I would, I suppose you never know, right? But they know I could. Just thought you ought to know."

Luca is looking at her, waiting for her reaction. She isn't sure how to arrange her face. Before she can make a decision, he leans forward and takes the kitten from its nest on her shoulder, untangling her hair from around its paws and putting it carefully into her lap.

"He's made a right mess of your hair, do you know that?"

His words are rough, but his caress is very gentle. Is he the boy he's describing, the one so violent he had to be sent away from home? Or is he the boy who's combing his fingers through the tangles in her hair, made by the kittens he summoned out of their nest to enchant her?

"But it's all right." She can feel his breath against her neck and cheek. She sits frozen and still, mesmerised. "You're safe with me. I wouldn't hurt you. I mean, I was violent and that. But I wasn't, like, *violent* violent. I mean, I was keeping someone else safe and it got a bit out of hand."

There's something odd about this story, as if he's reading from a script. She wonders what he means by *a bit out of hand*, and who he was defending. There's a lie in here. She can see it in the way he glances at her, checking to make sure he's being believed. But which part is he lying about? What did he do? Who did he hurt, and why? If only she could ask him some questions, shake him up a little bit and see what falls out. She turns her face towards him so their mouths are only a few inches apart.

"Fuck," he whispers. "Willow... I don't... I mean... I don't know..."

They're saved by a series of rustling thumps. Something is jumping and scrambling up the haystack towards them. As one, the kittens sit up and prick their ears forward.

"Hey, look," Luca says, leaning precariously over the bales. "Their mum's coming back. And she's got this massive rat and all."

Willow feels a slight tremble in the bale she's sitting on and a large tabby cat leaps from below. She's sleek and prosperous, muscled and strong, and an equally sleek brown rat dangles from her jaws. At first Willow thinks it must be dead, but then she sees the two front paws move weakly in supplication. When the cat lets the rat drop, it staggers to its feet and tries to drag itself away. The kittens watch intently, and creep closer.

"Teaching them to hunt," Luca explains unnecessarily. All five kittens are clustered around the rat now, dabbing at it with tiny paws, jumping back when it twitches. It would be charming if it wasn't for the poor rat, confused and desperate, its end inevitable.

"This is fucking awesome," Luca says. He's watching avidly, his face tight and intent. "Look at the size of it. Reckon it's pregnant?"

She doesn't want to look, but she can't make herself stop looking. The rat is a living thing, it's frightened and in pain and it wants to live. Luca is right, it looks pregnant, its belly distended, dragging against the hay. One of the kittens leaps forward, needle teeth closing on the fur at the back of the rat's neck. The rat screams.

"Yes then," Luca whispers. "Go on. Kill that fucking thing. Rip its throat out."

How can you watch this? Willow presses her hand against her mouth. Did the rat know when it woke up this morning that today would be its last day on earth? The other kittens are growing bolder, lunging for the fat curve of the rat's belly. Is Willow imagining it, or can she see the taut outlines of the babies, squirming inside the skin? Luca is transfixed, his eyes bright, his mouth wet. Moving carefully, he reaches forward and prods at the rat. Is he going to make her stay here and watch until they tear the rat open? Until the babies spill out onto the hay?

"Shit. You okay?" Luca suddenly seems to remember she's there. "Sorry, mate. I wasn't thinking. We don't have to stay and watch. You all right climbing back down?" He puts a hand on her shoulder, but it's the same hand he prodded at the rat with and she cringes away. "Okay, manage on your own then."

The worst thing is that she can understand why he's so fascinated. There's something enthralling about the small cruelty unfolding before them, the unborn rat-children meeting their end beneath the teeth and claws of the creatures she and Luca had petted to sleep. Is there something wrong with both of them for wanting to watch?

"Take it steady on the way down." Luca has a long strand of straw stuck in his hair. She resists the temptation to take it out for him. "You have to watch out for gaps. And don't pull too hard on the bales cos they might slip."

The last thing she sees before she slithers over the edge is the mother cat, quick and efficient, tearing open the rat's belly so that a long rope of pink shrivelly things spill out, slick and covered in blood. The last thing she hears is the small wet sounds of the kittens, taking tiny, hungry bites of fresh tender meat.

CHAPTER FIFTEEN

She's in the woods, and she knows she's dreaming because although it's night and she doesn't have her phone with her to use as a torch, she can still see. The trees open out in front of her like a strange corridor, and her feet skim over the ground without effort.

"I'm so glad you're here." Laurel is beside her, her face pale and her white nightgown stained with blood. "Please don't leave me. We have to hurry."

Where are we going? She can't speak, but Laurel is her identical twin, and in this dream, they share all their thoughts and feelings. Willow's chest aches where the autopsy saw opened Laurel up for inspection. The pain's gone on for so long that she's learned to live with it, but now it comes back to her, a brutal white flare that stops her breath and freezes her in her tracks. She's afraid to look down at her own chest in case she sees the same wound.

This is a dream, Willow reminds herself. *You never saw what they did. She was dressed when you saw her, they dressed her. You only know about the autopsy because you heard the funeral director talking to Mum about it. You don't know how it happened.* But she knows, of course she does. She's seen a million autopsies performed on TV, the Y-shaped incision and the slow peel of skin just a part of the grammar of the entertainment landscape, so routine she used to look away and check her phone. It's so familiar that by now she could probably do one herself.

"We're going to see him," Laurel says. "He can help us."

Instantly her feet grow slow and reluctant, but Laurel takes her arm and urges her on. At the fork in the path, Willow tries to turn down the track to the farmhouse, but Laurel shakes her head and pulls her on.

"That's the wrong way," she says. "They're nice, but they can't help."

And Laurel's right, because when Willow takes a step onto the path, it's like wading through deep water and quicksand, and Laurel is pulling at her arm and her chest hurts so much that she can't stand it. She follows Laurel, taking the path towards the Slaughter Man.

"Look," Laurel says.

The signs on the trees have been joined by the butchered head of a deer, flayed and eyeless and terrible, hung on its own nail at head-height so it appears to be watching for their arrival. Willow can smell it, a sweetly rotting smell that turns her stomach.

No, she tells herself. *This is a dream. I don't have to let anything happen that I don't want. I'm dreaming. I can't smell anything.* She wants to will the deer head away too, but she only has a certain amount of control here, and that terrible pink-and-white face continues to stare at her, muzzle thrust forward, flat thick teeth exposed. Laurel lifts the barbed wire and Willow ducks beneath it. She wonders if Laurel is going to make her go into the Slaughter Man's house, but instead they glide around the side of the house, to where a small built-on back room has a separate entrance.

"He won't mind," Laurel explains. "He's looking forward to seeing you again. He'll be here in a few minutes, but we've got time to look around first."

The door is slightly open, so they can both see inside. The cold blue-white light reminds Willow of all the TV morgues she's casually glanced into, barely bothering to watch any more because they all look the same. Clean white tiles on the floor. Bright lights overhead. An aluminium table. From the sudden fierce throb in her chest, she knows Laurel is remembering her own time on the table, the whine of the bone-saw and the respectful reach of hands inside her chest cavity, the first and last time she will ever be touched in these places, tracing out the secrets inside the chambers of her heart.

"It hurt," Laurel whispers, and presses the palm of her hand against her chest. There is blood seeping out into the soft frail fabric of her nightdress.

The room feels familiar. When she touches the wooden walls, the texture seems like something she recognises. Is she dreaming, or remembering? Has she been here in her sleep and forgotten? Laurel is sitting on the table now, her legs dangling, hunched over herself, one hand pressed to her chest.

"I don't feel well," she murmurs.

Was that what Laurel said when she died? Is this how it was? Willow has no idea. This is another reminder, if she needed one, that she's dreaming. She doesn't know exactly what happened to Laurel, because she wasn't there. She was sitting in her History class, trying to make herself care about Tsarist Russia while also considering whether her teacher was fanciable, or only a little bit earnest and baby-faced in a way that made her feel vaguely protective. Laurel was gasping and choking in the gym as her heart stuttered, then halted, but she hadn't known. Even when Willow heard the scream of the ambulance she hadn't known. Her first thought had been, *I wonder if Laurel knows what's going on?*

In her dream, she has joined her sister on the table. They are sitting side by side, holding hands, and the door is swinging open. The tall spindly figure stands in the doorway. He is wearing his bird head, but she knows now what his face looks like beneath. The Slaughter Man has come for her, and she is ready for him. Laurel clutches her chest and sobs, and Willow can see the life draining out of her eyes, the slow transition as Laurel becomes uninhabited meat.

"He can help us." Laurel's voice is a wet rattle in her throat. "Let him help us. Don't be afraid."

"Don't leave me," Willow begs, knowing it's too late and she's dreaming and Laurel has already gone.

"Don't leave *me,*" Laurel begs in return. "Come with me. Please. I miss you. I miss you so much I can't stand it. I want to be with you again."

And even as she begins the frantic rush into wakefulness, Willow feels the tears pouring down her cheeks, because she's listening to her own words in her sister's mouth.

CHAPTER SIXTEEN

She's sweating with horror, her pyjamas and her sheets clinging to her skin. She hopes it's only perspiration that's soaked her, but then her sense of smell wakes up too, and she realises wearily that it's happened again, she's getting worse again, and now she has to deal with the consequences.

Shaking from the adrenaline of her waking, she peels everything off herself and off the bed. The mattress is almost dry, apart from a small damp spot in the centre that will probably dissipate in the time it will take her to… to… She thinks of the walk to the utility room which will take her past the kitchen window, a wide uncurtained sheet of glass that the night will turn into a mirror, and shudders.

Come on, she thinks. *Don't be such a coward.*

She puts on clean pyjamas, then folds her sheets into a bundle. The stairs grumble and groan no matter how cautiously she moves, and she's convinced that any second now her Uncle Joe will wake. She can picture it perfectly. First the creak of his bed, then perhaps the snap of a light switch and the shuffle of his feet on the floor. The sound of his door opening, and then his footsteps on the landing and the stairs, and before she knows it she'll be caught, utterly and completely, when all she wants is to be left alone to lick her wounds in private. She can picture all of this so clearly that it takes her by surprise when she finds she's made it safely into the kitchen, and Joe is still asleep.

Can she get away with putting the light on? She drops the sheets on the kitchen table and thinks about the shape of the house, trying to guess if the light will leak out and give her away. In a house this old, who knows what's connected to where? She settles for opening the fridge door as wide as it will go. When she turns around – careful to keep her back to the window so she won't frighten herself with her own reflection – the light of the fridge glints on something on the table.

They stand straight and tall on the table, a matching pair, except that one is entirely empty and the other's half-filled. Their labels are neatly aligned and facing towards her chair, as if the drinker was trying to prove they weren't too drunk to observe the decencies. On the draining board, a single shot glass has been washed but not dried, and is now spotted with watermarks.

Of course it's vodka and not water – grown adults don't keep water in vodka bottles – but she unscrews a lid and sniffs it anyway. Then she takes a gulp and holds it in her mouth, letting it scratch at the root of her tongue. She wonders how much was in the first bottle.

No wonder Joe hasn't woken up. Does he do this every night? Or has she got lucky and caught him out the very first time? She unscrews the top again, tilts the bottle to her mouth, takes another hot white swallow. She hasn't drunk for months, and she's pleased to find she can still get it down without flinching. The warmth spreads out from her stomach and melts the tension in her muscles. Why hasn't she thought of this before? Maybe if she drinks enough, she'll be able to sleep without dreaming.

The thought that she has the whole house to herself and no need to worry about waking Joe makes her feel loose and liberated. She doesn't need to worry about being caught. She can take all the time she likes, and make her arrangements at her own pace. Vodka singing in her blood, she grabs clumsily at the bundle of sheets and pads through to the utility room. No need to worry about the accidental slamming of the cupboard doors. No need to worry about the washing machine waking Joe up. No need to worry about anything at all. When her feet begin to ache against the cold slate floor, she slips her feet into the oversized Crocs that live by the back door and seemingly belong to no one, enjoying the clumsy slither they make as she stumbles across the tiles.

Back in the kitchen, she takes another victorious swallow from the bottle. She's survived the terror, the night is hers, and as long as she doesn't sleep, she's invincible. As she replaces the bottle on the table, she finds a long slim white packet that makes her fingers tingle.

Don't touch it, she tells herself. *Leave it alone.*

She picks it up and turns it over and over in her hands, feeling the rattle and shimmy of the pills in their little foil-and-plastic prisons. She's heard the name before but hasn't seen it in the flesh: Temazepam. She can't quite believe what she's looking at.

They must have told you to be careful about stuff like this. Back at home, her parents policed their house as if she was a child once more. No painkillers in the first-aid kit, nothing sharp in the kitchen or the bathroom, all their own prescriptions kept in a padlocked cupboard with the key hidden somewhere she hasn't managed to find yet. And to be fair to Joe, up until now he *has* kept them from her. She had no idea he had anything like this.

She's managed to get the box open, and she can feel the tablets rolling a little in their chambers, begging her to push against the blisters and feel the satisfying *pop* as they tumble into her hands. The pack is almost full, just two missing from the blister. If she took these pills, the whole lot all at once, that would be enough. Of course she's not going to take them. She's only looking. But if she took these pills, she could be gone before Joe even woke in the morning.

And then what? Would she be with Laurel? Or would she somehow still be trapped inside her body, ready for her own time on the table, her own moment to be opened up like a puzzle-box?

She takes another mouthful of vodka. The packet is still in her hand, but she's not going to take them. She's only tempted by the feel of the packaging, so similar to bubble wrap. Just a quick press of her fingers and she'd hear that joyous little snap, inviting her to do it again and again and again until all the blisters were crushed and torn.

And then what? You'd have to hide the evidence, wouldn't you? You can't put them in the bin, he'd find them. You could flush them down the sink, but that's bad for the environment. So why not put them inside you?

Her resistance weakened by alcohol, she finally lets herself glance towards the window. Is that her own face looking back at her from behind frightened eyes? Or is it…

And then she knows she can't stay in the kitchen any more. She has to get out.

Please, Laurel's eyes beg her. *Please come and find me. I need you.*

It takes her a few tries to get the door open (*I'm not drunk,* she thinks to herself, *I'm a bit tipsy but I'm not drunk*). The night air rushes to greet her, sweet and cool and slightly damp. She slip-slithers past the empty chicken coop, past the little shelter that she now knows was built to hold pigs, telling herself that her clumsiness is because she's wearing borrowed shoes. It's less than an hour since she came this way in her dreams, Laurel by her side. Is she trying to escape her own destructive impulses? Or is she simply recreating her own nightmare? She pushes her way down the garden and over the fence that leads her into the woods.

If Joe wakes up and comes to check on her, he'll be worried. But he won't wake up and check on her because he drinks and he takes sleeping pills. She stumbles over a root, then staggers into a bramble bush, aware that this should hurt, but somehow immune to the pain. *I'm not drunk. I'm definitely not. It's the Crocs, they don't fit me*. The path is growing familiar, the distance getting easier, and when she reaches the fork in the pathway she has a curious sensation that the world around her is shrinking. Surely she shouldn't be here already? But no, this is definitely the place, she recognises the shape of the trees and the curve of the path.

Have I come here before in my sleep? Did I sleepwalk up that path? If I go there now, will I find a butchery room at the back of his house? And will he be waiting for me?

Perhaps he, like she, is a night creature. Perhaps he's expecting her. Perhaps he sits up every night in the darkness of his little shack, his gun lying across his knees, waiting for the intruders who may or may not arrive. If she doesn't visit him, will he be disappointed?

This is a stupid idea. I don't want to go and see him. But she does, she does, she does. *I should go home and go back to bed*. But she doesn't. She doesn't. She doesn't. *He can help us*, Laurel whispers. And he can. He can. He can.

The pull of his house is like gravity. She can't resist it any more than she can fly. She's turning towards him, her feet in their ridiculous Crocs shuffling through the leaves. Then, at the edge of the circle of light cast by her phone's torch, she glimpses a flicker of movement. Two round green eyes like lamps stare back at her from the darkness. She feels the sharp jump in her chest that is the closest she can manage these days to a scream.

It's not him, she thinks, forcing herself into calmness. *It's not him. He hasn't come for me. This is someone else.* Cautiously, she points her torch into the darkness, letting it feel out the shape of whatever's watching her. It's an animal. One of Katherine's goats? No, it's a deer, not the dainty delicate creature Luca described but a big sturdy beast with a strong thick neck and twin sprays of bone flowering from his head like a warning.

Oh, she thinks, and holds her breath.

His nostrils flare as he takes in her scent. Should she take a photo? No, this is a holy moment; taking a photograph would be greedy. The stag studies her, curious and considering. Then he turns away – not frightened, not aggressive, just ready to leave – and she hears the soft neat thump of his first few steps as he disappears in the direction of the farmhouse.

It's like the breaking of a spell. She turns away from the path that leads to the Slaughter Man and follows the stag. Not because she thinks she might catch up with him, but because the universe has sent her a sign.

At the edge of the forest, the sky is lightened by moonlight. Switching off her torch, she puts her phone in her pocket, climbs over the fence and drops into the grass. The goats are huddled in their shelter and do not come to greet her as she crosses their field.

She's not trespassing. Katherine said she could come here whenever she liked. Of course, even Katherine probably didn't mean for her to visit in the dead of night when everyone was asleep. But she's not going to do any harm, so why would it matter? She feels as if she's not entirely in her body. Maybe this is all a dream too, another kinder dream to make up for the torment of her nightmares. Or maybe if she gets caught, she could pretend to be sleepwalking?

Now she's by the vegetable beds, and she can smell the fresh green scent of late growing crops. She shines her phone on the bushes, finds a lone plump raspberry, its colour leached by the darkness, and lets it burst against her tongue. Now she's a thief as well as a trespasser. What would the penalty be for a single raspberry? She picks at a seed trapped in her front teeth.

She can see the long crouch of the farmhouse clearly now, each window dark, each pair of curtains tightly closed. The yard is missing its bustling background cast of bad-tempered geese and flouncy, pecky chickens, tidied away for the night to keep them safe from foxes. She crouches in the shadow of the chicken coop for a few minutes, listening to faint rustling inside as the hens shuffle and mutter and move closer to each other for warmth.

It must be very peaceful to be a chicken, surrounded by all the other chickens, shut safely away in the warm darkness. Could she get into the coop with them for a minute? And what's it like inside? Is it warm and comforting? Or does it just stink? She puts her face close to the door, takes in a deep incautious sniff, and backs away hastily. From inside comes a low broody chuckle as one of the hens calls back to her.

It's all right. I'm not going to hurt you. She wonders if they'd find her voice reassuring or frightening. She doesn't want to go in there, the smell is appalling, but she still covets the thought of stroking their loose ginger feathers. With them all tucked away like this, maybe she can reach in and pet one before it can argue?

The coop's dotted with boxes and hatches, each with its own little door, held shut with a fat metal peg. She fumbles with the nearest opening and puts her hand cautiously inside, picturing the hen arching her neck like a cat as she strokes her fingers over its back.

There's no hen, but instead she finds something smooth and cold like a stone. It's an egg, that must have been missed at the morning collection. The shape feels satisfying against her palm. She can hear the hens shuffling and crooning, aware that someone's raiding their nest box. Do they mind her taking the egg? Do they want it for themselves? Or is it something they forget about as soon as it's laid?

First a raspberry, and now an egg. She's a thief. She ought to leave it here for the morning. It's not her property. She has no right to it.

Katherine won't mind, she thinks. She lifts it out and tucks it into her pocket, but she's still not satisfied. She's come here to be reminded of all the things that are still alive and happy in this world, but everyone's asleep. Where can she go where someone will be awake?

In contrast to the eerie stillness of the yard, the haystack buzzes with activity. She can hear the scrabbling and rustling of what sounds like a thriving rodent city, and when she gets closer, a dozen rats pour out of the darkness as if someone's tipped them from a bucket. As she slips her feet out of their clumsy rubber shoes, she thinks about the sharp yellow teeth of the rat the kittens killed and hopes she won't be bitten as she climbs. And what if she falls?

It's okay, she decides. She won't fall, and even if she does, she won't feel it. She's cushioned by vodka. Halfway up the haystack, someone says 'roo' down her ear, and she finds herself face-to-face with the enquiring gaze of the mama cat.

No wonder you're so glossy, Willow thinks. *This barn must be like an all-you-can-eat buffet.* The cat sniffs politely at Willow's hand, but backs away from her attempt to pet her, making a long elastic leap downwards towards the feast waiting in the barn.

In the nest at the top of the haystack, the kittens are huddled in their burrow. She scratches lightly at the hay, and is rewarded with five little heads going up like signals, radar-dish ears turned towards her.

Come on, she thinks, and scratches again.

It takes longer than the first time, maybe because Luca isn't with her, maybe because it's colder and they're reluctant to move. Finally, a single kitten detaches itself from the ball and comes marching towards her with its tail quivering. She picks him up and holds him against her, trying not to crush him. The idea that comes to her has the brilliance of curved glass gleaming in the moonlight, arrives on a bubble of fiery inspiration that burns and hiccups in her throat.

The kitten is tiny and new, but he's starting to hunt. He must be almost ready to leave. He's Katherine's kitten, not hers, but Katherine has plenty of cats already. Surely she won't miss just this little one? If she could have him on her pillow, protecting her, perhaps she'd be able to sleep without nightmares. The kitten is purring and kneading painfully at her chest.

Spiney fucker, she thinks fondly, and kisses his tiny head as she tucks him beneath her top.

The strange contraction of space has reversed itself, and now the distance back home stretches endlessly outwards, until she begins to wonder if she's taken the wrong path. No question now of whether she's sleeping or waking. The ache in her legs and the chill in her flesh tells her she's definitely in the real world. The vodka tide in her blood is on the ebb, leaving her mouth sandy and sour. Her arm complains at the effort of holding the kitten in place against her chest. When she finally reaches the fence at the end of Joe's garden, the feeling of relief is so great, it's almost like joy.

She's made it. She's home. Her adventure is complete. Beneath her chin, the kitten stirs and stretches, as if he knows he's home too.

The delight in what she's done is overwhelming. She creeps into the utility room, slips off the Crocs and pulls the back door closed. Outside in the yard, her feet revel in the feel of the ground beneath them. Dancing carelessly up the stairs that lead to her bedroom, she steps on something so sharp she feels the impact in the base of her skull.

Shit, she thinks, hopping frantically on one leg and trying to get to her foot while still balancing the kitten. She can feel a warm ticklish trickle that must be blood. Her fingers, creeping gingerly across damp muddy skin, make contact with a sliver of metal. It's one of the blades from the razor she stole. *Shit, shit, shit.* She pulls it out, the pressure of her need to sob pushing back against the terrible compulsion that keeps her voice locked away. The blade is bright and sharp in the moonlight. She drops it to the floor in disgust, then picks it up again and puts it in her pocket. She doesn't want to step on it again.

Limping with every step, she makes it into her room and closes the door on the night. She puts her foot down on the floor, then lifts it up hastily. A bloody heel print stares up at her.

She doesn't want to deal with this now. Perhaps she could

put on a sock and let that soak up the blood and sort it out in the morning? But a moment's inspection shows her this is a terrible idea. Blood mingles with mud, dust and scraps of grass. She can't go to bed like this; and besides, she has this kitten to deal with, this kitten who's prowling curiously around her bedroom and sniffing at her mattress with his mouth half-open. She has to steal him some food, build him somewhere to sleep, and get her foot clean. Will this night never end?

Feeling as if she's trapped in a time-loop, she forces herself to go back downstairs to the kitchen. The fridge is humming and buzzing, frantically trying to replenish the cold air that's pouring out of it. Someone as organised as Joe is bound to have a first-aid box, but she has no idea where it might be, and she doesn't dare put on the lights. Besides, she has to keep as close a watch as she can on the kitten, who is currently mountaineering up the side of the sofa, tail whipping and claws clutching tight.

Instead of a first-aid kit, she fills a bowl with warm water from the tap, grabs the kitchen roll, and sits down at the table to clean up her foot. The cut's smaller than she'd first thought, but so deep it makes her ears sing. She takes three more sheets of kitchen roll, folds them into a pad and soaks the pad in vodka. Then she holds it against her foot and presses hard, biting her lip as the alcohol touches the opening in the skin. She takes another mouthful of vodka. She's almost sobered up from the first lot, and besides, she's not drinking alone. She's got the kitten for company, even though he's rolled into a ball in the corner of the sofa and is purring himself to sleep.

When she takes the pad away, the wound seems very clean, but has started bleeding again. She makes a new pad and holds that against her foot, counting slowly in her head to give the blood time to clot. Her initial plan is to count to five hundred, but by the time she reaches two hundred and seventy-three she can feel her head rolling on her shoulders and knows that if she sits any longer, she'll fall asleep at the table.

Come on. You can do this. Just a few more jobs and then you can go to sleep. She collects the various leavings of her emergency clean-up and drops them in the bin. She opens the cupboard beneath the sink, finds the kitchen cleaner and sprays a thin bleach-scented mist across the table, then wipes it clean with a cloth. She rinses the cloth and drapes it over the rail of the Aga to dry.

Next, the kitten. He'll have her for company, but he might get hungry in the night, and he'll need a litter box. In the fridge she finds a bag of cubed meat. She chops a few pieces gingerly into tiny morsels and arranges them on a saucer, then fills a teacup with water. The litter box stumps her for a minute, but a frantic rummage through the recycling uncovers several editions of the free local newspaper. She'll tear these into strips and lay them out on a piece of cardboard in the corner of her room. Hopefully the kitten is clever enough to work out that it's meant for him to pee on rather than sleep in. If only she could explain to him. If only she could ask him if he understood.

But at least she won't be alone now. There'll be someone else in the room with her, someone who will keep her company even without speaking. Someone small and young, who needs her. She'll have to get better now. She's got someone she has to look after.

That's how Joe feels about me, she thinks. *I keep him company. He talks to me and I don't say anything back. I can't talk so he has to try and guess what I want, but it doesn't matter. He likes having me here so he's got something to look after.*

She looks again at the bottles of vodka. Joe does this in secret, once she's gone to bed, and he always seems fine in the morning. But what will happen to him when she has to leave? Apparently, this kitten isn't for her after all.

She puts the meat and the water on the floor near the sofa, and the litter box in the corner. The kitten is fast asleep now, paws twitching as he dreams. She knows from experience how comforting it can be to cram yourself into the crease at the edge of a chair, how safe and protected you feel against the padded edge. But perhaps once he gets settled in, he'll come and sleep on her bed sometimes.

In her pocket, the egg remains safely nestled, warmed now by the heat of her body. She takes it out and lays it on the table, next to the vodka bottles, balancing it carefully. She's afraid it will roll and smash on the floor, but it simply waits there, smooth and enigmatic, a sealed chamber. She hopes the inside is as blank and empty as the outside, and she hasn't stolen away and then killed an incipient yellow chick.

Once she is sure the egg isn't going to roll across the table and hurl itself to the floor, she takes the razor blade from her pocket and lays it down beside the egg. There's a small smear of rusty brown around the point where she pulled it out of her foot, and she feels her skin itch and wince with the memory of pain.

She closes the fridge door and waits for the darkness to grow lighter again as her eyes adjust. There are no street lights here and the windows are too low for the moonlight to make much impact, but eventually she finds she can make out the shapes of things by the tiny red glow of the light from the socket over the worktop. She doesn't dare sit down. She's so tired she could sleep even upright in a dining chair; or maybe on the sofa, curled into an awkward semi-circle with the kitten tucked underneath her chin, a talisman against bad dreams.

All right, she thinks. *That's it. You've done everything you needed to do. You can go to bed now.*

She gives the kitten one final stroke, astounded by how infinitely tiny he has made himself. Then, reluctantly, she leaves the kitchen. She moves cautiously, not because she's afraid any more that she will wake Joe, but because she's afraid of disturbing the fragile arrangement of the things they have left for each other in the clean warm emptiness of the kitchen, huddled together like unspoken confessions.

CHAPTER SEVENTEEN

When she wakes the next morning – dry mouth and fuzzy head, swaddled in the quilt because her bed has no sheets – it's so late it's almost afternoon, and there are words hovering in her head, as clear as if someone has crept into her room and whispered in her ear. *You shouldn't have done any of that*.

She sits up cautiously and wonders what the chances are of her getting away with any of last night's antics. What was she thinking? The stolen vodka she might just about get away with (Joe seems to have a pretty good memory of what being a teenager is like, and besides, he left it where she could find it). He might interpret the egg as simply a bit of teenage weirdness. But the kitten? What on earth will he think about the kitten, which can only have come from one place? Last night, made brilliant with vodka, she had thought only of how perfectly the kitten would fit into Joe's home, a small piece of flotsam from the disorderly torrent of life that pours through the rooms of the farmhouse. Now, she can see that he'll know she went into the forest at night and walked all the way to Katherine's farm. And whatever position he takes – whether he's gentle and bewildered, or impatient and irritated, thrilled with his surprise present or insistent that it has to go back – everything is going to change, because the forest at night was something just for her.

Or will this be the start of something different? Will he want to talk to her about what *she* found out last night?

Through the floorboards, she can hear Joe talking to someone. She can't make out the words, but she can hear the cheerful rise and fall of his voice, the pauses for the other person's replies. Has his partner come back early? She strains to listen, but can't make out anything. When she looks out of the window, there's only Joe's car parked outside.

Still, if he *has* come back, Joe will be happy to see him, and perhaps they'll both be happy about the kitten (and maybe Willow will get to know Joe's partner's *name*). Maybe in the flood of greetings and explanations and unpacking, she might manage to escape any discussions. She can feel the pull of tender flesh in her foot as she goes downstairs, the seam threatening to burst open.

"No, you're not doing that. No. No. No!" Joe's voice is amused and scolding, as if he's talking to a small child. She opens the door to find him peeling the kitten off his sleeve where it hangs like a sloth, biting frantically at his elbow. "Let go now. Come on. That's right. No, don't grab on again. Sit there on the sofa and think about how you can do better in future. Morning, Willow."

The table is clean and bare. The newspaper box has been replaced with a plastic tray filled with white dusty granules. Where Willow left a saucer of meat-scraps and a cup of water, there's a dish filled with cat food and a metal drinking bowl.

"Sorry about that," Joe says as the kitten flings himself off the sofa and gallops over to pounce on Willow's toes. "He can't help it. I think he's a bit of an idiot. You might want to start wearing socks."

Aren't they going to talk about this? (Or rather, isn't *he* going to talk about it, while she listens, and nods or shakes her head at the right moments). She stands still and wary, waiting to see if this is a cunning way of softening her up. But from the way Joe is carefully not catching her eye as he hurries around the kitchen, sweeping non-existent crumbs into a cloth, it looks as if they're not.

She ought to feel relieved. Instead she feels a strange

little chill at the back of her neck, as if someone is pressing there with cold fingers, trying to get her to pay attention to something that matters.

"Anyway, the traffic wasn't too bad," Joe continues, which mystifies Willow until she realises he's talking about his trip to replace her cup and her saucer and her newspaper box with the real thing. She reaches down and scoops a hand around the tight little curve of the kitten's belly. He crawls onto her shoulder and bites at her hair.

"Right," Joe says. "I've got to get on." A small paw shoots out from Willow's hair, and Joe catches it between his fingers to give it a friendly shake. "He'll try and drink out of your cereal bowl, so you need to decide if that's okay or not."

She wants to challenge him. She wants to say, *Aren't you even going to ask me where I got him?* She wants to ask, *Aren't we going to talk about anything at all?* She wants to ask him, *What the hell is wrong with you?* Is anyone even in charge around here anymore?

"Right." Joe's smile doesn't quite meet his eyes. "See you in a bit."

And then he's gone, whistling to himself over the whirr of his laptop springing back into life.

Willow eats in a daze. She finishes her cornflakes – fending off the kitten, who does, indeed, think he ought to be allowed to share the milk – puts her bowl in the dishwasher, and goes back upstairs. In her room, she's confronted with her bare mattress, and remembers the sheets she left in the washing machine last night. They need taking out and hanging on the line in the yard, or at least bundling into the tumble dryer, so they can both pretend they don't know why they needed washing in the first place.

Her aim is to complete this task without Joe having to know anything about it, and she nearly succeeds. She's got the sheets into the dryer, and she's just turning the dial when he comes into the utility room, carrying the recycling crate that lives next to the bin. When he sees her, he jumps so violently that Willow jumps too, knocking off the box of washing powder. A long trail of bluey-white grains pours out.

"Sorry," Joe says. "My fault." The recycling box rattles and shivers as he puts it clumsily down by the door. "Um, I didn't realise you were – I mean, obviously it's – um…" His smile doesn't fit properly into his face. "I tell you what, shall I maybe go out and come back in again five minutes from now?"

Willow's cheeks burn. What's the matter with Joe this morning? Of course *she* feels awkward, but isn't he supposed to be the grown-up? She starts the tumble dryer, then takes the dustpan and brush and sweeps the powder off the grey slate floor, making sure to get all the residue out of the cracks. Then she goes to the recycling crate and takes off the lid.

The contents are as carefully stacked as if Joe has been playing Tetris. At the top of the crate, a thick layer of tall glass bottles nestle like jewels, their labels turned carefully outwards.

But this isn't fair, Willow thinks, knowing she's being childish. *He's supposed to be looking after* me. *What am I supposed to even do about this? Is he asking me for help? Or should I let him get on with it?*

Her foot's hurting again. She presses hard against the floor, feels the skin split and tingle, and then the spreading warmth stretching out towards her toe.

"We going to your place then? Or somewhere else? Do you even know?" Luca laughs. "Hey, if I, like, annoy you enough by asking you questions will you start talking just to fucking shut me up?"

Spending time with Luca is like a game of Shag, Marry, Kill. She doesn't like being laughed at for her silence, but it's better than his guilty awkwardness when he first found out about Laurel. She's not enjoying his company exactly, but she'd rather have him, with his bad past and his bad behaviour and his endless, endless monologue, than the awkwardness of her and Joe, stepping uncomfortably around each other as if they're afraid the other one might bite. If she was playing Shag, Marry, Kill and Luca was one of the options, which category would she put him in?

"Or are you going to, like, drag me off into the woods and stab me with a kitchen knife or something?"

Definitely kill, she thinks, and smiles to herself, and knows Laurel would agree.

"When you smile like that, you look just like a murderer." Luca laughs breathlessly. If he talked less, he'd be able to keep up with her without effort. "I'll probably meet some of them while I'm inside. Murderers, I mean. Maybe even a serial killer. Might as well get some practice in on dealing with them. Come on, mate, this is getting annoying. Give me a fucking clue or something."

She stops to let him catch up with her. They've reached the fork in the path. Luca blinks in surprise, then grins.

"And I thought you were a nice girl."

Is he going to refuse? She's not sure she dares go on her own. She needs someone who has a better grip on reality than she does. Someone who's properly anchored into their own life, committed to staying in it. Someone who will make her come back again.

"God, the face on you, woman! Like you're about to shit a brick. No wonder you wanted me with you. Don't worry, I'll look after us. Make sure you keep quiet and we'll be fine."

It's annoying to have Luca take charge as if this was all his idea, but there's something comforting about seeing him go up the path ahead of her. He's making no effort to be quiet. Does he know more than she does, or less? Has he been here before? Has he read the signs?

"Shit." Luca stops to look. "Visitors not welcome at any time. Nice. If you trespass on my land I will not be responsible for my actions. Possible armed response, what the fuck? You can't put a sign up with that on it. And there's barbed wire as well. This is insane."

Willow lifts the strand of wire and ducks beneath it.

"Hey, no. We're not going any further. It's not safe. Come on, don't be a dickhead, Willow. This isn't somewhere we ought to be. Look, come back here, I'm not coming in after you, it's fucking stupid. Oh for God's *sake—*" She hears the rustle of leaves and the scuttle of footsteps behind her as he follows her beneath the wire and catches up. "This had better be worth it, all right?"

She reaches up and puts a finger to his lips. She's surprised by how warm they feel, how plump and vulnerable when the rest of him is hard-edged and skinny. She can feel the warm flow of his breath down her finger.

"Okay, good point," he murmurs. "Christ, this is weird. This is so fucking weird." He looks at her sternly. "Have you been here before?" She nods. "When? Did you see him? What's he like?"

She stops his questions by turning away and leading him on. She treads as carefully as she can, conscious of each snap and rustle. Behind her, Luca is trying and failing to be quiet. Why can't he look where he's putting his feet, keep his arms still so they don't swish against his sides, try breathing like a human being and not a steam engine? Or perhaps she sounds as loud as this to him.

"Christ." Luca's voice makes her jump. "Look at that place."

She wants to tell him to shut up. She settles for a glare, but he's too enthralled by the house to notice.

"How did anyone build that out here? It's not like some shack, is it? It's a proper house. Come on, let's get a bit closer, I want to see more of it."

No, she thinks. *He might be in there.* But it's too late, Luca is already striding closer, the threatening signs forgotten, confident and loose in his stride, as if nothing bad can happen to him because he's a boy. He walks up to the door, knocks hard on it with his knuckles. She forces herself to follow him, trying not to cower, carefully not looking at the bare, burned place where once, there was a fire and a pot full of bones. What are they going to do if the Slaughter Man comes to the door? Can they pretend they're lost in the woods and need some help? Will he recognise her?

"Anyone in? Hello?" Luca knocks again, tries the handle. "Nah, it's locked. He must be out. It's just a bloke lives here, right?" She nods, and he grins slyly. "Thought so. No way a woman could hack it out here."

Fuck off, she thinks, but doesn't rise to the bait. Her skin prickles with the fear that they're being watched, from a window or from behind a tree. She strains her ears for the click of a gun.

"Hey, you know I'm kidding, right? I mean, I've been raised by my mum, I know how strong women can be. I reckon most blokes are pretty useless to be honest. You girls are better off without us." He scratches restlessly at his arm. "Reckon we can get inside?" She shakes her head. "God, I'm kidding. I'm kidding! What kind of a dickhead d'you think I am?"

I think you're the kind of dickhead who's probably just about nice enough to stop me if I do anything too stupid. A kind of dickhead canary-in-the-mine, but with worse conversation and more hats. She leads the way around the edge of the house, and dear God, there actually is something like the place she dreamed of, not exactly the same but close enough to turn her cold. A big box-like structure, no windows and a separate door, that in a more normal home would be the garage. Or maybe it is a garage, and not a butchery workshop at all? When she tugs at the handle, the door swings open.

"You want to go in there?" She nods. "Are you trying to impress me? We don't have to. I mean, if you'd rather go back—"

The air inside smells of bleach. The walls and floor are unfinished wood, but in the centre of the room the Slaughter

Man has laid a slab of white tiles and put a steel table over the top. The gleam of the steel and the whiteness of the tiles make her think of operating tables, until she sees the two chest freezers side by side in the corner, and the implements hanging neat and orderly on the hooks above, and then she thinks of the autopsy table and the scar that Laurel has and she does not and she can feel the blood beginning to pool in her feet, and before she can get a hold of herself, take the deep breaths that will anchor her back to reality, Luca has his arm around her and is patting solicitously at her shoulder.

"It's all right," he says. "I know what it looks like, proper serial killer set-up, right? But it's nothing to worry about. This is just, like, butchery stuff. All those survivalist maniacs have kit like this so they can process their kills." He grimaces. "I mean, not kills like murders, kills like animals. Rabbits and deer and that." He's talking a little too fast, as if he's trying to convince himself as well as Willow. "Have a look in those freezers. It'll just be a bunch of meat."

But we're made of meat, Willow thinks. *We're all of us made of meat. We think we're special but we're only animals with clothes on.* Luca is forcing open the lid of the freezer.

"Yeah. Look at this lot. He's got loads in here. All in parcels and wrapped up properly and that." He's trying to be brave, to style it out, but she can see the nausea in the lines around his mouth. "It's really big joints and all."

She makes herself get to her feet, hating the wobble in her legs, and joins Luca beside the freezer. Slabs and rounds of thick dark meat, some with bones poking out like sticks. Despite the cold she can smell it, a faint tang that stirs something primal in the base of her brain. She's glad of the cold air that pours out over their faces. Something clicks, and a motor begins to run.

"I mean, it's not anything, like, dodgy," Luca says, uncertainly. "Look at it, it looks like beef… or something…"

How would they even know if they were looking at human flesh? She doesn't want to touch it but she has to. She reaches into the freezer and begins to rummage, glad each piece is wrapped in plastic, cringing when her fingers brush against a knobble of bone. At the bottom, she finds something pale pink and naked with a long muzzle and blank holes where eyes would once have been, something that is unquestionably a head and unquestionably not human. Something she last saw nailed to a tree, in her dream. Something she last saw alive, gazing back at her without fear, before turning to guide her away from this awful place and down the path towards the farmhouse. What has he done with the antlers? Are they mounted on the wall of his living room?

"Is that a cow head?" Luca looks as sick as she feels. "No, wait, I reckon it's a deer." His laughter is forced and over quickly. "It's a deer, that's all. Told you it was all right. God, I thought for a minute though…"

He's loud and cheerful with relief, and he lets the freezer lid fall without any sort of caution. She feels the slam shudder through the floor. She wants to tell him to be quiet, because they're still trespassing (VISITORS NOT WELCOME AT ANY TIME) and the man who lives here still has a gun (I WILL NOT BE RESPONSIBLE FOR MY ACTIONS) and could be back at any moment. He's high with relief, messing around with the knives and saws that hang on the wall, trying them out in his hand for size and weight, taking one down that she thinks might be a filleting knife and holding it up to the light to watch it gleam.

"Look at these," he says, and she can hear the longing in his voice. "They could really do some damage."

She stands beside him and takes the filleting knife from his hands. She can feel her pulse beating in her wrist, in her neck, in her chest, all the blood coming to the surface, ready to escape. Her body is a cavity to hold organs, that's all. If she were to press into the right place, who knows what might happen? She tries it against her own thumb. The blood arrives first, then the white line of pain. She lays it down on the table.

"It's really sharp," Luca whispers hungrily. When he takes

her hands, her skin flares with heat. His caress dips into the line of blood that trickles from her thumb. She strokes his palms, then feels up towards his wrists, wanting to touch his pulse points, so she can tell if he feels the same as she does. He grabs hastily at her fingers.

"No. Stop it. Seriously, Willow, you have to stop. This isn't safe." He holds her hands tight within his own. She can see the movement in his throat as he swallows. "I mean, *I'm* not safe. I shouldn't be here with you. I might end up hurting you. I mean, it's not cos I don't like you. Because I *do* like you. And sometimes when I like girls – I get, like, confused – I mean, I don't want to hurt you, but sometimes I feel like—" He licks his lips. "D'you get what I'm saying? I think there's something wrong with me, inside my head. I feel like it might, like it might feel good to hurt you. I don't think I'm safe to be around you…"

They're neither of them safe. They're like two addicts huddled over a wrap, coveting the sharp cutting edge of the knife, waiting for the other to make the first move. She ought to be afraid. Instead she's watching the movement of his mouth, thinking about the way his lips felt underneath her fingers earlier. How would it feel to bite them? How would it feel if he bit her?

"Fuck." His voice is hoarse. "You're so fucking dangerous, you know that? You are the most dangerous fucking person I've ever met in my life."

His face is inches from hers. She can see the faint line of grease at his hairline and the small white smear where the wax he's used to sculpt his hair into shape hasn't quite melted away. He has a scab where he's picked a spot by the side of his nose. His eyelashes are long and thick. No one knows they're here. She's completely at his mercy. If he put the knife against her neck, if he slid his hands up her t-shirt or between her legs, would she be able to stop him? Would she even want to try? The freezer clicks, the distant generator rumbles into stillness.

"Shit. Can you hear something?"

All she can hear is the sound of their breathing. She shakes her head.

"No, shut up, quiet. I need to listen."

Funny, she thinks sourly, but she knows what he means. Sometimes just the sound of someone else thinking is enough to drown out what really matters. Like mice beneath an owl, she and Luca hold themselves in utter stillness.

Nothing. More nothing. Then, a slow breathy tune, coming out in bursts, the melody flattened by effort, as if the person singing is carrying something heavy and their breath is short.

"Yeah, Cape Cod girls… ain't got no… combs…
Haul away… haul away…"

The Slaughter Man has come back.

"What do we—" Luca begins, then stops when Willow shakes her head.

"They comb… their hair… with cod-fish—"

The breathy singing stops as abruptly as if the singer has dropped dead. Then, a solid thud. The Slaughter Man must have come around the corner of his house, carrying something heavy, and seen that the door to his back room is open. The heavy thing, whatever it is, has fallen to the floor. Now he's coming to find them.

"It's all right," Luca whispers. "If he tries to hurt you, he'll have to get through me first."

It sounds like something Luca heard someone say once and thought was cool, but her heart's beating too fast for her to laugh. What can Luca possibly do against a man with a gun? A shadow falls inside the door.

"Hello." The Slaughter Man's mouth is wide and toothy. He is tall and thin and his shaven head gleams.

"All right, mate." Luca tries to smile. "We're a bit lost."

The Slaughter Man isn't listening. He's studying Willow's face, his expression peaceful, his eyes mild.

"I know you," he says at last. "You… ought to know better." His gaze turns to Luca. "I don't know you. But you

179

ought to know better too. You both look old enough to know better than to come here."

"Hey, look, we're lost, all right? You don't have to be a knobhead about it. Hey, wait, don't you fucking come anywhere near us, mate."

"Do you know how terrified you sound?" The man takes a single step forward into the room. "How about you, little one? Are you going to say anything?"

"She doesn't talk," says Luca.

"So that's why you didn't scream the other night. Was it you watching me the next day, too? You were so quiet I wasn't sure if you were even there. I think I could help you find your voice. Shall we find out?"

"Don't you touch her. Don't you fucking dare—"

"Or else what? Or else you'll attack me with my own knife?"

Why hadn't they thought of the knives? She'd been so afraid he'd have his gun with him that she hadn't considered anything else. The knife fits into her hand as if it was made for her. She holds it up in front of her, willing her hand to stay steady.

The Slaughter Man leans against the doorframe. He seems amused.

"You do realise I could take that knife from you and put you both in hospital before you got anywhere near me."

"Come on then," says Luca. His voice has changed, as if he's found a different and darker part of himself. "Come on then. You think you're so fucking tough."

"Oh, you adorable little shithead. Was that what you came here for? To impress your girlfriend? *Come with me into the woods and I'll show you where the bad man lives?* Do you really think you're tough enough to take me on?"

It was me, thinks Willow. *It was me. I brought him here. You think I'm a poor little girl but I'm the reason we're here.* In lieu of the words she wants to yell in his face, she lifts the knife and lets it catch the light.

"That's a brave effort." The Slaughter Man scratches his chin. "But have you ever heard the phrase, *Never bring a knife to a gun fight*? It's a good thing I don't have my gun with me right now, isn't it? Because if I shot you out here in the woods, no one would ever find out. I could hide your bodies somewhere they'd never find them. They'd look in my freezers, of course, but I have other places where I process the meat I kill. Nice damp places where it can soak up the salt, and nice dry places where it can hang up to cure. And without a body, they'd have no evidence of any crime. They might think it was the weirdo who lives out in the woods, but they'd never prove it. You'd just be… gone. And I'd still be here." He licks his lips thoughtfully. "Then again, so would you be. In a manner of speaking."

This is pure fear, the kind that wastes no time on *what if* and *but maybe* and *shouldn't we try* and focuses only on survival. The same instinct moves them both at the same moment. Without pausing for thought, without worrying about what might happen next, without thinking about whether he might hurt them or catch them or if they might provoke him or make things worse for themselves, they bolt for the door.

CHAPTER EIGHTEEN

And incredibly, shockingly, they make it out. Perhaps the Slaughter Man is surprised by the speed of their run. Or perhaps he was only ever playing with them. Perhaps he simply let them go. They pound across the clearing, ducking beneath the wire in perfect synchronisation, leaping over branches and roots until they reach the place where the two paths join. Finally, they stop, whooping for breath and feeling the adrenaline trickle down through their feet and out through the soles of their trainers.

"That fucking bastard weirdo," Luca gasps. "I ought to go back there and fucking kill him. He needs putting down." He clenches his fist around an imaginary weapon.

Willow shivers.

"Hey, it's all right." Luca's hand around her waist feels hot and intrusive. "I'll look after you." He teases a strand of hair that has got stuck against her lip and strokes it back behind her ear. His touch is frighteningly gentle. "One quick smack on the back of the head and he'd be fucking gone. When someone hurts someone else, you got to hit them back harder." He looks at her and laughs. "Bet you've never hit anyone in your life, have you?"

As it happens, as far as she can remember, she never has, but she doesn't see how he could possibly know that.

"Course you haven't. I can tell by looking. Jesus, put that

fucking thing down before you hurt yourself." She realises she's still holding the knife. He takes it from her as if she's a small child. "What were you thinking, running with that in your hand? If you fell over you'd have your eye out. You want to store it somewhere, only get it out when you're ready to use it."

He sounds authoritative and convincing, as if he's passing on a lesson he's been taught by someone older than him. Where on earth would he learn something like that? When he sees the look on her face, he laughs.

"Now you reckon I'm some kind of knife-wielding gangster boy who's going to carve you up, don't you?" He lays the knife down on the ground. "Feel better now? You are way too easy to read, mate. Or maybe I'm getting to know you."

You don't know anything about me, she thinks. *But the Slaughter Man does.*

"I tell you what. I bet I can tell a lot about you just by looking. Sit down here while you get your breath back."

She sits gingerly beside him on the long trunk of a fallen sapling. It sags and springs beneath their weight, then settles.

"Okay. Now I'll guess three things about you and if I guess them all right then you lose and you have to…"

The last time he made an offer like this, he wanted her to flash her tits. Is that what he's angling for now? If he likes her, why can't he say that? Why does he have to make it into a battle, her body a prize to be awarded to the victor, as if she has no needs or desires of her own? Perhaps she should lift her t-shirt for him right now. No, of course she shouldn't.

"Actually, you know what? I'll do it for free. Because I'm just that good. Right, first thing. You're seventeen, right? Yeah, I know you are, that's not one of the things, Katherine told me. So, I bet you're doing A-levels." She nods. "Course you are. I'm resitting my GCSEs. Well, I'm supposed to be. For all the fucking good it'll do me. Right, sorry, I'm on about myself and we're meant to be talking about you, better go back to paying you some attention. Typical girl, you are. I'm kidding. I'm kidding!"

He's like a rabbit running from a fox, constantly switching direction so she can never quite pin him down to a single opinion. She keeps her face carefully neutral and waits for his next pronouncement.

"I bet you live… in a detached house… with at least one spare bedroom. Yes? Yeah, course you do. Holy shit, I'm out in the woods with a posh girl. Well, I live in a high-rise tower block. Drug dealers next door, working girls above us and everyone pisses in the lifts cos they don't work so they might as well be used for something. Your face! Can't you tell I'm kidding?"

Half the stuff you tell me turns out to be lies! How the hell am I supposed to know what's true and what isn't?

"We're in a terrace. It's a nice one. Old. Fancy fireplaces. Lots of trees in the street. Two bedrooms cos there's only the two of us. Well, three of us with the knobhead. I can't believe you thought I lived in a flat next to a drug dealer! That is actually quite offensive, that is. No, I don't mean it, of course I don't! Come on, Willow, stop taking everything so seriously. Right. Next thing."

I bet, Willow thinks, *I bet you got picked on at school. I bet they used to laugh at you when you got stuff wrong in class, and took your bag on the bus and threw it around, and you always got chosen last in PE, and that's why you act so tough all the time. How am I doing, Luca? How do you like it when I do it to you?*

"I bet your mum and dad are still together. Am I right?" He looks at her face, and laughs. "Yes! Three for three. I am the fucking king."

I bet your dad's a complete dick, Willow thinks sourly. *I bet that's where you get it from.*

"Must be nice, having your dad around." Luca's trying to sound casual. "My mum left my dad when I was about six months old. Apparently he was a complete twat. I mean, if the ones she's been out with him since are anything to go by…"

He's holding her hand now, their fingers laced together, raised up between them as if they're making a vow. She can feel the tension of the moment caught between their palms.

"Look, if I tell you this, you can't tell anyone, right? I mean, I know you won't *tell anyone* tell anyone, but, I mean, you can still write stuff down and that, can't you? So you've got to promise not to say anything about it. Like, ever. Especially in writing. Cos, you know, there's a court case coming up and that. I've got to be careful what I say, in case the other side find out about it and I get into worse trouble."

She nods. When he lets her hand go, she can feel sweat drying against her skin.

"Okay. So what happened was…" He's let go of her hand and is seeking out things to shred, picking off pieces of bark from the tree they're sitting on, tearing handfuls of ivy leaves and ripping them into pieces. "A couple of years ago, my mum met this bloke." He grimaces. "I mean, I love my mum. But she's an absolute *wanker* when it comes to blokes."

Willow is filled with a sudden longing for her dad.

"So this one was, like, such a tosser. He used to talk badly to her – to me as well, but I wasn't bothered for me – throwing his weight about. Not cleaning up after himself, expecting his dinner made, stuff like that, you know? Arsehole behaviour."

Why did she let him do that? Willow thinks incredulously. But then, how *do* you make a man do something if he really doesn't want to?

"Then," Luca says, and stops. Willow nods, not quite meeting his eyes in case she frightens him into silence. "One day. She was out. She'd gone shopping I think, with a mate or something. Like a proper day of it, going to a big shopping centre." He laughs. "I mean, that's a shit day out if you ask me, but anyway. And she was supposed to come back at a certain time and she was late. It wasn't her fault, she missed the bus and got the next one… but he just, fucking, he just lost the plot."

His fingers fidget about the log for something else to

destroy. If she took his hand in hers, would he grow quiet? Or would he start tearing at her skin?

"So they had this massive row. Screaming, swearing, the full thing. I thought the neighbours might call the police. I mean, I nearly did it myself but I didn't know if my mum… anyway. He was winding himself up to hit her. Squaring up to her and everything."

He's watching for her reaction. She isn't sure what he's expecting. The story he's telling her is both banal and horrible, dreadfully familiar and dreadfully predictable, like a story from a soap opera. What's the right expression for her to wear?

"And then…" he laughs. "Well to be honest, I don't really know what happened next. I mean, you know when people talk about the red mist coming down? It was like, I was *someone else* for that bit of time. I can't hardly even remember what I did to him, but I know it was bad because they made me look at the pictures afterwards and he was all bashed up and that…" There is a quiver of emotion in his voice that could be either fear, or remembered pleasure. "And I knew I'd done it, but I couldn't *remember* doing it. So I called the ambulance, and everything kind of snowballed from there. I mean, I thought for a minute I'd killed him."

He looks both ashamed and proud as he says this, and she finds herself staring at the skinny clench of his boyish fist in fascination. Surely he was acting in defence of someone else, so why is he the one who's been sent away? Why didn't the boyfriend have to leave? And how can a grown man be frightened of a boy?

"Thing is," Luca continues, as if he can read her thoughts, "he fractured his skull. Well, okay, *I* fractured his skull. And that counts as, like, GBH. If they find that I did it – I mean, obviously I *did* it, but if they say it wasn't, like, self defence – then I'll end up doing time. Which is going to be crap, but, you know, I'll manage." He shrugs. "Only I can't stay with my mum while we're waiting for the court case cos she's still with *him,* and he reckons he don't feel safe with me around. And if I get sent down…" His face contracts and she glimpses the frightened teenager who lives behind the tough-guy persona. "At least it'll be a chance to get some qualifications under my belt. I can do the classes and that. Keep myself busy. Not like there'll be much else to do. Might as well try and better myself while I'm in there."

Lucas adjusts his beanie hat and forces a cocky grin.

"Right, come on then. Best get back to you before you get mad about me not paying you any attention."

I bet, she thinks, *you have nightmares about being locked inside. About what might happen to you while you're in there. I bet you're terrified you won't be able to cope.*

"I bet," he says slowly, eyes bright, gaze sly, "the lads at your college were well into you and your sister. You know. With you being identical twins and that. I bet they all used to fantasise about—"

Before she can stop herself, she slaps him. The crack of skin against skin echoes off the trees like a gunshot. She regrets it almost immediately.

I'm sorry, she thinks frantically, and then, *No I'm not sorry, how dare you?* It's because she has no words, that's what it is. If she can't speak, how else can she express what's going on in her head? She reaches out to touch his cheek, but then Luca grabs her, his fingers hard and vicious in the meat of her shoulder, dragging and pushing her against a tree, and then his breath is in her mouth and his tongue is between her lips and his body is hard against hers, and this is not a kiss, it's an invasion, an act of war, and all she can do is let it happen.

"Shit! Sorry. No." As suddenly as it began, it's over. Luca lets her go and backs away, rubbing his mouth with the back of his hand. "Jesus, no. Fuck. Are you all right? Sorry, of course you're not, I mean, you shouldn't have hit me either, but I shouldn't have done that. Did I hurt you? God, I don't ever want to, I promise, I swear, I won't do that again."

She feels sore and battered, but she's not sure exactly

which part of her he's damaged. When she probes her lips with her tongue, her mouth feels swollen.

"I'm sorry. I am so sorry. But you can't just, like, touch me like that, when I'm not expecting it."

I didn't touch you, she thinks. *I hit you.*

"I mean, I really like you." His hand hovers over her shoulder. "But you've got to be careful around me, okay? We have to be – we can't – I mean, if we're ever, like, doing something and I push you away, you've got to let me do it and get right away from me cos otherwise I might—" His fingertips touch her face, light and delicate. "Are you scared of me now? Cos I wouldn't blame you."

The shameful thing is that she isn't, she isn't scared at all. While he was kissing her, she knew she was still alive.

"Here." He picks up the knife, presses it into her hand. "Maybe you ought to hang onto this after all. Might come in handy some time."

The handle feels good in her hand. She wants it and she doesn't want it. It doesn't feel like something she should keep hold of. With a sharp sense of loss, she lets it fall to the ground and kicks it away.

"Soft wench," Luca says. "Think of the damage you could do with that. Look, we should get back, yeah? God, it's hot, isn't it? Are you hot?" He pushes his sleeves up to his elbows, then pulls them down again. "I've got to get back. You coming?"

It's no good, she thinks as she follows behind him. *I saw.* He's hoping she hasn't noticed, but one quick glance was all it took to see that Luca's forearms are crazed with long silvery scars, tracing out the places where the blue veins lie beneath his skin.

CHAPTER NINETEEN

"How are you, sweetie?"

Willow stretches out long and thin, enjoying the luxurious tug in her muscles, the feeling of expansion as her arms and legs breach the edges of the chair and her back presses against the arm. Then she coils herself back into the crease of the chair-arm and surrenders herself to her mother's voice.

"I know you've been doing some work because your tutors email me when they've marked your assignments." Her mum's voice is uncertain, as if she isn't sure it's all right to say this. "It must be weird though, doing all that stuff by yourself rather than in a class."

The weirdest thing about it is how little time it requires. Alone in her bedroom, she can blitz through what she'd previously have considered a full day's work in a couple of hours. Of course, it's possible that without the goad of a teacher supervising and critiquing her, she simply isn't putting in enough effort, and her grades are falling through the floor.

"They send me the grades as well," her mother continues. "But we haven't been looking. I mean, we've seen them because they're in the emails, but we don't mind what marks you get. We're just proud of you for getting something done."

No, Willow thinks, *don't say that.* She wonders if her mother can hear her frown through the phone handset.

"College rang," her mother says. "To see how you were getting on." She laughs. "I thought we'd burned our bridges there good and proper. Your dad was a bit rude, before. They send you their best."

It's hard to remember that the college still even exists, that each morning everyone but her still gets up and packs their bag, boards the bus and gets off again, pushes their way through the crush of students in the central hallways. Do her classmates talk about her at lunchtime sometimes? Or has everyone simply closed up around the gap where she used to be?

"They miss you," her mother says. "That's what Mrs Bascombe said, anyway."

Yeah, right. There was no way her teachers missed her, not the girl she'd been these last few months, slow and silent and hopeless, physically present but mentally lost, a walking waste of carbon. Most of the time everyone forgot she was there. Then there'd be a moment when she'd become visible again, and with this remembering would come a sudden cold hush as everyone realised for the millionth time that they didn't know what to say to her. Who could miss that?

"D'you know, when I was at university we were always talking about twins," her mother says. "All the studies into nature versus nurture. And when we had our first scan and the sonographer told us, the first thing I thought was about all those papers."

For a frantic moment, Willow wonders if her mother ever considered conducting her own experiment.

"It's such a strange way to meet someone. A blurry black-and-white picture on a screen, and all these *organs* and the *teeth* and the massive heads…" her mother laughs. "And then there were two of you, my God, the shock of that. We couldn't speak at first. And then your dad said, *which kind is it? Are we having the weird kind? I mean, the kind like in The Shining?*"

She can feel the laughter bubbling behind her breastbone,

longing to be freed. She can imagine her dad saying exactly this.

"And the sonographer said, *You mean girls?* Like *girls* was the weird part, rather than *identical*…"

Willow's ribcage is shuddering. She hopes her mother can hear the change in her breathing.

"Willow? Are you all right, sweetie? I haven't made you cry, have I?"

No, that's not it, I was laughing. Why can't you tell? Except she's crying too, although she only realises when something tickles her nose and that something turns out to be her own tears. The thick sharp line between laughter and sorrow has vanished. She settles for blowing her mother a kiss instead, hoping the burst of air in her mother's ear will explain everything.

"It was funny though, knowing I'd only be pregnant once," her mother says. "I mean, not that being pregnant is so much fun that I wanted to do it again. But we'd always wanted two children, and then we were getting two at the same time. I remember thinking all the way through, *this is the only time I'll ever do this*. And I cried when they said I ought to have a c-section, because that meant I'd never get to go through labour. Can you imagine? That's what it's like though, the first time. You're so obsessed with getting to the finish line you sort of forget that's just the start."

Willow isn't comfortable with this conversation. She wants her mother to talk to her about things that don't matter, about the weather and the garden and her dad and what they had for dinner that night and her work receptionist, Helen, who's sometimes rude to the patients but whose rudeness is sometimes justified. She wants to get lost in stories about things she doesn't care about and people she'll never meet.

So tell her. Talk to her. Ask her a question so she'll talk about something else.

Willow switches the phone to her other ear, and turns around in the chair to get more comfortable.

"The other thing I remember," her mother says, her voice very hesitant now, "was thinking neither of you would ever be on your own. Joe told me once that before I was born, he always felt outnumbered. Because there were our mum and dad in the grown-up generation, and only him in his. He said he used to feel like being squashed. And when I saw the two of you on the screen I thought, *Well, at least we'll all be nice and even, right from the start*."

She's never consciously thought of it this way before, but Willow recognises the rightness of what she's saying. Even when she and Laurel were small, there was a balance in their family, their two-by-two configuration ensuring equality. She and Laurel squabbled, of course, fiercely and many times a day. But when it came to the big decisions, they spoke as one, taking advantage of their twinship to add weight to their arguments. *We don't want to go for a walk, we think we should go to the park instead. We'd like to have pasta, not potatoes. But we both like jumping in puddles.* Sometimes they won, sometimes they lost; but they both knew that, working together, they won more often than they would have done if they were one on their own.

"There was this one time when you were about six," her mother says. "You had a couple of friends round. You were all doing some drawing. And one of the other girls, she was being silly, the way kids are when they're somewhere new, and she said Laurel's drawing was rubbish. Poor Laurel was absolutely crushed. And you looked at the mean girl, and you looked at Laurel, and you said, *Well, I think it's beautiful*. And you started pointing out all these nice things, the colours she'd chosen and so on, and after a minute the other little girl, the one who hadn't been mean, started joining in as well, everyone saying how great Laurel's drawing was. Only soon you were both praising Laurel's drawing by saying it was better than the mean girl's, and the mean girl started crying."

Willow tries to remember these events – the colouring, the dining table, the girls from their class – but comes up empty. Did this really happen? How can her mother recall it so clearly when to Willow herself, it feels like a story about someone else?

"So your dad felt like he had to tell you off," her mother continues. "Because, to be fair, the mean girl *was* a guest, and you *had* made her cry. But as soon as he started talking, Laurel glared at him and said, *Don't tell Willow off, she was looking after me*. And he said afterwards he'd never realised until then how great it was to have a sibling. How much he'd missed out on, being an only child. He said he knew you'd be all right no matter what, because you'd always have each other's backs."

Then why did you stop talking to Joe? Willow hadn't cared about this for years, but now it seems all-consuming. But even if she could ask, would either her mother or Joe tell her the answer?

"I mean, I know no one could ever replace Laurel," her mother continues. "She was irreplaceable. People are irreplaceable. You can't swap one for another. And I don't ever want you to think you're not enough. If we'd looked at that ultrasound screen and seen just you, we'd have been so proud, so thrilled. And if you'd been the only child we'd been lucky enough to have, we'd have been the proudest, happiest parents on Earth."

There is a curious intensity to her mother's words, as if she's arguing with herself. Willow pushes herself upright, sitting forward and frowning with concentration, as if her mother's in the chair on the other side of the fireplace.

"But," her mother continues, "I am so, so sorry you've ended up with this. Being the only child, I mean. It's too much, to go through this life as one on your own. No one should have to do it."

Her mother's words drive a thin sharp hole into her. This is exactly how she's felt since Laurel left them. Unbalanced. As if there's too much weight on her shoulders, as if she has to carry a burden meant for two to share. She presses her hand tight against her chest, half-expecting to find some physical wound.

"Willow? Sweetie? Are you still there?"

She manages a deep noisy sigh.

Her mother begins speaking again, telling Willow about a rainbow she saw over the garden that afternoon, how rainbows have always been a symbol of hope and renewal, but Willow is lost in her own thoughts. How will she make it through all the months and years that lie ahead? How will any of them survive now it's her by herself, and if she fails, at something big or small, there will be no *Oh well, at least Laurel's fine, I'm sure Willow will be too soon,* no *Never mind, remember that time Laurel did that awful thing at the pub, and now look at her?*

And even if she does well, her parents will still be looking at her, because there'll be nowhere else to look. She'll be the only one who can deliver the things all parents want: a wedding, grandchildren, a parade of work and leisure accomplishments to trade with their friends. Their attention will beat down on her like the noonday sun. She has no idea how she will survive.

PART THREE

NOVEMBER

CHAPTER TWENTY

She's standing in the doorway that leads to the outside stairs, and she knows she's asleep because when she walks, her feet take her right off the edge of the landing and into the air. It's thick enough to support her, and when she stretches her arms up, she finds she can swim through it, up and up until the world lies below her like a miniature model.

We're safe up here. It's not her thought, but Laurel's. Laurel is pale, as she always is, but tonight her nightdress is stained, and there's something else about her that is different; when Laurel turns over in the air and propels herself earthwards, Willow can see the outline of the buildings through her sister's shape.

I'm dissolving, Laurel explains. The words come to Willow as a thought rather than a sound. Laurel's lips blue and still. *It's because I've been left on my own for too long.*

Willow reaches out a hand to catch Laurel's. The flesh feels spongy and yielding, and Willow is afraid that she's breaking Laurel just by touching her.

It's what happens to us when someone we love dies, Laurel says without words. *I'm falling apart. It's not my fault. I want to stop it, I want to be how I was, but I miss you so much.*

But that's what I feel, Willow replies, pressing her hand against her own pounding heart.

I know. Because I'm you. And you're me.

Does that mean I'm dead?

Of course you're dead. Laurel rolls her eyes.

No. That's not right. I'm not—

You died that day in the gym. Don't you remember? You were doing circuit training. You always hated it but you were doing it anyway because you wanted to get fit. Then your heart started beating really fast and everything went black. They said you were unconscious, but you weren't. You could feel and hear everything that happened. They crowded round you and the teacher was pushing on your chest and you could feel your ribs breaking. You could hear them snapping, and it hurt so much, and you wanted to beg him to stop, but you couldn't. And you wanted me to be with you, but I wasn't. I was somewhere else. You had to go through all of that, all by yourself, all the hurting and the terror, all by yourself. Laurel is crying, fat thick tears tinged faintly with pink, as if her eyes are bleeding a little. *And I didn't know. I should have known but I didn't. It was happening to you and I didn't realise. I'll never forgive myself for not being there at the end. Never.*

No, Willow says, desperate. *It was you. You died in the gym. That happened to you. I'm the one who can't ever be forgiven. I'm me and you're you. You're dead and I'm alive.*

What does it matter? Laurel presses her fingers to her cheeks and the tears soak into them like sponges. When she lets her hands fall, there are finger-shaped indents in the skin. *No one can tell the difference anyway. Maybe it was you who died, and they thought it was me. Maybe we swapped.*

We haven't done that for years, it never worked anyway. People can always tell which is which, because we're different people.

No, says Laurel, *we're not. We never were. They tried to tell us we were different people, but we both knew better. We're the same. We have one heart between us. And that's why we're both broken. We only have one heart, and you've got it.* She tears at the front of her nightgown. *Look.*

Willow doesn't want to look, but this is a dream and she

can't make herself turn away. The incision marches from each shoulder, two lines kissing in the middle of Laurel's breastbone and becoming one, held together with fat black staples that bite into her flesh.

That's why I need you to come and be with me, Laurel explains. *I need our heart back. But you're trying to give it away to someone else.*

What are you talking about?

You know, says Laurel, and turns her face away.

If the air really was water and they really were swimming, it would take them hours to get anywhere, but this is a dream, and they can move at whatever speed is necessary for its message to unfold. They soar and swoop, pushing themselves higher to escape the clutch of the trees that reach greedily for their ankles. In a minute, they're over the farmhouse, which sprawls out more expansively than in the waking world, all its windows aglow and welcoming.

There's a boy in there, Laurel says. *And you like him.*

No I don't. Not like that.

Don't be stupid. I know you better than anyone. Have you kissed him yet?

Has she kissed him? Trapped in the fiction of her dream, she can't remember. When she thinks about Luca, she can only find the feelings he summons in her: a tension that might be fear or excitement, a racing in her pulse, a feeling that something is about to change, for better or for worse.

You're remembering what it's like to die, Laurel tells her. *That's how I felt, right before it happened. I remember looking around the gym and thinking,* This is it, this is where it's going to happen. *I knew something big was coming, but I didn't know what. It felt like someone had sewed a bird in my chest. And now, when you think about Luca, you're thinking about death. That's how it feels to die.*

I thought you said it was me who died in the gym, Willow says, not because she wants to argue but because she doesn't want to discuss Luca. He's the first one who has only known her in her single state. The first person who looked at her and saw her without seeing Laurel's shadow.

Laurel rolls her eyes. Her eyeballs seem too small for their sockets and the surface looks dull and shrivelled.

It doesn't matter which of us it was. The point is, they separated us. You can't fall in love with him, it's too dangerous.

I don't know what you mean, Willow says. *I don't even know if I like him. He's just a boy I hang around with sometimes because there's literally nobody else around here to talk to.*

He's afraid of you, says Laurel, and as she says this they're outside one of the bedroom windows, looking in through the gap in the curtains. *He's afraid of you because you're dead. You fooled him for a while, you made him think you were still alive, but he knows the truth really. That's why he stopped kissing you. Because he's terrified.*

He isn't scared of me, Willow protests.

Of course he is, says Laurel. She takes Willow's hand and they melt through the wall and into Luca's bedroom. Luca is fast asleep, curled on his side with his hair sticking out at foolish angles.

Wake him up, then, says Laurel.

All right, Willow says, and reaches out a hand to touch Luca's shoulder.

But then she sees that Laurel's wearing Willow's pyjamas, her skin smooth and firm, her eyes bright. And now Willow feels the pain in her chest, feels the slow black ooze of fluid from the scar that splits her open.

Luca opens his eyes, and the look of utter terror on his face as he scrabbles to get away from her is almost enough to stop her heart. But her heart has already stopped. It stopped that day in the gym, and now she's simply a dead girl walking, waiting for her twin to come and join her.

She wakes to find herself standing on the stone landing outside her room. The slight breeze makes the door creak and the curtain whisper. She thinks she ought to feel cold, but she can't feel much of anything.

Maybe I'm still asleep, she thinks. *Maybe this is one of those dreams you keep trying to wake up from but you're so deep under you can't quite manage it. Maybe I can still fly.*

She creeps forward towards the edge of the landing and holds out one leg over the void below, testing the air with her foot to see if it might be thick and strong enough to hold her weight and allow her to soar into the sky.

CHAPTER TWENTY-ONE

Willow is supposed to be analysing poetry. She has all the requirements for this to happen: she is sitting at her desk, she has her set-text book open alongside her study guide notes, she has the worksheet her tutor sent through to her, she has two different colours of pen to annotate the text, a clean new sheet of lined paper to capture her observations. She has everything she needs, except the will to make a start.

What's the point of doing this, anyway? These words were written down hundreds of years ago, back when everyone believed in God rather than evolution and there were whole swathes of the globe that no one from the poet's country had even been to yet. What's she doing, reading about his nice boring walk in the hills and how happy the daffodils made him? What could a man who thought other people wanted to hear his views about daffodils possibly have to say to someone like her?

Joe is rattling around the kitchen. He's probably cooking. He likes to cook; great elaborate meals that generate mountains of leftovers, which she'd happily eat for lunch the next day, but somehow he disappears them into the freezer and replaces them with something new and exciting that makes her forget the dazzling tastes of the day before. She could be downstairs learning to cook, instead of up here with this useless essay. That would be far more worthwhile than taking poems to pieces to find out what makes them tick. No, she's got to try. This is the bargain she made with her parents, and she has to stick to it.

She drags her attention back to the page, but her thoughts are in rebellion. Who cares if this man likes daffodils? Everyone likes daffodils. What's not to like? They're pretty, they're cheap, they grow everywhere. This is a poem about privilege, is what it is. The privilege to go off into the Lake District and look at the view and think, *Wow, very nice*, and then come home and scribble some thoughts about it and mess around with them until they're nice and rhymey, and then go down to eat a dinner cooked by someone else and pretend you'd done a day's work. No, she can't put that, it's not the right answer. She stares at her study guide. If she learns this by heart instead, will she pass her exam? Is that what her teachers want her to do? What will she have proved when she's done it? She turns the pages impatiently, looking for something that might inspire her to do some work:

When we two parted
In silence and tears
Half broken-hearted
To sever for years,
Pale grew thy cheek and cold,
Colder thy kiss—

She throws the book to the floor and scoots backwards off the bed, as if the problem is with the words on the page rather than the feelings in her head. Why didn't she stick to the daffodils, to the stupid self-indulgent daffodils and the man who thought everyone wanted to hear about them? Is that what the daffodils poem is for? To fill everyone's heads up with smooth sweet bland niceness, drowning out the horrors of their lives? If she had her voice she'd be whimpering and maybe even screaming, and then Joe would come up the stairs two at a time to see what was wrong. But she knows by now that even terror isn't enough to call her voice back out, and Joe continues to potter around, accompanied by a faint murmur that could be him singing to himself or could be him talking to the kitten.

It's all right, she tells herself, *it's only a poem. You don't have to read it again. You could tear the page out maybe, then you know it's gone for ever.* She doesn't want to touch the book, but she makes herself do it, trying to see and not see the words so she can take out the right page. A quick rip and it's done, the page is gone and crumpled in her hand and all that remains is a thin raggedy edge of paper.

She stares at the space she's created, shocked and disbelieving. She's vandalised a book. She's never torn a book up, never.

You know better than this! You both do! The words come to her in her mother's voice, and she's very small, sitting on the floor beside Laurel and the tattered remnants of a book they were squabbling over. *You know better than to rip your books! What's the matter with you both, tearing it all to pieces like that? Books are precious. Now which one of you was it?* She can remember their joint puzzlement, their sense that neither of them had *done* it, and the book had somehow come undone through some process of its own. And the way their mother's rage melted into tears as she picked up the pages. *I bought you this for your first birthday.* She can't remember the book, she can't remember even if it was hers or Laurel's. She can only remember the shame, and the knowledge that neither of them would ever damage a book again.

And now she's broken their promise. Another step away from the person Laurel knew. But it's just one page. She won't do it again. She puts the crumpled page in the bin in the corner, balancing it precariously on the top, but she can feel it staring at her over the rim of the basket.

What she really wants to do is burn it, but she doesn't have any matches. She'll have to think of something else instead.

In the bathroom, she tears the paper into scraps and drops

them into the toilet. They float, take on water, then finally slip beneath the surface. She takes her time, adding more pieces gradually, hoping they won't clog in the pipe. There's far more paper than seems feasible for a single page. Eventually, she flushes, holding her breath. Will the water keep rising? No, it's sinking, and the wad of paper's disappeared like magic. It's as if she never did anything wrong. She can pretend the book was always missing the page. If anyone asks, she can say it was like that when she got it.

She's feeling so good, so relieved and free, that she forgets to be careful of the mirror. Her reflection snags her as she passes. Before she can stop it, she's caught.

There it is, that face she used to share but that now belongs to her alone. She wants to look away, but the face in the mirror has her gaze now, and all she can do is stare into the frightened eyes that look back at hers. Once she knew the million small differences that made this face hers and not Laurel's: the blemishes that came up at the same time of the month but in different places, the freckles that emerged in slightly different patterns under the almost-identical rays of sunshine, the small hair and make-up choices that marked them out as individuals. Now, all she can see is her sister, as if Laurel's fighting Willow for possession of their single remaining body. Her face is white, the skin under her eyes bluish, her lips are dry. When did she turn into her sister's ghost?

She raises a hand to her face, and then lets it fall. She's afraid to touch her own skin, afraid it will feel spongy and yielding, and her finger will leave a permanent indent. She's a walking corpse, she's dead and doesn't know it yet, this body died that day in the gym and now the only decent thing to do is—

What happens next is a mystery. Her hand's raised; Laurel disappears; there's a crash; the floor fills with bright splinters. She's sure she must have had something to do with it, but she can't make herself believe that she's taken her uncle's mirror, his beautiful silver-framed antique mirror, and deliberately smashed it on the floor of the bathroom. She stares at the spines of glass, the exposed wood where the silver veneer has split, and feels only confusion. She can hear Joe's shout of alarm, asking if she's all right. She could go and meet him, save him a few seconds of panic, but the mirror's spread across the floor in a glorious silver starburst, and she isn't sure if it's safe to move.

"Willow?" Joe knocks on the door. "Willow, I'm going to open the door, okay? If you're in the shower or something I promise I won't look." The door peels open slowly, and Joe glances cautiously in, trying to see as little as possible while still trying to see what's happened. "Oh no, not the mirror…"

She can see her mother in him as he kneels, in the way he reaches tenderly out to the frame as if he's picking up something alive and vulnerable. For the second time that morning she remembers the book that was destroyed. Guilt thumps in her stomach.

"Maybe… no, the frame's gone too, it's cracked." He's trying not to mind, but she can tell that this has hurt him, hurt him deep in his heart in a way she hadn't imagined anything ever could. She ought to say something, one of the things you're supposed to say. *I'm really sorry. I didn't mean to. It was an accident. I'll clean it up.* The things you say when you're a child, words that work like a spell to get you out of trouble. If she could say these things, perhaps he'd reply with the counterspell, *It's all right, I know you didn't mean to. I'll clean it up, it's not safe for you. Don't worry.* Instead, all she has is silence, as her uncle kneels at her feet and picks up the jaggedy shards of mirror as if he might somehow piece them back together.

"We were on holiday," he says, almost to himself.

I'm sorry, she thinks. *I'm sorry. I'm sorry. Please believe me.* If he'd only look at her, if he could only see the words that she's longing to speak, he'd understand. But he doesn't look.

"What were you doing with it? Did you try to take it off the wall?" She shakes her head. "You must have been, it was on there securely enough. Seriously, Willow, there's a mirror over the basin if you needed a better light for your make-up or whatever."

I'm not even wearing any make-up, Willow thinks. *I can't. I can't look in mirrors any more, all I see is…* She needs to do something to remind him who she is, that she's allowed to break things and wreck things and make mistakes, and it's his job to forgive her because he's the adult and she is broken, and that's how this is supposed to work. Perhaps if she cleans up the mess she's made, he'll forgive her? She lifts her foot, looking for a safe place to put it down again.

"For Christ's sake," he says wearily. "Don't be ridiculous. Stay there and don't move. I'll need to sweep up first before you walk on that floor. Oh, you would pick right now to learn to climb the stairs, wouldn't you?" He grabs the kitten, who is sniffing curiously at the broken frame, and passes him to Willow with an artificial smile. "Look, it's all right, it's only a mirror. We can always buy another one. The important thing is you're okay. Stay there and keep him out of mischief. I'll get a dustpan and brush."

These are the words he's supposed to say, but she can tell his heart isn't in it. He's going through the motions. She hadn't thought of him as a man who treasured possessions. It occurs to her that she doesn't really know him at all. She waits exactly where she is, holding herself perfectly still, the kitten riding on her shoulder. Joe comes back up the stairs.

"Okay," he says, squaring his shoulders as if he's recommitting to the right behaviour. "First things first. Willow, are you all right? You're not cut anywhere?" She shakes her head. "You're sure? Glass cuts can be funny, you don't always feel them straight away." She holds her hands out to him, turning them over and over so he can see the pristine envelope of her skin. "How about your feet? Did it get you on the way down? Yes it did, look at that. No, keep still and let me—"

He grasps her ankle firmly, and plucks a small bright

splinter from her foot. She only feels the pain as he takes it out of her. She watches in fascination as a fat ruby cabochon grows on her skin.

"Don't move," he says again, and this time he sounds as if he means it, as if he really cares about her not hurting herself. The anxious knot in her stomach begin to unravel. There's something almost soothing about watching the mirror being cleaned away, knowing there's one less reflective surface where Laurel can hide and peer out at her.

"It wasn't expensive or anything," he continues as he works. "The mirror, I mean. It was only from a junk shop in Stratford." Nonetheless his movements are careful and slow, as if even the fragments that spark and tumble in the sunlight, gathering like glitter on the bristles of the brush, are precious. "Have you been there?" She shakes her head. "It's pretty. Full of pictures of that hideous Shakespeare portrait, but the buildings are nice. Anyway, it wasn't like we'd had it for years, we only got it last October. We were there for his—" The brush, which has been making slow careful arcs of the floor and gathering up miniscule looking-glass fragments, stutters to a halt. She's in the presence of something very precious, and if she moves at all or even breathes, it will shatter and disappear.

Keep talking, she wills him. *Please. I want to know. Tell me about this bit of my family. Tell me his name, that'd be a start, and then I could Google him and find out the rest.* She can see he wants to talk. She knows what that looks like, what it feels like to have the words piling up inside of you with nowhere to go.

"Anyway," he says, and shakes the glass briskly down into the dustpan. "You're sure you're not cut anywhere else?" She nods. "Good. Are you ready for lunch? Give me twenty minutes and I'll give you a shout when it's ready."

Alone in the bathroom, she pauses to take stock. There is one piece of glass still remaining, a lone survivor that slid beneath the doorway to hide in the corner. It's well-concealed, but she sees it glint when she moves. She picks it up, careful not to cut herself. When she holds it in her hand, she can feel the potential dripping from its edges.

She shouldn't keep this. She ought to take it downstairs and throw it away.

Instead, she takes it back to her room and stashes it in the drawer beneath her underwear. After a moment, she takes the torn poetry book and puts it with the glass spike.

Feeling light and free, she hurries downstairs to the kitchen where Joe's doing something fiddly with plum tomatoes and basil and a long flat loaf of ciabatta.

"How's the school work going?" Joe is himself again, breezy and contented, in control of his world. Willow shrugs. "I know, stupid question. I used to hate people asking me when I was your age as well. What were you working on today? Nod when I get it right. French? History? English?" She nods. "Okay, Shakespeare? Dickens? Oh, hang on, poetry?" Another nod. "Bet you're doing the English Romantics. I remember absolutely hating them. Flouncing around in their huge white shirts, always starving to death or getting TB or drowning or, I don't know, having sex with their sisters or something. Am I allowed to say that in front of you?"

I'm seventeen and I've got the Internet and even if I didn't, the teachers go out of their way to tell us this stuff, to try and get us interested. She resists the impulse to roll her eyes. It's not his fault he's so innocent.

"And then the way they make you take all the poems to pieces," Joe continues, gloomily scooping out the seeds from another tomato. "How they expect anyone to enjoy a poem they've spent weeks ruining… You know, if you and Luca want to study together, he's more than welcome. I know he's doing resits and you're doing A-levels, but, you know, if you fancy some company."

The sudden change of direction takes her by surprise. She doesn't have time to arrange her face into a suitably neutral expression. Luca is just for her, and she isn't even sure what they are to each other, but she doesn't want to ruin it with textbooks, to see his weaknesses and failures exposed. She likes him wild and rebellious, out in the woods doing things they both know they shouldn't do. Joe is watching her as if he can read everything she's thinking in the shape of her face.

"Yeah, I thought not," he says. "I don't blame you. Why ruin everything with work? I promised Katherine I'd ask, is all. She's worried he doesn't spend enough time studying. But if you want to have him round here and hang out together, that's fine too." He shreds basil leaves with his fingers. "Be careful, though. He's a bit of a wild boy apparently."

I know he is, Willow thinks proudly. *He's a criminal, sort of. He beat up his mother's boyfriend to keep her safe and now he might go to jail for it.* Does that make him the hero of the story, or the villain? She isn't sure if she approves of what he did, exactly, but there's something appealing about his recklessness, the way he charged straight in without stopping to think of the possible consequences.

"I mean, not that there's anything objectively *wrong* with a wild boy," Joe adds, almost as if he's talking to himself. "But I promised your mother…"

What? What did you promise her? She thought she knew everything her mother had told Joe about keeping her safe, shamelessly eavesdropping on as many conversations as she could. *Don't let her have knives or scissors. If she needs any medicines, make sure she only gets one dose at a time and lock the packet away afterwards. Listen out for her sleepwalking. If she wets the bed in the night she'll try and clean it up herself. I think it's best to let her but I'm not sure, I don't want to embarrass her but I don't want her feeling like it's something she's got to hide. Make sure she eats regularly, she tends to starve herself and then steal all the biscuits…* Nothing at all about boys.

"Mind you," Joe says, putting the complicated sandwich down in front of Willow with a smile, "you should have seen the rough trade she used to drag home when she was your age."

She knows what he means by *rough trade*, but she's never heard anyone use the phrase out loud before. She likes its slightly out-of-time feel, like a piece of vintage clothing scrummaged from the back of a second-hand shop. *Rough trade*. Is Luca rough trade? Did her mother know that queasy feeling he induces in the pit of her stomach, as if she isn't sure whether she finds him attractive or repulsive? The sandwich is impractically fat, oozing olive oil and tomato juice. When she takes a bite, scarlet shells tumble from the sides and onto the plate. It's delicious, but she has no idea how she's meant to eat it with anyone watching.

"There was this one guy when she'd just turned sixteen," Joe says. "He dropped out of school – because that was actually a thing you could do when we were kids – just stopped going a couple of months before GCSEs and didn't bother turning up for the exams. I don't think anyone was really looking out for him and he was kind of flailing around, hoping things would work out somehow. But at the time she thought he was this huge rebel – well, we both did, really – and I think that's probably why she liked him. Our parents were shitting themselves in case he messed up her exams."

Willow tries to imagine her mother besotted with an unsuitable boy. She thinks of the certificates that hang on the wall behind her desk, of the carefully stored rolls of exam results, year after year of academic perfection.

"And," Joe continues, "he had this denim jacket with a dragon hand-painted on the back, and he gave it to her as a present." Willow chokes on her sandwich. "I know. It was a different time. She used to wear that jacket all the time, and he used to take her out on these really long walks, and they'd hang around in old graveyards and by the side of disused railway lines and so on." He's smiling, but she can tell from the look in his eyes that this is a sad memory too. "And she used to come home with little bits of flowers and grass in her hair. She looked so pretty and wild."

Willow picks up three tomato shells between her fingers

and pops them into her mouth one at a time. There are times when she's glad she's not able to speak.

"It was a bit hard to watch from the outside, though," Joe says thoughtfully. "I mean, I didn't mind her fooling around with boys or anything." He laughs. "I was probably just jealous because it wasn't me."

He's talking to her in the same way he talks to the kitten, as if nothing he says can ever be repeated, as if she doesn't matter. Her mother must hear confessions like this all the time. She must know how to move and breathe and respond in a way that doesn't interrupt the flow of self-analysis. What would her mother do? Willow sits as still as she can, keeping her breath slow and even and quiet. If the kitten wakes up and starts begging for attention, she'll wring his neck.

"She'd go out with all these cool boys, wearing their clothes, and they'd be looking at her, in that way. And I'd feel this awful *despair,* you know? Because she was my little sister and she was having proper relationships, and I'd never even kissed someone I liked. I mean, none of us were out then, you know? Absolutely none of us. Hopefully it's better for your generation."

Back in the days before, she and Laurel would have long, deep conversations, with each other, with their friends, with the occasional boy who had been temporarily admitted to their friendship group. At these times they all knew they could be completely honest, offering up their naked souls to the group and receiving only love and validation in return. She'd thought this was a unique quirk of their generation, something they had invented that would one day change the world as they came into their power and built a kinder society. She'd never imagined adults, fully formed and in their final lifetime shape, would do the same.

"I mean, I loved her to bits, of course I did, she's my little sister. But when you like the same boys they like, and it's blatantly obvious which of you they prefer... do you know what I mean? Feeling like you'll never quite live up to your...

Wait, no. Shit. Sorry, I didn't mean... God, did I leave the oven on? Hang on and I'll check and see if—"

She's never seen an adult blush like this. His face is scarlet, his neck is flushed, even his hands are shaking and blotchy. He pushes his chair away from the table, leaving his sandwich oozing and abandoned on the plate. She can see the pinky-red mush at the edges of the bread where his teeth have crushed the tomato into the dough. When he bends over the stove, pointlessly checking a dial that she can see from where she's sitting is firmly in the 'off' position, she can see the mottling on the back of his neck.

Tell him it's all right. Tell him you understand. Tell him it's not the worst thing anyone's ever said to you about Laurel. Tell him people say stuff like that all the time. Come on. You can do it. You broke his mirror. Now make up for it.

She gets off her chair and stands beside him, laying a hand awkwardly on his arm. When their eyes meet, for a moment he looks like her mother.

"I am so fucking sorry," he says, and the obscenity reinforces to Willow how strange this moment is between them, as if she is an adult now and he is the lost child. "I am the most thoughtless, stupid man on the planet and I can't believe I said any of that to you. I don't know what was going on in my head. Jesus. If I was a dog they'd probably have me—" He shakes his head fiercely, as if his thoughts are insects he's trying to dislodge from his hair. "No, no, no, I didn't mean that either. Sorry, Willow. You've officially got the world's worst uncle."

He's trying to claw his way back into the safety of adulthood, but it's too late now, she's seen the real person underneath.

"And while I'm at it, I'm truly, truly sorry I wasn't around for so long. I mean, six years of your life, Jesus. And it wasn't your mother's fault, not at all. The door was always open. It's just I was too stubborn to walk through it. She doesn't like

Shaun, you see, and I got the hump and said we came as a package or not at all, and then before you know it—"

She wants to ask him, *Was it because Shaun's a man?* She wants to ask him, *If Laurel hadn't died, would you have come back at all?*

"And I wish I hadn't missed so much of Laurel," he says, so soft and hesitant she can hardly hear him. "If she was anything like you she must have been lovely. I feel like I'm getting a second chance here, getting to know you a little bit. And I know that however sad I am, it's not even the tiniest little scrap of what you're going through. I don't want to be this crashing idiot who keeps putting his foot in his mouth and mentioning stuff that upsets you. I'll try and do better from now on. And I'm sorry I made such a bloody fuss about the mirror."

She's had enough of this conversation now. He's kind but clumsy, and he talks too much, and she isn't sure she can take the pressure of any more *sorrys* from him. Wondering how to make it stop, she's inspired by the thought of her mother, who would close a conversation as if closing a book – a quick folding of her hands, a smile and a turning away towards the next task – which in her case is the unfinished sandwich waiting for her on the table.

"You are so much like your mum it's almost spooky," Joe says, and Willow feels as comforted as if her mother has joined her for a moment at the table, caressing the back of her head with gentle fingers.

CHAPTER TWENTY-TWO

"There's something I wanted to ask you about."

Listening to her mother's voice is like sinking into deep warm water. With no need to reply, she can simply drift, letting the words cocoon her in love. Sometimes her mother talks to her about what she's done that day, a slow rundown of household tasks accomplished, interspersed with *and then I went to work and I saw sixteen patients, admitted one and discharged two, then spent the afternoon talking to the CCG about a project I want funding for*. With no visible evidence to contradict, they can both pretend Willow's a baby again, her silence the silence of the pre-verbal rather than the traumatised. Last night her mother read to her, the first chapter from *Moominvalley In November*, and Willow only realised she was being woken up when she felt Joe take the phone from her hand with gentle fingers, heard him murmur the words "I think she's asleep" and heard the faint tinny echo of her mother's chuckle.

But tonight there's something different, something she can sense even through the electronic distance separating them. Her mother sounds, well, how does she sound? She considers her options. *Angry*. No, that's not it, it can't be. She hasn't been there to do anything that might make her mother angry. *Stressed*. That's not it either. When under pressure, her mother's outward demeanour becomes very calm, and her voice becomes clipped and tight, as if she's commanding a military operation. *Upset. Anxious. Embarrassed.*

"Your dad and I were thinking about holidays," her mother says, to Willow's total surprise. "A holiday to go on, I mean."

Are they going away without her? She and Laurel had been negotiating for a trip without their parents next summer after their exams, but that was on the strict understanding that her parents stay at home, where they belonged, anxiously waiting for their chicks to return to the nest.

"Somewhere hot, if you like," her mother continues. "Or maybe something adventurous, Iceland maybe, we could go whale watching and see the Northern Lights."

Is there a *but* coming? Might this be some sort of bribe for good behaviour? *But we can only do it if you try this therapy, make this amount of progress, go back to college next term, get these grades in your mocks.* Will this only happen if she starts speaking again?

"This isn't a bribe, by the way," her mother says, and Willow wishes, for what must be the millionth time in her life, that her mother was less intuitive. How could anyone get in a decent teenage strop with a mother who was so insightful? "We thought it might be nice. Because…"

Yes?

But nothing comes after *because*.

"Oh, sweetie." Her mother's sigh is so sweet she imagines she can feel the warmth against her ear. "I wish you were here instead of there. It would be so much easier to talk to you."

That's not true. Willow, knowing she can't be seen, lets herself frown and shake her head. Communicating this way is a thousand times easier. A golden thirty minutes at a set time each day, and all the distance she could ever want in between. She finds it so satisfying that she's wondered if they could replicate it once her time in her uncle's house comes to an end. Could she call her mother once a day from her bedroom?

"We were thinking of doing some redecorating," her mother says. "Not your room, we wouldn't dream of doing anything in your room without you choosing, and not Laurel's room. But the spare room could do with a bit of love. Don't you think?"

Willow has absolutely no opinion about the spare room, but she's happy to hear her mother talking lightly about things that don't matter.

"When we bought the house, we had this mad idea we needed a guest room," her mother says, with a laugh in her voice now. "I mean, can you imagine? When have we ever had guests? And I never liked that sofa bed either. I think we bought it because it was on sale. But it's hideous. And unused. If it's still got its labels on, I'm giving it to charity. And if not, it's going in a skip."

When she was about thirteen, Willow had gone through a phase of creeping into the spare room and closing the door. She'd liked being somewhere unfamiliar in her own home, the sensation of exploring somewhere forbidden. Then she'd grown up a little bit more and lost interest. She'd never asked Laurel if she'd done the same thing.

"And we can get it furnished nicely," her mother continues, and that quiver is back in her voice again – what does it mean? Is she excited? Confused? Frightened? – "and make it properly welcoming."

Welcoming for who? Willow wonders wildly if this is meant for her. Perhaps they're thinking that if she moved rooms, got away from the space where she was always one of a pair, she might be able to speak again.

"And for the holiday," her mother says, as if this is a perfectly logical connection, "we could do something properly grown-up if you wanted. I mean, we could go somewhere cultural like Rome, or somewhere with great shopping and nightlife, maybe Barcelona, that might be great in the spring. Or if we were quick we could maybe fit it in before Christmas. But we thought maybe not *at* Christmas. Or, I don't know, we might do something else at Christmas, if you wanted to I mean, but not the holiday. I think what I'm saying is, let's play Christmas by ear and see how we're all feeling."

What's wrong with her mother? She's almost babbling now, talking and talking in a way Willow recognises because she used to do it herself. When there was something she desperately wanted to say or to ask for, instead of asking directly, she would talk all around the subject, until eventually one of her parents (usually her mother, sometimes her dad) would ask the right question: *Willow, are you trying to tell us you want to go out and get pizza for lunch? Would you like a microscope for your birthday by any chance? Do you want flashing lights in your trainers like Amy?* But she stopped that years ago. Her mother's a grown woman. Why would she be doing this? And what can the right question possibly be?

"I'm babbling, aren't I," her mother says. "Sorry. I don't know what came over me. Shall I read to you again? I really enjoyed reading to you the other night. Um. Sorry. Maybe if you don't want me to read to you, just, I don't know, press one or something."

This is the mother she needs, the one who can make jokes even though there's nothing really to laugh about. There's a faint rustle of paper, the hollow swooshing sound as her mother re-adjusts the handset, and her mother's voice pours out like a recording. She's a superb reader, never stumbling or hesitating, turning the pages without breaking the flow, and thank God, not attempting special voices for the characters. If she's not careful, she'll be asleep again. She keeps herself awake by picking at the places on her toes where her nail polish has grown out like a tideline. The polish is astoundingly durable. When did she last paint them?

("You know what I've noticed?" Laurel sits on Willow's bed, her toes splayed out by pink foam toe separators. "It's harder to polish your own fingers, but it's easier to do your own toes, because your feet are more ticklish... Want to try this red?")

Willow's hand falls to her side. She forces herself to breathe slowly and quietly.

"Willow?" Her mother, anxious and tender. "Sweetie? Are you all right?"

She's not all right. She's burning up with rage. This isn't fair. She should be past all these stupid reminders.

"Willow? Willow? I can hear there's something wrong. Darling, can you please give the phone to Joe so I can talk to him?"

She doesn't want to move, but she knows she has to, or her mother will become more and more panicked. She slumps out of the chair and goes to the kitchen, handing the phone to Joe. She will not let this conquer her. She will get herself back to a place where she can't be caught out. She will be strong.

"Hey there. Sorry, I didn't realise it was time… Oh, right. No, no, nothing to worry about, I think she's fine. Willow, are you fine?" She nods. "She's fine, she's nodding. Yeah, a bit, but you know what she's like, she can't stand a fuss… Um, so does that mean you… oh. Okay… No, I didn't mean that, God, what would I know?… No, not a thing…"

Willow has the volume of her phone turned up loud so that if she lays it down on the arm of her chair to get more comfortable, she can still hear her mother's voice. It also means that if she concentrates hard, she can listen in to what her mother's saying to Joe. She ought to do that now, because there's a puzzle here that she hasn't yet got to the bottom of. But the kitten's bouncing around her feet, begging to be picked up, and it's easier to go upstairs and lie on her bed and let him bite at her hair and snuggle against her ear, while she stares at the line of polish on her toes and lets the guilt gnaw at her insides, for daring to live while the girl who once sat beside her and painted her toenails in a colour called *Dragon's Blood* is gone.

CHAPTER TWENTY-THREE

When Willow wakes, she's aware that something's missing, and its absence feels good. She fumbles for a minute, then finds it. For the first time since it happened, she's woken without the terror that she'll have forgotten, somehow, that Laurel is dead.

She hadn't been aware until now of the fierce guard she set over herself, continually reminding her what she'd lost (*Laurel's gone okay she's gone make sure you remember, she's gone and she's never coming back*), to avoid the deeper pain of waking up forgetful, and having to walk into the fire of new remembrance. And now, without her realising it, the watcher has been stood down. Her sleeping self was unguarded, vulnerable to forgetting. It feels like a loss rather than a gain.

How did this happen? Is this the first step towards forgetting Laurel? She wants to get better, but she doesn't want to lose her sister. She stares at the ceiling and sorts carefully through her feelings, trying to rediscover her fear, but it's no good, there's nothing there, only the sense of relaxation, as if she's beginning to recover from a long illness.

Her phone tells her it's just after five in the morning, and when she pulls her curtains back the sky is blue and starry, but her body feels bright and eager to begin. She tiptoes into the bathroom, relieved that there's no mirror, relieved that today she won't have to wash her sheets. It's too early to start the day, but she gets dressed anyway, kisses the kitten's head as he stirs and stretches on her quilt, then opens the door to the outside staircase and gulps down the newness waiting outside.

It's too early to get up, too early to go for a walk, but nonetheless that's what she's doing. Her feet know the path past the empty chicken coop, the immaculate pig-pen where no one lives. There's something eerie about these places where animals ought to be, but are not. Someone should do something about it. She broke Joe's mirror, but maybe she can make up for it. She climbs over the fence and into the forest, enjoying the crunch of the beech-casts beneath her trainers.

In their shelter in the field, the goats stir as she passes, blinking yellow eyes toward her and considering whether it's time to leave their warm straw bedding and venture onto the cool damp ground. Are the bottoms of their feet more like bare feet, or shoes? She's seen the underneath, with their long bifurcated shape that makes her think of a hawk's talons, but she doesn't know how sensitive they are.

It's all right, she thinks to herself, as the billy leaps up and mounts a straw bale, his head raised in challenge. *I won't hurt you*. Her instinct is to hold his gaze, but she makes herself look down and away, turning her body soft and casual so he'll understand she isn't trying to threaten him. After a minute, he climbs back off his bale and folds himself back into the neat goat-loaf shape he was in when she arrived. And now she can go closer, to where the strong young kids – startlingly large now, and full of themselves – are already awake and ready to play, butting into each other and bleating.

Come here, she thinks, and rummages in her pocket where she has a packet of mints. The smaller kid tosses her head and leaps away, but the little billy prances forward, dips his head and nibbles the mint from her palm. His lips are clever and muscly. His lower jaw makes small neat circular movements as he crunches the mint between his teeth. Then he launches himself vertically into the air, all four feet extended, and tears off across the field, bounding over his little sister in a single strong leap.

Shit? Have I poisoned him? The little goat seems overwhelmed with his minty experience, leaping from side to side and tossing his head. *What if he keels over and dies? Will Katherine know it was me?* The little kid's squaring up to the billy goat, who doesn't even bother to get up, but simply turns his massive head in his son's direction and lowers his horns for a moment. *Never mind Katherine, what if he dies and the other goats know it was me?*

It's all right. It's not drugs. It's a sweet. Stop that now. Willow thinks this thought as hard as she can, willing the little goat to calm down and act more normally. *You're going to be fine.* The little goat lowers his head and paws at the ground. *No, don't do that, you'll get murdered.* The billy closes his eyes and turns his head away.

The little goat takes one more huge vertical leap, then trots back towards Willow and shoves his nose back into her palm, butting and nuzzling as if this will make another mint appear there. From the shelter, the kid's mother is watching attentively.

There, Willow thinks, feeling limp with relief. *It's all fine, see? Nothing wrong with him at all. He's asking for another one. No need to worry. I haven't hurt your baby.*

Either goats are telepathic or the mother goat is too lazy to get up, because she does nothing to stop Willow making her next move, which is to begin luring the kid across the field. He's clever enough to work out there are more mints in her pocket than the single one in her palm, and she has to work hard not to let him stuff his busy little muzzle in there. But with some coaxing and the occasional hard shove, she eventually gets them both over to the fence.

Now for the difficult part. Her instinct is to grab, but a sudden lurch will startle the goat, who is quicker and more nimble than she is. She placates him with another mint, then begins to scratch at the spot between his horn-buds. Now he's used to the sudden burst of heat from his snack, he seems happy to stand still and savour the experience. Still scratching at his head, she works her other arm slowly along his neck, down his flank, and then with a swift movement, scoops her arm behind his front legs. While he dangles over her arm, startled but accepting, she lifts his back end with her other arm. He's warm and comforting to hold, and much heavier than she remembers.

We're going on an adventure. Would he enjoy it if she could whisper these words into the long twitch of his ear? Perhaps he finds silence more reassuring. He's never heard her voice, after all. She heaves him over the fence somehow, sweating with fear that she'll drop him and hurt him, then follows as fast as she can. What will she do if he takes off into the trees? But he seems content to stay by her side, gazing back at his field on the other side of the fence with his yellow eyes wide with wonder.

We're going to my house now. You're going to have a new home. She tells him this not with words but with further offers of mints, walking a few feet down the path and holding out her palm until he joins her. As the field recedes, he becomes less interested in mints and more interested in the new foliage, darting from her side to pluck mouthfuls of bramble and cow parsley. But he's always watching her from the edges of his vision, making sure she doesn't leave him alone in this strange place. When she turns away to walk further down the path, he pings after her as if there's a piece of elastic stretched between them. Sometimes he trots neatly by her side like a dog. Sometimes he butts his head against the back of her knees.

Her original plan had been to shut the little goat in the pig-pen, but he leans so confidingly against her, and looks so small and alone, that she can't make herself do it. She could take him up to her bedroom, but she doesn't especially want a goat in her bedroom. Has Joe left the back door unlocked? Yes, he has, and the small sofa in the kitchen window seems the perfect place for a small goat who's taken the longest walk of his life to fold himself up for a rest. She leaves the back door open so he can get out into the yard if he wants to, settles him down with the rest of the Polo mints, and goes back to her room with the satisfied feeling of a job well done.

She's drifting somewhere warm and hazy between sleep and wakefulness when she hears Joe's steps on the stairs. She sits up and tickles the kitten behind his ears, her smile big and unstoppable. The kitchen door scrapes. She hears footsteps, the spurt of a tap, the click of the kettle, and then a sudden shout and a skitter of feet.

"Willow." Her uncle's voice comes to her as clearly as if he was standing in her doorway. "Would you know anything about this baby goat—" a little pause and another exclamation – "about this oddly minty baby goat that's standing in the kitchen?"

The joy is splitting her face in two. She jumps off her bed and pads downstairs, trying to arrange her face into a shape that doesn't instantly give away her complicity. In the kitchen, Joe and the goat stare at each other from opposite sides of the kitchen. When the goat sees her, it dashes to her side as if only she can save him from this sudden monster.

"He's very sweet," Joe says, sounding as if he really does think the goat is very sweet. "Is he one of Katherine's?" Willow scratches at the spot between the goat's ears. "Um, why is he here?"

How can she explain? *He's a present. He's to say thank you. Katherine's got too many goats anyway, she won't mind. He's to celebrate, because this is the first morning since it happened that I've woken up and not wanted to die.* She shrugs.

"So did he walk all the way? No wonder he was asleep when I came in. Oh, now, come on, fella, that's not playing the game." The goat spreads his back legs and pees, a startlingly huge and pungent puddle that splashes out across the tiles. Willow cringes and looks apprehensively at Joe, afraid he's going to yell at her, but her uncle's laughing, a deep low rumbling chuckle that makes everything all right and more than all right, and the goat pops his feet up on the table to steal an apple from the fruit bowl, and Joe, still laughing, opens the back door and shoos the goat out into the yard, where he crunches his apple and watches the two people inside mopping the floor as if it has nothing at all to do with him.

Willow spends the morning turning the pig-pen into a palace. There's no straw, but she improvises with a blanket, making a soft place for him to lie down. She fills a bucket with water from the tap, then wonders if he'll be put off by the chlorine, pours it out again, and refills it from the water butt. She raids the fridge and finds three carrots, a head of lettuce and a red pepper, which she mixes with an assortment of dandelion leaves to make a luxurious salad. The goat eats the salad, ignores the blanket, cries when she shuts the door on him and follows her around the yard like a dog.

In the utility room, she finds an actual dog bed, stuffed behind the drying rack and apparently forgotten about, which she carries triumphantly out to make the goat's blanket nest more welcoming. He climbs into it for a minute, pees, then hops back out and settles down next to her to go to sleep. Looking after him is more work than she'd imagined, but presumably it gets easier with time. After a few minutes, Joe arrives, armed with two plates of thick fluffy pancakes that ooze syrup and drip cream.

"Breakfast," he explains as he folds himself up beside her. "Well, brunch. Don't give any to the goat or he'll be sick."

Willow isn't sure how she's supposed to stop the goat from eating food that's right there in his face, but he seems exhausted by his busy day, and is obliviously asleep with his head in her lap. When he breathes in, his whole body inflates like a balloon. Trying not to drip cream on his head, she slices through her pancakes with her fork.

"You know we have to take him back," Joe says.

The goat's muzzle twitches. Willow wonders what he's dreaming about.

"Look at me so I know you're listening. That's better. Willow, he's very sweet, but he's not ours, okay? He's a farm animal, he's worth money, and Katherine's going to want him back."

We could buy him. I could buy him for you. How much can a goat possibly cost? I've got money.

"And even if I bought him, we can't look after him properly."

She looks disbelievingly around at the pen they're sitting in.

"Yes I know, but it's not just about having a proper enclosure. He needs to be with other goats. They're herd animals. They don't like to be on their own. Why do you think he's following you around?"

He could be a House Goat.

"And he can't live in the house, if that's what you're thinking. He'd pee everywhere." Joe reaches gently out to the goat's long silky ear, pulling it between his fingers. "And he's a billy. He won't stay this cute. He'll get huge and he'll stink and he'll be territorial. If he hasn't got any females to look after, he'll go looking for some, and he'll get down to Katherine's place and start fights and try and mate with his relatives."

Willow's pancake is sticking in her throat. She swallows hard to get it down, feeling as if she's eaten a stone.

"But thank you for bringing him. It was a really nice thought."

Why do you have all this space for raising animals, when you don't have any actual animals? The question fills her mouth, begging to be set free. *Come to think of it, why have you got a dog bed but no dog? What's the point of living in the country if you're not going to do country stuff?*

"We were planning to raise some livestock," Joe says. "Me and Shaun, I mean. Nothing complicated, but enough to feel like we were joining in. Some chickens. A couple of pigs."

So where are the chickens? Why has Katherine got the pigs? Perhaps her silence is an advantage. Perhaps he might feel he can tell her, knowing she'll never tell anybody else. The pen's very hot and the concrete's very hard, but nonetheless she feels safe and comfortable, surrounded by her own improvised miniature herd. Doesn't he feel it too? Doesn't he want the safety that comes in numbers?

"Right," he says, and gives her that smooth bright smile that tells her she's shut out again. "I'll give Katherine a call. She's probably wondering where this chap's got to. Don't worry, she won't be angry with you. She never really gets angry with anybody." He reaches out for the goat's ear again, and laughs when the goat twitches it away from his fingers. "He can come in the house if he absolutely must, but only the kitchen. No goats in the bedrooms, you understand?" Willow nods reluctantly. "Of course, if you happened to leave your outside door open, and if he happened to climb up the outside staircase, I probably wouldn't ever have to know about it."

Her first heroic plan is to sit with the goat for as long as he wants to sleep, but he's much heavier than he looks, and after a while her legs begin to hurt. When she drags herself out from underneath him, he staggers blearily to his feet and follows her out of the pen, pausing for a long drink from the bucket.

Revived by his drink, he needs no coaxing to climb the stairs, skipping into her room as if he's done this every day of his life. Within seconds he has his face in the bin. When he raises it again, he's chewing smugly on a crumpled tissue. She tries to take it out, but he responds by hoovering the tissue into his mouth at double-speed, his jaw rotating faster and faster as he devours his treat. The kitten scrabbles onto the chest of drawers, arches his back and fluffs up his tail.

Tissue consumed, the goat looks around the room with interest to see what else he can steal. They lunge simultaneously for her history notebook. Willow's fractionally quicker, but the goat takes his revenge by lifting his tail and expelling a stream of pungent black pellets onto the rug.

He's been in her bedroom for under three minutes, and he's already causing chaos. She leads him back out onto the staircase, then tries to shut the door in his face, but he guesses what she's planning and barges his way back in again, determined not to be left alone. She has to drag him away from the cable of the lamp before he electrocutes himself. The kitten watches in appalled fascination.

You can't stay here, she admits reluctantly to herself. She still doesn't see why he can't live out in Joe's pen – possibly joined by his little sister, which surely won't be a problem since apparently the herd's getting too big – but her half-formed secret-goat-in-the-bedroom plan is never going to happen. He's nudged open a drawer and is nibbling thoughtfully on the string of one of her hoodies. She tugs it out of his mouth, trying not to mind that it's now covered in slime, and leads him back into the yard.

The goat shit will have to wait until he's left. He clearly can't be trusted on his own. She pulls up a handful of dandelions, stuffs them into her pocket, and feeds them to him in scraps. His capacity for food seems never-ending.

She's expecting Katherine to arrive through the woods, and isn't prepared for the loud rattling arrival of the Land Rover, complete with a thing on the back like a horsebox. Suddenly the yard is very small and full of diesel fumes, and she and the goat hide behind the empty chicken coop as Katherine and Luca climb down from the cabin. For the first time, it dawns on Willow what she's done. She stole from Katherine – not an egg that would be replaced the next day, or a kitten that Katherine didn't want anyway, but a whole goat. Is she in trouble? She watches Katherine's face apprehensively. There's a certain tightness around the corners of her mouth, but when she sees Willow, the smile she gives her before disappearing into the kitchen is as friendly as ever.

"Did you seriously get that thing to follow you all the way through the woods?" Luca looks at the goat in disbelief. "What the fuck, mate?"

Willow isn't sure if he's asking her *how the fuck did you do it*, or *what the fuck were you thinking*. She settles for a shrug.

"You didn't have to carry it or nothing? So how did you get it over the fence? Mate, you did *not* lift that thing over the fence. You did not." He looks her up and down. "Your upper body strength must be absolutely mad."

Is he looking at her arms? Or at her breasts? When their eyes meet for a moment, they both look quickly away again. She scratches lightly at the goat's back. When Luca reaches out to do the same, their fingers meet.

"How'd you make him follow you?" Luca asks her. He's holding on to her fingers, his touch light and casual, but she can tell from the way he won't quite meet her gaze that this contact matters, more than either of them want to admit.

Moving awkwardly because she only has one hand free, she takes a scrap of dandelion from her pocket and holds it out. The goat takes it from her, then follows as she leads him and Luca down the path towards the fence.

"You're a goat whisperer," Luca says. "The Magical Goat Girl of Great Britain."

It's only because I feed him, she thinks.

"That's your superpower." His laugh is a little too loud, the voice he chooses afterwards a little too soft. "Goat Whispering. Makes up for the not-talking thing."

He's being a twat, but he's nervous and talking nonsense to cover it up, so she'll forgive him. His hand moves over hers, their palms kissing as he takes a firmer hold. They're unquestionably holding hands now, there's no possibility of passing it off as anything else. His other hand falls to her hip, pulls her closer, in a clumsy parody of confidence so raw and vulnerable she feels her heart crack a little bit. They're going to kiss and they both know it, but they still have to pretend they're not, in case the other one backs out at the last minute.

Is this the best bit? The moment before his mouth comes down on hers? No, the best bit is the part that's happening right now, the sweet moment of contact and the dizziness in her ears and the touch of their tongues and the leap in their chests and their bodies moving closer. His movements are clumsy, as if he's only seen kissing acted out on a screen. She's very aware of the rhythm of his breath, of how tense he is, as if he's still expecting her to push him away. His hands tremble on her waist, and he breaks the kiss so he can look into her eyes. He looks terrified. *It's all right,* she thinks, *this is good.* How can he not understand that she wants this?

"I shouldn't be doing this," he says. "I mean, you can't exactly tell me if it's not all right, can you? I mean, I could do fucking anything to you, I could go on and on, and you wouldn't be able to tell anyone, would you?"

But what if I want you to carry on? His kiss is in her bloodstream, racing and looping through her body. Does he not like her after all? Is he trying to let her down gently? Does she dare to reach out for him? She takes his hand, takes a step closer. He smells of deodorant and clean sweat, and it should be repulsive but it isn't. She lifts her face towards his. His body trembles like a wire filled with electricity.

"Hey, you two." Katherine calls down the garden. "We're coming for the goat now. So if there's any shenanigans going on, now's your chance to hide the evidence."

"Best stop there then," Luca mutters, and they break apart, not quite daring to look at each other, as if they've each caught the other one doing something private and shameful, and now they both need some space while everyone forgets what they've seen. When Joe and Katherine arrive, Willow finds she can't look at them either.

"Come on then, mister." Katherine holds out a handful of pellets to the goat. He tosses his head and looks disdainful. "I see. Too good for pellets now, are you?"

"He likes dandelions." Luca's voice has the artificial ring

of someone trying to sound comfortable. "That's what Willow gave him."

"Spoiled beast," says Katherine, without any rancour at all. "All right then, we'll go for something green instead." She plucks a handful of bramble leaves. "This way."

And to Willow's faint disappointment, as if he'd never clung to her side and followed her every move as if she was his queen and his goddess, the goat trots after Katherine.

"Fickle creatures," Joe tells her. "He knows which side his bread's buttered."

At a safe distance, they follow the goat down the path to watch Katherine load him into the trailer. She climbs in; the goat follows; he spots the hay net hanging limply from the back of the trailer; he begins to tug at the hay; Katherine climbs out again and shuts the door. The whole procedure is impressively neat. Willow wants to applaud, but she's afraid it would be taken as sarcasm.

"Sorry again that my niece stole your goat," says Joe.

"It's all right." Katherine smiles at Willow. "At least he had his last hurrah before he gets shipped off."

Where is he going next? Perhaps to become the godfather of his own new herd, to sit majestically in his own field and let his beard grow thick and his horns grow long. He'll mate with all the females, and boss their kids around, and watch over the growth of his own family. She's aware of Luca close beside her, just as he must be aware of her. What's going to happen between them now? The kiss is like an anchor, holding them to a single moment. One of them needs to decide what comes next.

"Come over later," Luca mutters, sounding almost reluctant, almost angry. "If you want, I mean. Nothing heavy."

His words are ungracious but his body's telling her something else entirely, not touching her but not staying in his own space either, his eyes bright and eager, his hand half-reaching for hers. She nods.

"About four maybe? I've got stuff to do this afternoon."

She nods again.

"Come for tea if you like," says Katherine, startling Willow, who hadn't known Katherine was listening. Her smile includes Joe. "Both of you, I mean. I'll feed everyone at about six. So you'll have a couple of hours to mooch around first."

"That's so nice of you," says Joe. "Willow, you go for tea if you like. But I can't."

"Course you can. Come and keep me company while the young 'uns are climbing all over the hay loft."

Her words are casual, but there's something oddly urgent in tone that Willow, feeling as sensitive as if she's been peeled, is suddenly aware of. Katherine really, truly wants Joe to come over for dinner. What does this mean? What has Katherine seen that she hasn't? In the moment when they're not being looked at, something takes hold of her fingers and strokes them gently. It's Luca, his fingers warm and clammy against hers. His index finger makes a brief, shy circuit of her palm. She holds her breath.

"I've got to work," Joe says, and now he too sounds reluctant, as if there might be something in Katherine's request beyond a simple offer of a meal.

"It'll keep. It's not good for you to be alone."

"All on my own for three hours in the evening. Whatever will I do?" He sounds as if he's mocking someone. Himself? Surely not Katherine, who's made the offer in kindness and doesn't deserve to be laughed at. "Besides, I've got that kitten Willow lifted from your latest batch. He'll keep me out of trouble."

"Ah, is that where he went?" Katherine smiles. "I thought maybe a fox had him. Is he staying?"

"Apparently." He ruffles Willow's hair. She forces herself to let him. "You have to stop nicking livestock from Katherine though, all right? Absolutely no more stolen animals."

"Oh, I've always got kittens to spare," says Katherine. "Have the lot if you want, we're overrun. I'll probably have to drown the next litter. And if you change your mind about dinner, just turn up. There'll be enough." She's climbing into the cabin of the Land Rover as she says this, and Luca finally breaks free of Willow's hand and hoists himself into the other side, and then there's the awkwardness of feeling endlessly in the way as Katherine turns the car and trailer around, a complex manoeuvre even though she seems to know what she's doing, and then they're gone.

Drifting back up to her bedroom, her body still awash with Luca's presence, she remembers that the goat has shat all over the floor.

CHAPTER TWENTY-FOUR

She's ready long before it's time, but then when the time comes for her to leave, she's suddenly not ready at all. In the moment when the clock turns over towards twenty minutes to four, all her clothes become the wrong clothes, her body becomes the wrong body; her face is ugly and laughable, and her hair's too long. What's the matter with her? He's just a boy. He liked her enough to kiss her earlier. And why does she even care? After what she's been through, after everything that's happened, what does the opinion of one fairly ordinary boy matter?

It's healthy to move on. She's never been a patient in her mother's office, never chosen between the comfortable sofa and the office chair, but she hears these words in her mother's voice. She can picture her expression: warm, supportive, professional. *Try not to feel guilty for feeling normal.* If she confessed that she and Luca kissed that morning, would her mother be pleased?

If she wants to get there on time, she needs to go now. Does she want to get there on time, though? Will that look too eager? Does she have time to change again? No, she doesn't, and besides, she needs to get over this. It's Luca. No one special. She clatters down the stairs to the kitchen.

"Are you off?" Joe is cleaning the already-clean kitchen worktop, his cloth making slow smooth swooping circles across the wood. "I'm not coming, I've got some stuff I need to get done. But if you get a chance can you thank Katherine for—" He shakes his head impatiently. "Sorry, sorry, ignore me. Have a good time, all right?"

Katherine will be disappointed, but Willow's relieved. She needs the walk to get her face and thoughts in order. She doesn't want company.

She's eager to go, but now Joe's hovering, looking her up and down as if he wants to adjust her somehow. Does this mean she's worn the wrong clothes? She knows it's a cliché that gay men are good at clothes, but nonetheless...

"Will you be all right coming back? Do you want me to come over and get you and walk you home?" She shakes her head. "No you don't want me to come and get you?" She nods. "Okay, sorry, I know this is annoying but I need to check, do you or don't you want me to come and get you?" She shakes her head, trying not to let her annoyance show. "So you're definitely coming home on your own then. Good."

There's something else he wants to say, but she doesn't have the time to listen, and besides, she's allowed to be oblivious to other people's wants and needs. She gives him a quick little hug.

"And no goats coming home with you, all right?"

In their field, the goats are anxious, milling around as if they're expecting something to happen. When she climbs over the fence, the billy puts himself between her and the rest of the herd, not threatening her exactly but definitely keeping an eye. Well, she did steal one of his children earlier. She'd thought about stopping for a quick cuddle with the goat she borrowed this morning, but she doesn't like the way the billy's looking at her, and she's afraid he'll bowl her over in the mud and make her filthy. It's not the mud she minds so much as the thought that Luca will know the goat went for her. She's glad when she reaches the other side of the field safely.

"Hello there." Katherine is in the vegetable beds, picking the long brown bean pods from the tatty-looking vines. "Luca's around somewhere. Do you want to give me a hand with these?"

Willow climbs cautiously between the long strands of string that form a rudimentary fence, and begins to pluck the pods, enjoying the crisp snap as they break off between her fingers.

"Get them all," Katherine says. "Then the vines can come out and make some room. Oh, hello, Luca. Can I leave you two to get on with this? Once you've got them picked you can rip out the vines too if you fancy it, but don't worry if you've got things to do."

And like that, she's gone, and she and Luca are alone, but with a task to do that makes the moment pass comfortably and smooths out the leftover awkwardness. Perhaps Katherine did it on purpose. Perhaps she knows everything that's happened between the two of them. She spends her life breeding animals, after all. She must know the signs. The bean pods feel crisp and dry, like paper. She slits open a pod and squeezes one of the beans. It's hard and dry and solid, like a little stone.

"I can't fucking stand vegetables normally," says Luca. "But Katherine does this thing where she soaks them and cooks them with spices and that and they're actually pretty good." The low autumn sun is behind him and she has to squint to read the expression on his face. "Look, Willow, about this afternoon…"

She plucks another pod, drops it into the bowl, reaches for another.

"I mean, I like you. I really do."

But, she thinks. Why are boys always so predictable?

"It's just," he says, and hesitates. "I'm not safe. You know what I mean? I mean, I don't know if I can trust myself."

He doesn't need to tell her this. She's seen that side of him already, that day in the woods. Why does he think she cares? She'll take her chances.

When someone tells you who they are, believe them. One of her mother's many life mantras. *And specifically, don't ever go out with a man who boasts about being violent*. But that doesn't apply *now*, surely. There's no future in this, and they both know it. She simply wants to know that he likes her. She simply wants to feel alive again, the way she felt when he kissed her. The way she used to feel before Laurel died.

"I mean, I'm not proud of it," Luca says, even though he sounds proud, as if sudden uncontrolled violence is a sign of manhood. "It's just. I mean. That's why I sometimes might be a bit funny with you. Because sometimes when I'm, you know, thinking about sex, or when I look at you, I mean, I want to kiss you, but there's… other stuff I want to do, too."

If she kissed him, would he stop talking and give in to the moment? Would he hurt her? Or would he push her away? Shameful though it is, she'd prefer roughness to rejection.

"I mean, it's not you, it's me. Something wrong with me, I mean. Well, I mean, you know, don't you? You remember what happened. In the woods. And I don't want to – you know – if that bit of me comes out again, I don't want to be hurting you—"

Maybe that's what I like about you, she thinks. *Maybe I like that you're dangerous. Maybe I want someone who might hurt me.*

"Besides," he says, tugging a handful of pods and leaves so hard the whole plant shakes and trembles, "I'm probably going to prison soon. So, you know, not much future in it or anything." He lets the pods fall to the ground. "But, you know… if you… I mean… it doesn't have to be anything heavy…"

Shut up and kiss me, she thinks.

"I should fucking shut up now, shouldn't I," he says, with an embarrassed laugh. "Right pair we are. I talk too much and you don't talk at all. I mean, how am I meant to get consent and that when you can't even tell me—"

Whatever he was going to say next is lost because Willow,

tired of the sound of his voice, puts the bowl of dried bean pods down on the ground and kisses him, firm and sweet, and it's better than it was this afternoon because they've already learned so much about how this works. The earth comes up to welcome them, as easy as if this moment is why they were born in the first place, and everything is simple between them; they're one animal in two bodies, no more words needed.

Katherine has prepared a feast in small portions, spicy and sweet and colourful, spreading out across the tablecloth in a profusion of bowls and platters. There are two kinds of curry – a sweet one and a hot one as Katherine explains – fragrant rice, thick chewy flatbreads, vegetables drenched in flavour and gleaming with oil. There's a dish of beans, not shrivelly and hard any more but plump and mealy, with more vegetables added and cubes of crumbly, wet-looking cheese nestled among them. There's something not quite real about it all, something not quite real about the entire world, as if she's looking at it through glass. She has to press her hands against the sides of the chair to remind herself that she's still in contact with the earth.

("Fucking hell," Luca whispers against her ear, and she feels herself melt as surely as if he had told her he loved her. They're lying in a long dry space between the bean-rows, the sun poking curiously at their eyes and skin, dry crumbs of soil scratching at their cheeks and crawling into their hair. Willow's t-shirt is tangled around her neck and her bra is unfastened. Luca has taken off his top. They're adrift on the heady thrill of exploration, a pause for breath as they consider what they might do next.)

"Eat," Katherine orders, and hands them each a plate. "If you're not sure what you like, have some of everything."

Willow isn't sure if she's too happy to eat, or too hungry to wait. Her body's appetite has become a sweet mystery. She dips her spoon into the curry Katherine said was sweet, and licks at the long drip of sauce that traces its way around her thumb. When she glances at Luca, she sees him watching her and thinks she might dissolve into the floorboards.

("Just look at you," Luca mumbles. His gaze as it moves down her skin is so hungry that she thinks it might leave a mark. His hand follows, trailing shyly around the curve of her left breast.)

The food bursts with the kinds of flavours she would once have rejected, but now finds herself savouring. How strange to think that a couple of months ago she would have eaten only bread and rice from this carnival of taste. The meat in the curry is chewy in exactly the right way, rich and delicious and satisfying. She thinks of the word *gamey,* and wonders if this is what it means.

"Clearing out the freezer," Katherine says with a smile, and helps herself to another spoonful. "Take some home to your uncle when you leave. Oi." She glances down at the pair of cats who have come into the dining room to twine longingly around her legs. "You don't eat curry. Too much garlic. No, there's no point looking pretty and confiding, you're still not getting any."

The cats give up on Katherine and move on to Luca. He pushes them away with one leg, then takes a spoonful of the bean dish, picks out a cube of cheese and lays it on the edge of his plate. A beat, two beats, and then the cube of cheese is between his fingers, pinched in two and dropped onto the floor, while he makes a clumsy attempt to cover up what he's doing by reaching for another piece of flatbread. Willow can hear the purring of the cats from right across the room. She licks sauce from her knife, wondering how a boy who'll feed two plump farm cats just because they asked him to can also be a boy who beat a man almost to death with his bare hands.

(Between the bean-rows, Willow basks in his touch. Her skin is hot and tingly, her limbs heavy. Luca's mouth is full and rosy with the kisses they've exchanged, the brush of their bodies against each other. The press of his erection against her thigh makes her feel drunk. Soon they'll have to go inside and sit side-by-side at Katherine's shining wooden table, in the dim comfort of thick walls that hold the cool air and form a blessed respite from the low sunlight, and their lack of satisfaction will become a kind of satisfaction in itself. What's happening between them will remain unfinished business, a question not yet answered.)

The cats, who are cleaning their whiskers and watching Luca intently in case more bounty drops from the sky, turn their heads in unison towards the window. Katherine chuckles.

"That'll be Francis," she says. "They can probably hear his truck coming down the lane." The cats are on high alert now, their ears straining forwards. They look both funny and frightening, as if they're either putting on a two-handed comedy act or being possessed by the same demon. Now even Willow can hear the faint rumble, growing closer and more distinct, resolving into the sound of a large vehicle being bumped down a rough track. "You two stay here and finish your food. Don't clear the table, you might want to pick at it later. Put your plates and forks in the dishwasher when you're done."

There's something very comforting about Katherine's clear, flat instructions about what chores are expected of them. On visits to friends' houses, Willow has tied herself in knots over the correct procedure. If she takes all the plates to the kitchen, will she look weird and overeager? If she takes only her own, is that rude? And when they tell her *No, don't worry, we'll clear up, you're the guest*, is she supposed to take them at their word, or ignore it? She's eating out of greed rather than hunger now, scooping up globs of sauce with her bread and letting the spices unravel on her tongue. Outside Katherine is talking to Francis, whoever Francis might be. Perhaps he's delivering something to the farm. Or is it too late for deliveries? She has no idea what kind of schedule farms operate on. Katherine never seems to fully come to rest, her days a continuous transition from one task to the next.

"This is bloody amazing," says Luca, picking up a nugget of meat from his plate with his fingers. "I had something like this once at the Carnival. You know the Notting Hill Carnival? It's, like, this huge cultural celebration, loads of floats and dancers and music and stuff, all out in the streets." Willow rolls her eyes. "Well, I don't know what you know, do I? Anyway, the street food there is amazing. Properly, properly amazing. But this is even better." He sucks the sauce off the final piece of meat, breaks it into two pieces and drops it to the floor. The cats stalk over with their tails high and quivering. "I got the stuff off. Should be all right… Shall we, um, get the plates cleared and that?"

Without the barrier of the table, now there's a chance to be close again, they're suddenly shy with each other. Getting through the door becomes a challenge. Navigating the dishwasher is almost impossible. She can feel the imperative singing through her bones. *Kiss him again. Touch him again. Get lost in how it feels.* Is this love? She doesn't know or care. In all the endless stretch of time since Laurel died, this is the only thing she's found that's made her feel good, and she wants more of it. Luca is bending over the dishwasher, the small tight shape of his buttocks outlined by the pull of the denim. She thinks about sliding her hand along the curve, finds she's already turned her thought into action.

What is she expecting? To feel his body come to stillness like a cat being caressed in just the right spot, to hear him sigh with desire. To see him turn towards her. To smell the spices that have stained his lips, taste his tongue against hers. She's ready for all of these things, her body softening, her skin awake. She's not at all ready for Luca to shoot suddenly upright as if he's been given an electric shock, his eyes black with rage, his hands held up in front of him. She staggers backwards.

"Shit," Luca says. "Shit, Willow. I'm sorry. Are you all right?"

She can't tell. She's too busy holding onto the tears that

are gathering in her chest. *You will not cry over this,* she tells herself sternly. *This is nothing. Don't let him get to you.*

"I didn't hit you, did I?" Luca looks as shocked as she feels, as upset as she's trying not to be. "Jesus, Willow, you've got to be careful around me. I'm not always going to be a nice guy."

It sounds like a line from a bad movie. It sounds like a terrible truth that she needs to take into her heart. *When someone shows you who they are, believe them.* Is this who Luca is? And does she want him badly enough to accept the risk?

"Oh Jesus, come here." He holds his arms out to her. "I'm sorry, okay? I'm sorry I frightened you."

She goes into his arms and lets him hold her, but this is almost worse than nothing at all. She doesn't want to be petted and calmed and stroked smooth. She wants the clumsy tenderness of his hands on her naked flesh, the feeling that he's bringing her back to life. She lets him hold her and wonders if this is the end as well as the beginning.

"It's like there's this other guy who lives inside me," Luca mumbles into the top of her head. "And he gets out sometimes. I can't help it."

His hands are on her back, but they don't feel the way they felt before. His body is wooden and sexless. It's like holding onto a mannequin. She's so hungry for something she hardly even knew she needed, but he doesn't seem to be aware of it. How far will she go to get that feeling back again? If he asked her to have sex with him, would she say yes? She turns her face up towards him and kisses him.

"Willow," he says, and it sounds like a warning.

She kisses him again.

"Willow. Shit. I can't... we can't—" She can feel the quiver in his body. "I mean, Katherine's right outside. She might come in any minute."

Then let's go somewhere else. There are so many places. They could go back to the bean-patch and lie down in the dry, grainy soil. They could climb the haystack, hide in the hot dusty space between the bales and the roof. They could go out to the woods. They could even go up the stairs to Luca's bedroom, which is the closest and most comfortable option. But she's not sure she's ready for the intimacy of seeing his private space yet. She takes his hand and leads him towards the door.

"What d'you fancy doing?" Now they're on the move again, Luca seems happier, although he frees his hand from hers under the guise of petting a passing cat. "Want to see the little goats and give them a farewell cuddle?" She looks at him blankly. "It's their last day out. We're bringing them in tomorrow afternoon, then they're off the next morning."

Of course she knows not every animal can stay on the farm for ever, breeding and breeding. But still, she's saddened by the thought of the young goats climbing onto the truck, not knowing they'll never see their family again. Will their mother miss them? Will they miss her? How long will it take them all to forget? She's pretty sure the billy won't give a damn—

Luca is still talking to her, something about room in the freezer and Katherine's cooking, but she doesn't have time to listen to it, because now she can see Katherine in the yard, talking to the person she named as Francis, and she can see his face and she understands everything, because Francis is the Slaughter Man.

He's leaning on the bonnet of his van and nodding as Katherine talks to him. The van is small, the kind used by tradesmen to transport small amounts of equipment. It can't be the one he uses to take away the animals and kill them. That's what Luca is talking about. That's what Katherine meant by allowing the goat his last hurrah. That's why she was clearing room in her freezer. The Slaughter Man is going to do his job.

"You all right, mate?" Luca pats her shoulder. "You look a bit funny."

She's always known this is where meat comes from. Animals are made of meat and meat is what she eats. But she's only now making the connection between the stuff that fills her plate and the living breathing creatures who have eaten food from her hands, leaned against her for comfort. Francis and Katherine are laughing together, her hand on his arm. How can she stand to touch him? Doesn't she know who he is? *We eat meat. It's what we do.* She remembers the kittens learning to hunt in the hayloft, the confusion and fear of the rat as it stumbled blindly from side to side, desperate to escape.

The conversation goes on and on. There must be more to this butchery business than simply *Can you please kill my little goats for me*; there must be decisions to be made and agreements to be reached. Francis is watching and nodding as Katherine draws her hand around the top of her hip-joint, then diagonally across her chest to her armpit. She must be explaining how she wants her meat dressed. *We eat meat. This is what eating meat means.* Now Katherine's gesturing to her ribs, and Willow remembers the beat of the little goat's heart as she lifted him over the fence, the warmth of him as she slept in her lap. What will happen to that heart now? Will it be eaten? Or does that part get thrown away?

"Fuck!" Luca is beside her now, his eyes wide. "Is that—? God, I never knew he had, like, an actual *job*." He laughs. "Although I suppose working in, like, a slaughterhouse is pretty much the perfect position for someone like him." He stretches out his fingers until the knuckles crack. "Creepy fucker. Should have fucking punched him when I had the chance. If he comes anywhere near us I'll kill him."

But you can't kill him, Willow thinks. *None of us can. Because he's the Slaughter Man. He's always going to win in the end.*

Katherine shakes Francis's hand and says something about seeing him the day after tomorrow. Francis glances around the yard, his gaze slow and assessing. What will happen if he sees her? She shrinks back into the doorway of the farmhouse and prays his gaze won't fall on her.

He looks in her direction for a moment, but she can't tell if he's noticed her or not. He climbs into his van, folding up his long lanky self into the driver's seat. He starts the engine. He turns the van around. He's gone.

Stop it. You're being ridiculous. We eat meat. This is where meat comes from. She disentangles her hand from Luca's.

"You look like you've seen a ghost." Katherine's hand is firm and kindly on her shoulder. "That's Francis. He runs the local abattoir. He's coming to collect the young goats the day after tomorrow for slaughter."

Katherine says this as if it's natural, as if there's nothing to be ashamed of. Willow blinks up at her, trying to recognise the kindness she thought she knew.

"They're a by-product of the milk production," Katherine says. "I keep the best of the nannies for milk but they can't all stay, there isn't enough land and they'd fight. We have to eat, Willow, and most of us like to eat cheese and meat, so that's what's going to happen to them. Francis is quick and humane, and he's local, so they won't have to travel far. And I promise, every part of them gets used. The chefs who buy goat meat come from cultures where you don't waste anything. Okay?"

Of course it's okay. What else did she think farmers do? Of course it's not okay. How could anyone raise an animal and then kill it before it even reaches adulthood? She wants to shrug and be cool and say, *I know, it's just life, isn't it?* She wants to shake Katherine by the shoulders, to tell her *But you can't, they're so young, can't they have a little bit more time?* She wants her voice back. Katherine's already gone, wheeling a barrow and muck-shovel in the direction of the chicken coop.

"Come on, mate." Luca is shaking his head at her as if she's being adorably funny. "I know it's a bit horrible seeing that fucker from the woods round here, but you can't tell me you didn't know where meat comes from. You ate that curry at dinner, didn't you?"

She'd thought they shared a connection, she and this boy she's just remembered she hardly knows. Now, he's standing beside her with that stupid grin on his face, laughing at her as she comes apart in front of him.

"Forget about it, okay? I know it's not nice to think about, but it'll be fine. Once they're in the freezer you can forget all about it and enjoy some nice dinners."

The worst of it is that she can still taste the tenderness of the curried goat in her mouth, just as she can still feel Luca's hands on her body. What good would words do anyway? She ought to slap him round his stupid face. She ought to stab him through the chest with a pitchfork. She ought to…

"Please don't look like that." He's trying to hold her. "I don't like seeing you upset."

As if he can make her feel better. As if physical contact could wipe out the knowledge that the animals she has played with and handled are now going to their deaths. Even as she thinks this she can hear the contradiction in her own head. What was she doing with Luca earlier, if not trying to blot out the memory of death—?

She was only young too, Willow thinks. *She was the one that got picked out of the herd and killed off.*

She's running before she's even aware that she's decided to leave, not bothering to look back because she knows Luca won't follow her. She runs until she's tired but not exhausted, then lets herself slow to a walk so she can cool off before going back into the house. She doesn't want her Uncle Joe to look at her and wonder what the matter is. If she could, she'd like to creep back up the outside staircase and hide herself in her room.

But she can't do that, it's not fair. She owes it to him to at least show her face and let her know she's back before vanishing into her lair. She wants to see him for a minute, to know that there's still someone in this world who's the person he seems to be.

She runs her hands over her face, hoping that any streaks will look like sweat, which they definitely are, and not tears, which they definitely aren't. At least he won't ask her why she's so quiet. Perhaps he'll be in the kitchen, making supper for himself. Perhaps she might be able to sneak a glass of wine.

But he isn't in the kitchen. Instead she finds a totally uncharacteristic mess of spilled oil and crumbs littered all over the surfaces, a glass shattered into fragments left unswept on the floor, the fridge humming frantically as it tries to compensate for the wide-open door, a slop of congealing cream trailing down the front of the freezer compartment and onto the slate tiles, and something burnt and shrivelled on the blackened grill-pan that lies flooded in a fat-flecked sink. It's not just the filthiest she's ever seen this kitchen, but the filthiest she's ever seen any room ever.

Her first thought is that something terrible must have happened to her uncle, because there's simply no way he would walk away and leave such a mess. She tears through the tiny house, checking the living room, the pantry, up the stairs to the bathroom where the door gapes innocently open. At the door to Joe's room, she hesitates. What if he's ill and doesn't want to be disturbed? She raises her hand to knock, lets it fall again. She can hear someone talking.

"No, please." It's her uncle's voice, made strange. "I'm sorry. I'm sorry. I just, I wanted to—"

He must be on the phone to someone. She knows better than to listen, but she stays anyway, because what if there is something really wrong with him? What if he's on the phone to the ambulance service? What if he needs her help?

"I know, I know. I know! But you don't know what it's like. It's easy for you, you've got someone there with you. No, I'm sorry, I shouldn't have said that, I know it's hard for you too, but you don't know how lonely it gets…"

Another pause.

"No, I have not, actually. What? Do I? Well, okay, but not much. A normal amount. You know bloody well what a normal amount is…! Oh for God's sake, what do you care anyway? I thought you said you didn't mind what I did any more… Then why did you fucking leave? We were going to be for ever, that's what you promised, get the youngest off to university and we'd be together, that's what you said... No, please, don't hang up, don't, I'm sorry, I'm sorry, I'm so sorry—"

Why is he making a fool of himself like that? Doesn't he know how he sounds? He's still talking, but in that hopeless way people do when they know the call has already ended, a querulous *Hello? Hello? Are you still there?* Then there's the slow, defeated creak of the bed, the protest of the floorboards, and Joe is standing in the doorway, a bottle of vodka clutched tight in one hand.

"Hello," he says, unsurprised to see her even though she wasn't supposed to be home for hours yet. "Sorry you had to hear that. It's just that he's left me, you see. Gone back to his wife. Rose always said he would, right from the start. But we were so good together and we made each other so happy and I really thought he'd pick me over her in the end, when the time was right."

That's why she didn't like him. Because he was married. Willow wants to grab Joe and shake him by the shoulders. *My God, you were someone's bit on the side. How could you be so stupid?*

"He was very nice about it really." Joe's voice is quite calm but the tears are pouring down his cheeks. "We bought this place together, we even got a dog, and when he left he took the dog so I wouldn't have to worry about it, and paid off the mortgage with his quarterly bonus, and gave me some money to tide me over while I got back on my feet. Did I mention he's ridiculously rich? I suppose you'd have to be really, to run two households the way he did." Joe seems to remember he's holding a bottle. "Do you want some of this by any chance? I've already had more than I ought to so you'd be helping me out really."

Don't be like this, she thinks. *I need you to help me. Why are you doing this tonight of all nights?* It must be because he thought he was going to be alone. Is this what he's been doing on all the other days when she's spent her time over at the farm? Is nothing and nobody stable and reliable any more?

"I'm so sorry about this," Joe continues. "Not much of an example to set a young girl. I wouldn't have done this if you hadn't gone out. You've been keeping me sane, to be honest. I mean, I can hardly do this while I've got you to look after, can I?" He wipes his nose on the back of his hand. "I didn't mean you to see this, I thought you'd be out until later... Did you have a row with that boy of yours or something? God, they're nothing but trouble. I think I'll ask Katherine to castrate me. Then maybe I'll get all fat and contented and stop bothering so much."

He's perfectly polite and sweet, the way he always is, but he's also so drunk he can hardly stand up, and his eyes keep closing as if he's barely holding onto consciousness.

He needs her help. There are things you're supposed to do – get the person to be sick, put them on their side, give them water to drink and sit with them and keep them awake until they sober up – but she can't seem to put her thoughts in order. She's alone in the house with a drunk man, no voice to call for help if she needs it, her bridges burned with the only people she knows to go to, and no idea what to do for the best.

"I'm really sorry," Joe says again, and smiles a loose, sloppy smile. "I'll be back to normal in the morning. You'll see. Going to get some sleep now." And then he's gone, and she's alone on the landing.

She stands for a minute in dull disbelief. Soon someone will be along to help her make sense of all of this. But there's no one but the kitten, slinking out of the shadows to claw his way up her legs and onto her shoulder. He's grown just in the short time he's been with them. Already his weight is enough to throw her off-balance.

She goes into her room, which still smells residually of goat, and shuts the door, and lies down on the bed and waits for sleep to take her away from all of this.

CHAPTER TWENTY-FIVE

She's in the waiting area of the funeral home, and she knows she's dreaming because it's become an opulent hotel bedroom. The thick white carpet is the same as in real life, immaculately clean, and so thick her feet sink into it a little bit, as if she's walking on wet sand. But the long white sofa and the little gilt coffee table have been joined by a cream vanity with its own padded stool and mirror, and instead of the reception desk with its well-kept potted plant, there's a huge double bed, its gold coverlet turned back to expose crisp white sheets.

When they came to this place in real life, she'd sat between her parents, the three of them tense with unshed tears and terrified. She remembers the box of tissues on the table, and the scent of air-freshener, and above all the whiteness of the carpet and the gleam of the glass, as if they're here to book a cleaning service rather than a funeral and the room they're in is designed to showcase their skills. She'd wondered why the dead would be so particular about housekeeping.

"We have an appointment to discuss a funeral," her father says, exactly as he did the day this conversation took place for real. His voice is tight and determined, ready to do the last thing he'll ever do for Laurel.

"For our daughter," her mother says. Refusing to leave the burden to her husband; sharing the pain equally.

"I'm so sorry for your loss," the funeral director says. Did he say this at the time? Willow can't remember, because she'd convulsed with grief, grabbing great handfuls of tissue to catch the river of snot and tears that poured out of her, as if something had broken inside her head. Today, tearless, she looks the funeral director in the face and sees that he is the Slaughter Man, dressed in a dark grey suit and co-ordinating grey tie.

"Her name's Willow," her mother says, and takes Willow's hand between her own.

"I see." The Slaughter Man looks Willow up and down, a careful assessing glance that's the opposite of lascivious, his gaze both discreet and penetrating. When he catches her eye he gives her a slow grave nod, as if they're equal partners in some important enterprise.

"And how old is she?"

"Seventeen." Her father answers this time. "The same as her sister Laurel. They're twins."

"I see." The Slaughter Man nods again, as if this is what he was expecting. Willow remembers seeing this gesture in real life, from the woman who they met on that terrible day. She remembers wondering if part of her training was to learn to hold her face in a neutral expression no matter what strange stories her clients brought to her.

"In fact," her mother says, "we came to you last time. I wondered if you'd recognise us."

But, Willow thinks, *this is that last time. I'm dreaming.* This is just a reworking of the past, her mind niggling away at the pain, picking at the scab left by Laurel's absence.

"I remember," says the Slaughter Man. "It's a great privilege to see to both of your daughters. I'm very honoured that you chose us a second time."

This is the first time, Willow thinks. *This is my dream and I can say how it goes, so this is the first time. We're here for Laurel. Not me.*

"If you could lie down on this bed for me," the Slaughter Man says, and he's definitely talking to Willow; his face is turned towards her and his eyes are bright and he's even holding out a hand, as if Willow is a small child. Her mother and father nod encouragingly. Their faces are sad but composed. When she stands, her father takes her mother's hand.

"It's for the best," her father says. "It's hard for us, but we'll be all right."

"There's a season for everything," her mother agrees. "This is the time for the harvest. But we can always grow a new one."

Willow tries to scream, and for a moment she thinks the force of her effort might drag her out of sleep and back into the real world, but then she's sinking again, reality melting around her, and she's standing beside the huge gold-covered bed with the Slaughter Man.

"Up you go," the Slaughter Man says.

This is a dream, Willow thinks. *This is all made up out of stuff in my head. None of this is happening. I'm in control and that means I don't have to do what he says.* But they aren't in the funeral parlour any more, the soft white carpet and the beautiful lighting have vanished, and now they're somewhere else.

"Do it, please," says the Slaughter Man. "It's what we agreed."

But I didn't, Willow thinks, *I didn't agree to anything.*

The bed is tall and hard to climb. The thought of falling back onto the ground suddenly becomes terrible, as if she is climbing a cliff and might fall to her death. When she finally makes it onto the top, she feels relieved.

"That's it." The Slaughter Man smiles and presses his hands together. "That's perfect. Now lie down for me and we'll see how long you are."

The bed's become cold and hard. She can feel the chill through her clothes. She lies down, keeping her eyes wide open, afraid of tumbling off. They're in a room with almost no furniture, and the lights above her are bright and unforgiving.

"I'm going to take some measurements now," the Slaughter Man says, and takes a tape measure from his top pocket.

"Would you prefer burial, cremation or butchery? We offer all three options here."

But I'm not dead, Willow thinks. *It's not me that needs a funeral. You've got me confused with Laurel.* She tries to sit up, but her body isn't under her command any more. Her limbs are heavy and still. The best she can do is to turn her head.

"We were thinking cremation," her father says. She wishes she could see them. If she could look at her father's face, catch her mother's eye, she could let them know she's still alive.

"The same as her sister," her mother chimes in. "We always tried to treat them as individuals, but they were the same person really. So it makes sense to do things the same. You could even get all the old files out and use Laurel's notes if you like."

"She might have grown since Laurel died," the Slaughter Man says doubtfully.

"Oh, no." Her father sounds sad, but resigned. "She hasn't grown or changed at all. She died too, at the same time as Laurel. They're the same person, you see, and their bodies both stopped working at the same time. We've just been keeping her around until we were sure."

"And you're quite sure you wouldn't prefer butchery?" The Slaughter Man gestures to the wall where his knives and cleavers hang in rows. "Plenty of good usable protein here, help keep you nice and strong." He grips Willow's wrist, raises her arm high and squeezes at the meat of her arm. "Look. She's young and tender, in her prime, perfect for the table. It's always best to eat the young. The older ones are tougher, you see."

"But doesn't it distress the parents?" her father asks.

"Only at first. And if you take away their babies at about the time they'd be moving out on their own anyway, after a while the adults forget about them and get on with making some more."

Her mother is stroking her stomach and looking at Willow hungrily. Her lips are wet and full.

"Perhaps it would be nice," she says. "I have such a craving… such a craving for fresh meat…"

"And we want you strong," her father agrees. "You're not as young as you were. It's going to be a strain."

Willow's trying so hard now to move that the Slaughter Man becomes aware of her struggle. He turns towards her and puts out his hand and she thinks he's going to hurt her in some way, but instead he strokes the side of her face.

"It's all right," he says. "You won't have to worry. The killing process is instant. You won't feel a thing."

No, she thinks, but her body is not under her command any more, and all she can do is stare weakly at him as he continues to stroke her hair.

"This is how it's supposed to be," he continues. "Some young ones are bred for milk, and some for meat. It's best to go now, while you're in your prime. And you don't want to stay here, in this world, do you?"

With a mighty effort, she shakes her head, not sure even in her own mind if she's arguing, or agreeing.

"You know what your mother was trying to tell you earlier," he says. "You tried not to listen, but you're too clever to get away with that. And once the new one's here, they won't need you any more. They'll grieve you for a while, but then they'll get better and be happy again. Can you imagine how confusing it's been for them, having to look after you? Seeing you walking around, wearing your sister's skin?"

This is a dream, she reminds herself. *This is just your head talking to itself.*

"Of course it is," he says. "I'm not really here at all. This is you telling yourself what you've known all along. You want to die. You've wanted to die for a long time now. And when you're dead, you'll be with her again. That's what you've wanted since she left you, isn't it? It's all right, you can tell me. I won't be shocked. I deal with death every day. It's nothing to be afraid of. I'll help you. Say the word and I'll help you. All you have to do is say the word."

And to her utter terror, she realises that this is the true cause of her silence; because she lives in terror of the words that she might speak. *I want to die.* The words she's held locked up behind her breastbone like jewels. But now the lock is springing open.

"This is a dream," he reminds her, "but when you wake up, you can make it come true. I'm waiting for you. You only need to follow the signs. The rest is up to you."

Her parents have vanished. She's alone with the Slaughter Man. There's a blade in his hand now, and a smile on his face that reminds her of her own, and all she has to do is to say the words. But even if she stays silent, the words will remain on the tip of her tongue, waiting for their moment. *I want to die. I know how to die. And now I'm ready to make it happen.*

CHAPTER TWENTY-SIX

She wakes in a single smooth motion that lifts her from the bed and onto the floor, riding the wave of adrenaline like a surfer returning to shore. She stands strong and solid on her feet, her body alert and ready for action even as her eyelids unglue and her vision swims into focus. She's still alive. She's still alive. Her heart is bursting out of her chest, her hands are shaking, the muscles of her legs quiver, and she's still alive, the one who lived, the anomaly, the freak, the mistake. The control in the experiment. The spare part. She's done something terrible. It's time for her to atone.

"Would you maybe be willing to consider Laurel donating some of her organs?" The conversation took place in the room they hadn't left since they'd been given the news, the room they'd been told they could use as long as they needed. Willow can still see the sickly peach colour of the walls, the strip of wallpaper separating the lower half of the room in a dreadful approximation of a once-fashionable decorating style. And her mother and father had looked at each other, that terrible glance that told Willow this was real, it was really happening. The first decision of their new life that no longer had Laurel in it. They have been in this room for less than two hours and already the world is demanding that they move on.

"I think," her mother began, and then stopped. Closed her eyes. Pressed her hand against her stomach. "I think…" And then, without warning, she was sick, quickly and neatly, a smooth turning of her head to one side and an efficient retch into the bin, as simple as emptying a coffee cup.

"Do we have to…" her father began, and then stopped. "Sorry. Of course we do. Of course we do." His gaze jittered wildly between his wife, his remaining daughter, looking for guidance. In his household of strong women, he was used to being the outsider, gladly outnumbered and happy to be told what to do. "I just… I mean… I don't know…" His gaze fell on Willow. "Willow, do you know if Laurel – if she – if she would have wanted—?"

And she knew. She knew. They'd talked about it sometimes, a lazy conversation where all moral decisions where simple because none of them would ever apply in real life. *I'd never have an abortion, but I wouldn't judge anyone who did. I'd never cheat on someone, even if I'd stopped loving them. If anything happened to me, of course I'd want to donate my organs. I mean, I wouldn't be using them any more, would I?* And the slow lazy hum of agreement as they lay luxuriously in the sunshine, two young healthy creatures among the rest of their healthy herd.

"Willow?" Her mother, white as a sheet, took her hand. "What do you think Laurel would have wanted? Would she want to—?"

And Willow, without thought, without guilt, without hesitation, shook her head.

I killed them, Willow thought wonderingly. *I killed all those people. I let Laurel's body go to waste. Why am I even still alive?* She opens her drawer, finds the broken piece of mirror she stole from the bathroom, and presses it hard against her wrist. All she needs to do is let it happen.

But she can't do it. Her hand won't obey her orders, and

her skin flinches away from the sharp pressure. Just a thin little line, that's all she can manage before she drops her hand again. Why is she so pathetic? The kitten, tightly coiled in the rumpled blanket and undisturbed by her sudden waking, lifts his head and blinks at her with green-gold eyes, then stretches out one long paw towards her, claws splayed. She swallows hard. How could she let herself be beguiled by such surface prettiness? He's a carnivore, the same as she is.

Start with that, she thinks. *Pick it up and wring its neck. Grab, twist, pull. All over. Think of it as practice.*

Her hands stretch out. He comes to her willingly, purring as her fingers reach under his chin, not knowing that death is seconds away.

That's right, she thinks. *Stay calm. It'll all be over in a minute.*

She grabs him hard around the neck. He squeaks in protest, struggling to right himself, as if she's playing a game and has gone too far. He still doesn't know what she's going to do.

Now twist. Twist and pull. Break its neck. Get it over with.

But her hands won't move. She's weak. She can't kill the kitten. She can't kill anything.

The kitten is still dangling from her hand, writhing and struggling. The claws of his back feet rake at her hand. She shakes him off onto the bed and opens the door to the darkness.

The woods welcome her as if she's part of them. She wonders if she could get lost in them, lost so completely that death might find her before anyone else could. Perhaps she could find the willpower to hide herself away until she died of thirst. But she knows already that she's weak – couldn't kill the kitten, couldn't cut her wrists, couldn't walk off the steps, couldn't take the tablets, couldn't take any of the chances she's been offered – and there's no way she can do this alone. She needs someone who can help her; someone who has already welcomed the darkness inside himself. He has a name, he has a job, but he is also the Slaughter Man, a man who kills for a living and hunts for his own amusement, and if she catches him in the right mood, she knows he'll help her.

And then what? Will he bury her out in the woods? Will her flesh and bones dissolve into earth and a tall green sapling grow from the place she lies? Or will she disappear into his freezer, so he can eat her flesh?

Here she is, at the foot of the path she needs to take. The last time she came this way, a deer led her in a different direction. What will she do if he comes to her again tonight? She can almost hear something moving towards her, almost feel the vibrations of his footsteps in the earth. Hastily, before she can once again be seduced by the beauty of another living creature, reminding her of everything she's about to leave behind, she turns up the path that leads to the Slaughter Man. She's not going to be talked out of this, no matter how many gifts the universe sends her to try and bind her back into its fabric.

She's not making any effort to be quiet – after all, it hardly matters if he hears her coming this time – and her breath is loud in her ears. Nonetheless, she's faintly aware of the sounds that follow in her wake, as if she's being stalked by something small and stealthy, who doesn't want to be seen. Perhaps there are rats in the woods? She remembers the squirming of the rat that the kittens had stalked and gnawed on, the distension of its belly and the sickening spill of little pinky-brown shapes like beans. How big is the bean in her mother's belly? Does it have a heartbeat yet? Arms and legs? If someone cut her mother open, would it unfold and stretch in agony before it died?

Two or three times she stops and looks back over her shoulder, strafing the air behind her with the beam of her phone. But there's no sign of anything. Why would there be? Surely nothing would follow her down this path. Animals aren't stupid.

At the barbed wire fence, she pauses to study the notices in the trees. *Follow the signs,* the Slaughter Man said to her in her dream, and she wants to do as she's been told, to show him that she's listened to what he's told her and she's coming to him willingly. *Possible Armed Response*. Is that how he'll do it? Will he shoot her through the heart, so that she matches Laurel? Or will he cut her throat and let her bleed out onto the floor? *I will not be responsible for my actions*. Of course he won't. She's the one in charge here. He's been telling her, all along he's been telling her. He can help her, but it has to be her choice, and now she's ready to make it.

She ducks under the wire, feeling the tug on her scalp as the barbs grab at her hair. If they come looking for her, this will surely be one of the places they'll look first, and if they find her hair, they'll know she's been here. But will that matter? Surely they can't convict someone over a strand of hair. Luca will tell them the story of the time they came before, two rebellious teens taking the path they've been specifically told to stay away from. As long as the Slaughter Man has properly hidden what's left of her, that should be enough to keep their secret.

Or perhaps he's clever enough to come this way afterwards, looking for any faint traces of her final journey that might give them both away. If he finds the strands of her hair, what will he do with them? Will he burn them? Or will he let them blow away on the breeze?

She can see the shape of the house ahead of her now, the long smooth shadow of it, too regular to be anything natural, and the burned patch of ground where the cauldron boiled and stank over the fire. She's hoping he'll be waiting for her, standing on the veranda with his gun by his side, waiting for her to come to him. But the Slaughter Man's house is dark and silent, its windows blank, the door closed.

Of course not, she thinks. *He can't make it too easy. He has to know for sure that I mean it. He's not going to come and find me. I have to go to him.*

Her skin prickling, she makes her way across the clearing towards the workshop, with its separate entrance and white light and equipment lined up on the walls with a remorseless neatness. The door is ajar, and she can see the white light slipping out through the gap. He knows she's coming tonight. Death is his business, and he's prepared the way for her.

The butchery room is exactly as she remembers, perfectly clean and with that terrible sense of order and ritual purpose. The apparatus of death and dissection is arranged on the wall with care and attention, as if this is a holy place and everything in it is to be treated with reverence. And if she had any doubts at all, any question in her head that the Slaughter Man might not be the one she needs, he has left her one last sign. On the table, gleaming like ebony beneath the harsh overhead light, a huge spread of antlers branch out from the dome of the bone-yellow skull.

So the deer wasn't following her in the woods after all. He was already waiting for her, in the place where she's going. He's gone the way of all flesh, shot through the head or the chest, then jointed and wrapped in plastic, preserved by the deep cold, not a part of him going to waste. Out in the woods, he'd been beautiful enough to stop her breath with the proud lift of his head and the deep muscled curve of his throat. When she'd found him in the freezer the day she came with Luca, her fingers had brushed against his dead flesh and she'd been sickened. But now, seeing him in his final form, the form given to him by the Slaughter Man, she sees beauty once again. A life completed isn't ugly, not at all. The ugliness is only in the transition.

She's done it, she's done everything right. She's followed the signs and understood their message. And now she can hear his footsteps on the ground outside, quick and eager, growing closer. He's almost running, as if he's waited for this so long he can hardly stand it. Is she ready? Yes, oh yes she's ready. *Come on and get me. I won't flinch. I won't look away. Come and do this. Please.*

But the figure who stumbles in through the doorway, wide-eyed and panting with fear, is Luca.

"Willow. What the fuck are you doing?"

No, she thinks wildly. *No, no, no. You can't be here.*

"I saw you in the woods," he gasps. "I mean, I wasn't following you or anything, not at first anyway, I was… Well, obviously you know what it's like, yeah? When your head's full of shit and you need to get out and think, and I swear to God, it was so weird seeing you there too. I mean, I thought I was the only one who… Sorry, I know I'm going on and on, I just —" His eyes are black with fear, or perhaps excitement. "What's that? Is that a deer skull? It is. It's a bloody deer skull. He must have shot it himself. What the fuck are you doing in here, anyway?"

She has to send him away, right now, before anything bad happens. She can't trust herself near him. He's going to end up hurt, or killed. No, it's already too late; her hands are reaching for his neck, pulling his face down against hers so she can taste the inside of his mouth. He resists, gives in, kisses back, then pushes her away.

"Seriously? You want to do – that – in here? You know, you're freaking me out a bit."

She feels like a freak, loose and wild, unbound from any convention. Why can't he see that he needs to leave? His eyes are black in the harsh light.

"I mean." He's almost laughing now, and his fingers are tight around the flesh of her arms. "You and me. Alone in the woods. With a freezer. And a wall covered in meat cleavers. And a huge fucking steel table. Don't ever let anyone tell you you're not a romantic at heart, yeah?"

She's come here for death, and she needs him to leave before her body remembers what it's like to be alive. If he stands there any longer she won't be able to stop herself. She reaches upwards, takes hold, and kisses him again, pressing him against her. His movements are clumsy and sudden, as if he's fighting with his own body. When she strips her t-shirt off over her head, he swears.

"Fuck me," he whispers. "Willow. You are just —" His

hands are traitors, grabbing for the clasp of her bra. "We can't do this here. What if we get caught?"

She wants to stop, she wants to send him away, but her body's a traitor too, and it wants her to live. With a quick strong press of her wrists she lifts herself onto the table, feeling the sharpness of the edge even through her jeans. Luca takes a step towards her, then stops, then takes another step. His arms go around her. The wall beside her is lined with instruments of death. *Cleaver,* she thinks. *Bone-saw. Filleting knife.* She isn't sure if these are the correct names, but the chime of the words in her head, the cold metal under her fingers as she runs her hands over them, is dizzying. They're what she came for. Not for the sweet warmth of Luca's breath on her neck, not for the press of his fingers against her skin. She's here for the clean cold sharpness of the blades.

"Christ," Luca whispers, his mouth against hers. "Will you leave those bloody knives alone? This is so messed up."

Yes, she thinks wildly, *I know. You can't be here when he comes for me. You have to leave, now. Stop kissing me so I can let you go.* The tremble in his flesh makes her think of the hum of a live wire, tempting to the touch even though it sings with danger. He presses against her, then with a sudden rush of movement, takes off his top. She has to stop him, but she can't, she can't. Her body is singing with joy, a siren call reminding her of the pleasure of being alive. Luca's skin against hers is delicious, scorching.

"I told you the last time we met." The voice in the doorway is calm, conversational, a little bit weary, as if one of their parents has walked in and caught them eating biscuits before dinner, as if they've tipped Lego on the floor and not picked it up. "You're not allowed to be in here."

They're both so still that Willow imagines for a moment that she can hear Luca's heartbeat.

The Slaughter Man's face is calm and terrible, almost meditative. She wonders if this is the expression he wears when he's working. She imagines a smooth conveyor belt of death, animals standing obediently still as they make their way towards him, the raising of the gun, the single crack and then the boneless drop to the floor. Is this how it will be for her? Luca's breathing is rapid and panicky. The lights gleam off the glossy brown stock of his gun.

"I'm sure I told you what would happen to you if you came back here. I did tell you, didn't I? What would happen to you? If you came back here?" He doesn't raise the gun, not yet, but his grip on it becomes a little tighter, as if he's readying himself for action. He must have fired it so often that the mechanics of taking aim are second nature to him. Probably he can simply raise it and pull the trigger in one simple movement. "I wouldn't want you to think I was being unfair. By not warning you what would happen if you came back here."

Do it, she thinks to herself. *Do it. Do it now. Oh, Luca, I'm sorry, I didn't want this to happen to you too.*

"If you fucking dare try anything, I'll come over there and fucking kill you," Luca whispers. "With my bare fucking hands, you hear me? With my bare fucking hands."

"Or maybe you could use some of my butchery equipment," the Slaughter Man says. "I'm sure you've been looking at it again. Yes, I can see your fingerprints from here. You shouldn't handle it without washing your hands first." His gaze slides from Luca to Willow. "Or was that you? Do you like my butchery equipment? Because that's not a nice thing to take an interest in."

Get on with it, she thinks. She hadn't imagined he'd play with her; she'd thought it would be a quick clean thing, a flash of pain and then over. She wants it done, before she has time for second thoughts.

"The two of you," he says, sounding almost indulgent. "Standing here in my butchery room, sweaty and scruffy and half-dressed. Come here to fool around with each other, in a room made for taking animals to pieces. There's something wrong with both of you children, isn't there?"

If she could be granted one wish before she dies, it would be to find her voice at last, so that she could scream at this awful, patronising man that of course there's something wrong with her. She wants to scream that she's not a child, she hasn't been a child since the day they told her what had happened to her sister, and the least he could do is to treat her with dignity before he kills her. The words are huge in her mouth, like those gobstopper sweets that you have to force in past the reluctant stretch of your cheeks, so huge you think you might choke, spit and panic accumulating in the spaces around the edge, before you remember that you can breathe through your nose. What will it take to unlock her voice, if not this moment? She's holding her breath in stark contrast to Luca, who pants like an animal beside her. Perhaps if she can make herself breathe out, the words might come with them? What if she tries to plead for Luca's life?

"I suppose I'd better get on with this, hadn't I?" The Slaughter Man shakes his head. The gun-stock gleams as he lifts it to his waist. "It's a shame, but sometimes these things have to be done."

Yes, she thinks, *yes yes yes*, and then, wretchedly, *no no no, just me, not him, please, I didn't mean this for him too*. But it's too late. There's no more time. This is it.

CHAPTER TWENTY-SEVEN

The bang is so huge that it takes her a moment to realise she's still alive. She's braced so hard for the impact that she can't quite process that her body's intact, no blood, no missing limbs, no slow dissolve into silence as all her time leaks out onto the floor. But the noise echoes in her head. What, then? Is Luca—? When she turns to him she sees the same bewilderment on his face, the same foolish bracing for a trauma that isn't going to come.

"What the fuck? What the fuck? Fucking hell, what the—?" Luca is gasping for breath, looking wildly around for evidence. "Where is he? Has he gone? Did he get you? Did he—? No? So what the... Did he shoot and miss?"

There are no signs of a shot. No splinters, no cracked tiles, nothing damaged or disturbed except the two of them, clutching at each other. It takes them an absurdly long time to understand what has happened. The sound they mistook for the blaze of the shotgun was simply the slamming of the door. They're not dead but imprisoned.

"Jesus," Luca whispers. "I really thought—" He shakes his head. "That absolute bastard. I'll burn his fucking house to the ground." He grabs the door handle, shakes it as if he's trying to kill it. "He's jammed the door with something."

He's locked us in, Willow thinks. *That's what he's done.*

"Come on, you fucker. Open up." Luca is pulling so

hard on the door handle that it's as if he's forgotten how it works. "I'll get us out of here. Give me a minute, just another minute, and—"

With a nasty little metal crack, the door handle comes away.

"All right," Luca says. "All right. Now we're getting somewhere. We just have to keep going and it'll come open by itself. Won't it?" He pushes against the door with his shoulder.

No, thinks Willow. *Now we're definitely shut in here until he lets us out.*

"I mean," Luca continues, and aims a kick at the base of the door, "people do this shit in movies all the time. You need to kick it in the right place and—"

The lights go out at the same moment that the slow background hum of the generator dies away, leaving a silence and a darkness so profound that Willow feels the pressure against every inch of her skin.

"Willow?" His voice is shaky. "Willow, are you still there?" He laughs. "Sorry, stupid question, obviously you're still there. Are you all right? Come on, this isn't funny. Talk to me so I know you're all right. Willow, you are all right, yeah? You've not, like, fallen off the table and cracked your head open or nothing?"

Don't you think you'd have heard me fall? Are you so frightened you've forgotten I can't—? Perhaps if he shut up for a minute he'd hear her breathing.

"Christ, sorry! Sorry. I forgot. Okay, keep still and I'll come over there." She hears his slow clumsy movements as he gets to his feet, the scrape of his hands as he makes his way around the wall.

"This place is twice the size in the dark. You ever notice that? Everywhere gets bigger in the dark? Is this the table? No, it's the freezer. Oh shit, is all the meat going to defrost and start stinking and that?"

No, Willow thinks. *It takes hours. It's all frozen solid. It'll be fine.*

"Willow." Luca's voice is ragged. "Can you please make a noise or something so I know roughly where you are? I mean, if you want to start talking, then this'd be a fucking marvellous time to do it, but can you move around or something so I can find you?"

She gropes upwards through the darkness, finds the knives hanging on the wall, runs her hands over them so they clink together.

"Jesus Christ." Luca's laugh goes on a little too long. "That's got to be the most creepy thing I've ever heard." He's beside her now, fumbling at the edge of the table, finding her knees and feeling along them as if he isn't sure what part of her he's touching. "That's better. I know it's stupid but for a minute I thought—"

She reaches out for him, feeling blindly in the dark. She'd thought her eyes might adjust, but there's no light for them to adjust to. She finds the skin of his chest, makes her way up to his shoulders to get the shape of him.

"You scared?" Luca asks, sounding calmer now they're next to each other again. "You're all right. I'll look after you. Come here."

The kiss is slow and tender, even sweeter because she's not expecting it. Then his hand leaves her waist and finds the curve of her breast and everything becomes harder and more frantic.

"Yes," he mutters. His hands knead at her flesh as if he's trying to mould her into a new shape. "Yes."

His hand fumbles downwards, presses hard between her thighs. It doesn't feel like anything much, neither hurting nor feeling good, just pressure in an unusual place; but he groans against her neck.

"Yes. Oh, yes. Willow, please. Now. Right now. Oh God, yes, please…"

Is this what she wants? That doesn't matter. This isn't about what she wants, it's about what she owes. She's brought him here, he's been locked in the dark by a stranger, and it's all because of her. The least she can do is let him do what he wants with her body. Why not? She won't be needing it any more.

His hands fumble with her jeans. When the denim slithers to the floor, she can feel the places on the aluminium table top where she was sitting. Warm where she's touched it. Cold where she hasn't. She strips him in return, feeling his clumsy movements as he kicks them off over his shoes. The skin of his erection feels shockingly young and tender.

"Oh God," he sighs, hoarse and sweet. "Oh my God. Willow. Willow. Wait. I don't know if I—"

She wriggles forward, pulls him closer towards her, feels the first tentative contact. She's fairly sure he hasn't done this before either, but they'll figure it out. Human beings have been figuring this one out for thousands of years.

And then, unexpectedly, gloriously, she can feel how it's all meant to work. He's pressing against her, eager little jabs that are almost in the right place, and then she slips her hand down and guides him and she hears his sharp intake of breath and it's going to happen, all of it.

"Willow." He sounds as if he's on the verge of tears. "I'm sorry. I'm so sorry. Please don't make me do this. I can't. I want to but I can't. I just – fucking – I just—"

He's still close to her but he's not touching her any more. Something has changed in the energy between them. Without the heat of his skin against hers, she feels cold and exposed. She's glad he can't see her. When she slips off the edge of the table to fumble for her clothes, her foot makes contact with him. He doesn't move towards her. He doesn't move away. Her touch is no more to him than the leg of the table.

"Are you angry with me?"

She doesn't know what she feels. She feels empty, aching. She feels ugly and brazen. She feels relieved. She wishes she could disappear.

"Willow? I'm so sorry. Please don't be angry with me."

He sounds so young. She sits down on the floor and inches

her hand out towards him, finds the shape of his ankle. When she touches him, he flinches, but doesn't pull away.

"I thought it might be all right." Luca's fingers close over hers, take her hand away from his ankle, holding on tight. Almost too tight. "I mean, I'm really into you, you're amazing. Way too good for a knobhead like me. I want to. So much. Swear to God, you are so fucking gorgeous and I'd like nothing more. But, you see – I – I need to—"

She feels her own neediness throbbing in her veins, her own longing for completion. She's the broken one; she's the one who needs help. If she could speak now, that's what she'd say, an unpleasant little whine, *What about me? What about what I need?* She's glad she can't speak.

"If I tell you," he whispers, then stops. "If I tell you this. Can I tell you – I don't know if I – okay. Okay. But I mean it, Willow. If I ever get even a fucking hint that you told anyone this, like even a little *sniff*, like if I even *suspect* you might have breathed a single fucking word to anyone – then I swear to fucking God, I will – I will—"

No, she thinks. *You won't.* She keeps still. Waits to see what he's going to say.

"So," he says. His voice is slow and halting, as if each word is something he has to cough up with great pain and effort. "What it was, right. My mum used to work Saturdays, not like every Saturday but like two in four or two in five, something like that. They had this rota so everyone got a fair share of Saturdays off, only sometimes it got messed up with holidays and that, cos people booked weeks off and it had their Saturday in it, so then they'd have to call people in. There was a big argument about it once, like whether it counted as overtime or just extra hours."

She has no idea what he's talking about, but at least the words seem to be coming more naturally, as if he's found a rhythm that will let him get out what he has to say.

"It was really hot. I remember that. My mum had this bee in her bonnet about me going out into the sunshine and getting some fresh air. I mean, fuck off, you know? I don't want to go outside and get all sweaty and skin-cancery, it's disgusting. I knew this Spanish lad once, he told me the best thing to do in Spain in August is go to the cinema, cos it's all air-conditioned. Back-to-back movies, as many as you can afford, then go home in the evening. They don't piss about getting *fresh air* and that. If outside's so great then why did they invent the internet?" He takes a long, shuddering breath. "I can't believe I'm telling you this. If you tell anyone I'll fucking kill you. Are you even listening? Be a right laugh if I told you and you'd gone to fucking sleep or something."

Her fingers are going numb with the pressure of his hand closed around them. She wriggles them as much as she can manage. He responds by clamping down even tighter. She wonders if she might end up with gangrene.

"Anyway," he says, "I had the place to myself so I was on the Xbox, because that's what normal people do, right? It's too hot outside, you shut the curtains, you go on the Xbox. Well, boys do, anyway. I mean, I know girls can be gamers and that, I'm not fucking sexist or nothing. I just don't really think of it as something girls do. I mean, I'm thinking, I don't know, pissing about on Insta or something? I don't know."

With her free hand, she feels blindly for his arm. She works her way up towards his face and lets her fingers rest against the back of his neck. Perhaps she can convince him to let go of her other hand, which is going from uncomfortable to actively painful. The muscles of his neck are tight and rigid. She feels the faint movement as he swallows hard.

"So I played for a bit, nothing serious, just a bit of mindless slaughter," he says. "It got a bit boring after a while. So. Yeah. Anyway. I was bored."

He seems to think this should convey something to her, but she has no idea what he's getting at.

"I mean," he continues. "You know what boys are like, right? Fucking animals, the lot of us. Leave us on our own in the house with an internet connection, it's what we're going to do, yeah? I mean, I should have gone up to my room and that, but I was feeling really relaxed. Got the place to myself. Got my laptop. I mean, shit, it's not like it's illegal or nothing, is it? I don't know why people even get so hung up about it. Animals do it all the time and they don't think it's weird."

Can he feel her blushing? Perhaps he's holding her hand too tightly for the blood to reach her fingers.

"Do girls do that too? I mean, when you're on your own and you're a bit bored, is that like your default activity? Or is it just us filthy pig-boys that think, *Yeah, bit bored, why not have a wank?* Oh shit, it was my fault, wasn't it? It was my own fucking stupid fault."

They're talking about The Day. She should have guessed that already. The day when he attacked his mother's boyfriend. The day that turned him into a dangerous criminal. Except he's not dangerous. He acts as if he is, but he isn't.

"Thing is, our front door's, like, the least discreet way of getting into a house you can imagine." For a blessed moment, he lets go of her hand. She flexes her fingers frantically. "It sticks all year round, but in, like, different places, so you have to change where you push it depending on the weather. So, when it's hot and dry, you have to shoulder-barge it. And when it's cold and wet, you have to kick. And it's really small. I think people in the olden days must have been much thinner or something, cos you can't get through it properly, not if you're carrying a bag or something. I mean, what's that all about? Didn't women used to have these fucking massive dresses and stuff? Were they like unfeasibly tiny or something? Sorry, I'm rambling, it's just…"

He sniffs, long and deep and disgusting, then takes her hand again. She tries not to mind that the fingers are slightly damp.

"But we always use the front door because the back door's such a fucking pain to get to. It's down this shared alley where all the bins are, and our neighbours are all right and that but they have this shitty little dog, like one of those ones that go in handbags and look like rats? And they put its shit in scented bags in the green bin and it absolutely fucking stinks. Specially when it's hot. Mum always says the smell would gag a maggot. And it would and all, I mean it was repulsive. So we don't use the back door. I don't want to tell you this, I don't know why I'm even fucking talking about it. What the fuck did you ask me about it for anyway? We were all right as we were…"

The darkness presses against them like velvet.

"Anyway," he says, as if he's following a path in his mind that only he can see. "That's why I didn't hear him come in. Because he didn't use the front door."

She's starting to see the shape of it now, the true monster that lurks in the dark places in Luca's mind. She's starting to glimpse the way it moves, see the sharp smooth gleam of its claws.

"And he came in, all quiet, like, and I—" Luca stops. "No, sorry, I don't think I can. I really don't think I can. You've got no fucking right to ask me this, no fucking right at all."

She can feel the train wreck inevitability of it, the words that have been building inside him, waiting for their moment to slink out and make themselves known. She wants to tell him, *Stop, please stop, don't do this*. But it's all too late. Everything that was done, was done long ago. She's only here to bear witness. The one thing she's learned about Luca in the short time she's known him is that he can't, absolutely can't, keep quiet in the face of her silence.

"And when he came in," Luca mutters at last, "I didn't see him at first. I mean—" he chokes with embarrassment. "I kind of had my mind on other things."

She can't picture the other person in this story, but she can picture Luca. She makes herself think not of his hands, the swift furtive working of his palms and fingers, but the look on his face. The way all his young-blood toughness softens and dissolves under the pressure of wanting, the sweet blankness in his eyes, the swelling of his lips. He's like her, just a kid.

"I thought I was going to fucking die," Luca mutters, and she can feel the heat of his shame making its way down into his palm, the sudden sweat springing out from his pores. "Getting caught, doing *that,* that's got to be, like, the worst thing that can happen to you, right? I mean, that's what I thought at the time. I thought that was the worst fucking thing that would ever happen to me in my whole life." He squeezes her hand. "Don't you fucking laugh at me, Willow. I know it sounds funny but this isn't funny to me. Please don't fucking laugh at me or I'll have to kill you."

She pictures her fingers as a row of dead piglets, fat and swollen, ready to split their skins. She won't let him know it hurts. This is the least she can do for him.

"Shit. Sorry." He lets go of her hand. "I didn't mean to... Have I hurt you? Shit, I didn't realise I was. Shit. Shit."

She stretches her fingers, then offers him her other hand instead.

"Fuck off," Luca says, sounding exhausted. "I can tell you this without holding your fucking hand, all right?"

He takes it anyway, crushing it against his chest as if it's all that stands between him and the void.

"It was the way he said it," Luca blurts out at last. "Like it was the most normal thing in the world. Like he'd come in and found me, I don't know, eating chips or something, and asked for one. *Mind if I have a look too, mate?* That's what he said. And he sat down beside me and got hold of my laptop and turned it towards him and then he fucking, he fucking, he just, you know, he unfastened his jeans and he just, he just -" he laughs. "Like it was *nothing,* you know? Like it was normal! The normal thing to do. Sit down next to your girlfriend's kid and get it out and start... start -"

This is the most awful, grimy, destructive thing she's ever heard. She feels soiled just listening to it. She wants to wipe her hands on her t-shirt, then jump in a bath and scrape at her skin with a pan-scrubber. How must it feel to live with this memory lurking behind your eyelids, waiting to pounce?

"I thought that was all he was going to do," he said. "You know, sit there and, you know, give himself a fucking treat. But then he looked at me, and he said... No, I don't think I can—"

She doesn't want him to. She doesn't want to hear this. She wants him to stop. She can't bear the weight of his pain on top of her own.

So say something. Because if you don't, he'll keep talking.

She opens her mouth. She feels the smallest sound take shape in the back of her throat, a soft little *uh*. Then, nothing.

"He fucking did it to me," Luca mutters. Something warm and wet drips onto their hands. "He fucking reached over and he pinned me down with one hand and he grabbed onto me with the other and he fucking... he fucking..."

Oh God, she thinks. *Oh God. How could anybody let that happen?*

"And," Luca whispers, sounding almost at the end of his strength, "I fucking... I mean, I couldn't stop myself. I hated it, I utterly fucking hated it, I don't *like* fucking gay stuff, I was watching a video of a *girl,* but he was fucking *touching* me and I couldn't stop it. And he said... he said... *See? You like it, don't you? I knew you would.*"

These are the last words that come out of him for a while, but not the only sounds. She holds him against her chest and strokes his hair. *I'm sorry,* she thinks. *I'm so, so sorry. Forgive me.* This is the key that unlocks all his strangeness.

"And that wasn't the only time," Luca goes on, as if what he's told her already isn't enough, as if he could have shrugged off a single rape and gone about his life. "I mean, I tried to be out as much as I could, but there's only so much you can do, right? It was like he was *watching* me, like he was *enjoying* watching me trying to stay away. And all he had to do was pick a fight, clothes on the floor or pots in the sink or something, and I'd be fucking grounded, you know? I didn't know how to... And the worst thing was, I'd get *hard,* you know? He'd be doing that to me and I'd get fucking hard. I mean, what the fuck is wrong with me? Who'd believe me when I said I didn't want it if he told them—" He shudders against her chest. "I think that's the worst bit. Wondering if maybe I *did* like it. I mean, boys can't fake that stuff, can we?"

She strokes his hair, unsure if this is the right thing to do or not. She's wondering how he got from there to here, if perhaps there's some truth in the first story he told her after all. Did he turn on the man who raped him and beat him to a pulp?

"Anyway," he mutters. "I was proper off the rails at school. Fuck knows what they all thought was going on. Probably thought I was reverting to type, you know? Kid from the rough part of town, single mum. They didn't exactly have high expectations. But I had this one teacher, he was a good bloke, and I don't know if they get special training or something, but he took me to one side one day, and—" suddenly there is a tinge of wonder in his voice. "It was like he already knew all of it, you know? He knew exactly what to ask me. It was like having someone open up the inside of your head and look inside. And I thought maybe—"

Is this what Willow's mother does for the people she sees? Is this how it feels for them as they sit in her office and look at her over her desk and let her peek inside their heads? And if this is how it is, how does her mother stand it?

"So then there was the police involved," Luca sighs. "I mean, I knew they'd have to be. I was sort of prepared for that. I mean, not like you can be *prepared*, it was just awful, but, you know, I knew I had to. But then, my mum—" He's crying again. "They told her. They told her. And she didn't… she said… she wouldn't… she said he was a good bloke, and I was trying to… Like I'd make that up, for *attention*—"

She's been so sad and angry about her own life for so long that she'd forgotten how it feels to have these emotions on behalf of someone else. If she stands up, she'll be tall enough to take the roof off, tall enough to stalk across the countryside and find her way to the house where Luca's mother lives. She will open up the top of her house, bend down and pluck her from the bed where she sleeps, bring her up towards her mouth and tear off her head.

"I miss her," Luca whispers. "All I want is to go back and be with her and have our lives the way they were before. And there's no way that's ever going to happen. Even if he goes to jail. Even if they say I can go back and live with her again. It's never going to be the same. Because she doesn't think he did it. So whatever happens, this is what it's going to be like from now on. Every single fucking day from now on, me and my mum, we'll be further away from *all right*. I can't even remember what *all right* looks like any more." He pushes himself fiercely away from her. "That's why I like you, you know. Because you're like me. You're on the wrong side of *all right*. But you're so fucking tough, you know? I mean, I know you don't talk, but you don't fucking have to. You keep going. And you make it look easy."

His words break over her head like cool water. She feels them soak into her skin. She's always assumed everyone sees her as broken.

"I mean," Luca says, "so many times I've thought about… but then I think, *Well, if Willow can*… I mean, I don't want it getting out that some girl's fucking tougher than me, do I?"

She can't move for the wonder of it.

"That's a joke, by the way," Luca says. "I don't actually mind a girl being tougher than me."

He's trying to sound like himself again, so they can both leave behind the story he's told. Very gently, because she knows now how raw and tender he is beneath his shell, she puts her arms around him. After a minute, he does the same, and lets his face rest against the top of her head.

"God," he sighs. "I'm so tired. I feel like I've run a marathon. Well, I'm saying that. I've never actually run a marathon. D'you think that fucking headcase is ever going to let us out, Willow? Or is this just where we live now?"

She doesn't know what the Slaughter Man is going to do. Nothing about this evening has gone the way she imagined it would, nothing except the dark. She'd thought she would come into this darkness and be with Laurel, but instead she's with Luca, leaning against her, warm and needy, as lost or as found as she is.

Pressed together, blind and wordless and exhausted, surrounded by their own ghosts, they sit for a length of time they have no way of measuring, and feel the gradual synchronisation of their breathing.

CHAPTER TWENTY-EIGHT

She's in a car park outside a hospital, and she knows she's dreaming because every inch of the landscape provokes a strange sharp nostalgia that makes her heart sing and swell like a bird.

She's alone, but somehow she isn't lonely. There are other people in the car park, but if she looks too closely, they'll melt into the concrete and disappear, because they're not really here at all, they're simply additional set-dressing for what she's going to see. She is alone, and this is how it has to be, because although she's dreaming, when she wakes she'll be in the place where she's no longer one of a pair, and it's time for her to accept it.

The few cars she sees are ones she remembers from her childhood. There's the Audi estate from when she and Laurel were small, the one that brought them home from the hospital, folded into car seats that looked like enormous shells holding a too-small pearl. They'd had that car until they were six, and she can still remember the number plate, which was Y626 KMK. She'd liked the double symmetry of it, had spent many happy hours on long journeys trying to work out the pattern that connected the 6 to the K, the 2 to the M. A little further on is the car that came after, the Range Rover they'd both disliked because it was hard to climb into and out of. The black Ford

SUV. Finally, the car they have now, the fat wide Audi that brought her home from the hospital without her sister.

She stops by the window and looks inside, wondering if she might catch a single final glimpse of Laurel. No sign of her sister. Not even the sweet wrappers she'd left in the side pocket that they could none of them bear to remove, not even the half-drunk water bottle that rolled around in the footwell. Instead, she sees a discarded plush bunny, its fur white and pristine, its nose an impossible adorable pink. She yearns towards this toy so fiercely she thinks she might be able to reach in through the glass and pluck it out.

Another sign that this is a dream, as wish becomes will becomes action. The window's now open, or perhaps simply not there, and her hands close around the plush bunny as if this is the treasure she's been searching for all her life.

She's too excited to walk to the hospital entrance. Instead she floats upwards into the air, pulling herself along with smooth strong movements. She sees the tops of the trees that grow around the edges of the car park, fat green clumps of dark green leaves that look almost artificially healthy, as if they're models rather than the real thing. She wonders about sitting in one for a while, to savour the strange comforting warmth of this place that reminds her of the soft safe space beneath her duvet, scented with her breath and body, a cocoon built only for her. But then she remembers the plush rabbit in her hands and knows she doesn't have time for this now. There's something she has to do.

She comes back to earth outside the doors, which lead into a tall atrium filled with lifts. This is a place she remembers from the real world, and she feels dizzy with apprehension and for a moment the lights dim and she hears the clacking of beaks, the slow hum of the Slaughter Man as he prepares his instruments.

"It's all right, love." There are arms around her, a warm white expanse of bosom so welcoming that Willow thinks she might fall asleep even in her dream. "It won't be like the last time. You've moved on."

But I didn't want to move on, Willow thinks, *I wanted to stay where I was. I wanted to be with Laurel.*

"It's like having a scar that never quite heals," the woman continues, and her voice is maddeningly familiar, so that Willow longs to be able to turn her face upwards and see who's talking to her. Is it her mother? Is it Katherine? The vicar from Laurel's funeral? Could it even be Laurel? "You'll never be the same again. Some days it'll give you trouble, and you'll feel as if you've gone right back to the start again. But some days, you'll be fine. You'll never love anyone in the same way you love Laurel, but that's all right. You'll meet other people, and you'll love them in the ways that are right for them."

I don't know what you're talking about, Willow thinks. If she freed her face from the comfort of this woman's vast pillowy breasts, would she be able to speak at last?

"You'll get it eventually. Now it's time for you to go upstairs."

The woman disappears, and now Laurel's in front of the lift. The doors slide open. Inside is a gaudy bronze space with tinted mirrors and a wide white velvet bench with twirly gold legs. A chandelier hangs from the ceiling.

This isn't a hospital lift, Willow thinks sceptically. *This is stupid.* She goes in anyway, and sits down on the bench, balancing the plush rabbit on her knee. The doors slide closed, and the lift begins to move, even though she hasn't chosen which floor she wants to go to.

"Don't worry." There's someone standing in the corner of the lift, but she can't quite resolve their shape into a definite person. They must be one of the background people, who she's painted into the landscape to make it less eerily empty. "This lift only goes to one place."

She wonders if she's made a mistake after all, and this is a dream not of moving forward but of dying. Perhaps the white and gold and bronze colour scheme, the pristine purity of the white velvet, are signs that she's making an ascent to some sort of afterlife?

"It's all going to be afterlife from now on. That's how life works. People die, but you keep living. Then one day it's your turn to die and then they're the ones living in the afterlife."

That's awful, she thinks.

"Death is only a change of state," the figure says, and now she can see clearly enough to make out that he's a man, tall and cadaverous, and with a hood pulled up over his face. "The energy we had locked up inside of us is released, but it can't ever be destroyed. It's just remade into something new."

Something better?

"Who decides whether something's better or worse than another thing? Is a fox better than a rabbit? Is a maggot better than a cow? Are you better than the wheat that made your bread?" He's talking at her now rather than to her, as if this is a speech he's given many times before, and now she thinks she knows who he is, but she doesn't dare look too closely, because she wants to hear what he's got to say. "We're all simply expressions of energy. Life is the rejection of entropy, and we fight to live for ever, knowing the battle is futile and the war unwinnable. We were born in the hearts of stars; one day we'll decay into low-grade heat. Everything that happens in between is a brutal miracle of life's resistance. We can't win the battle. Ragnarok waits for us all. The point isn't to win. Only to try."

You sound like my physics teacher, Willow thinks. *Entropy and stars and low-grade heat. You sound like that day when he went off into this weird lecture and halfway through he started crying and then he told us his mum had died the week before.*

"Well, of course I sound like him. I can only work with the materials you've given me. Nonetheless, I'm telling you something important. The universe rebels against its own destiny, and *homo sapiens*, being children of the universe, are rebels too. Fight it or accept it, we all know how the story ends. It's what we do with the part in the middle that makes it all so interesting."

And as the doors slide open, she catches a glimpse of his face beneath his hood, and she sees that he wears the bare bone skull of a crow that covers his head.

"My face isn't important," he says, seeing her trying to glimpse the face beneath the skull. "I'll see you again one day. Until then, my advice is to try and find as much joy as you can." He sweeps his arm out in a long, elegant gesture that verges on a bow.

Now she's standing in a bright empty space with a polished linoleum floor. Ahead of her is the door that led into the Family Room.

No, she thinks, *I'm not going back in there, I'm not.*

But she has to. It's the place where it all began, and it's the place where it all begins again. The merry-go-round of love and fear, the joy of having perfectly counterbalanced by the pain of losing. She clutches the rabbit tightly by its ears, daring it to come to life in her hands and protest, to wriggle and kick and set itself free. But the toy remains lifeless and passive, and she knows there's going to be no last minute reprieve. She pushes hard on the door.

She's expecting to find her parents in there, perhaps sitting on the sofa or pacing impatiently around and waiting for her to join them. Instead she finds a room that's almost entirely empty. There's no sofa, no chair, no kitchen countertop with a microwave and kettle and tiny camping fridge. The only thing in it is something she doesn't really have a word for, a thing like a giant rectangular sandwich box with its lid off, mounted on wheels and containing a small wriggling thing, pink and unformed. Stuck to the end of the box is a gigantic ribbon, a crude visual reminder that the thing inside is meant to be a gift.

No, she thinks, and closes her eyes so she won't have to look.

Yes, she thinks, and opens her eyes again so she can peer inside.

The baby inside is fat and luscious, his chins quadrupled, his wrists and ankles plump little folds of flesh. When he sees her, he opens his eyes wide and flaps his arms and legs. The gesture is familiar even though she knows she's never seen it before.

This isn't what newborn babies look like, she thinks.

No, she thinks, *but this is a dream. You're making do with the materials you've been given.* In his cot, the baby blinks solemnly, as if he can hear her thoughts.

And now she can feel her chest and stomach swelling, making room for all the love she'll need for this new little one who will soon burst into her life, not to take Laurel's place, but to make a new place, reshaping the world around him to accommodate his presence. Can she live with the terror of losing him? Her mother and father do that with her every day, so she'll have to try and do the same. And besides – besides – those little arms, those huge eyes, the trusting way he's looking at her.

She holds out the toy rabbit to the baby, watches as he takes it in his hands and brings one ear to his mouth, covering it with milky spittle, marking it as his own. Her fingers come to rest on his little chest, feeling the flutter of his tiny heart. Will it be strong enough to last? What if it breaks before he's grown? What if…

I can't do this, she thinks.

I can do this, she thinks.

Until the moment comes for real, she'll have no way of knowing if she can do it or not. For now, there's a new sensation, one at once strange and gloriously familiar; the sensation of her voice unlocking within her throat.

You're going to need a name. Of course, it's not for her to pick; her parents ought to be allowed to choose. But who said the universe was going to be fair? She's stealing this one, and the hell with anyone who wants to stop her.

"Ash," she says, her voice clear and bright in her throat. She closes her eyes so she can imagine the words taking physical form, like birds perhaps, fluttering around the cot and coming to rest against his skin. "Your name's Ash."

And the part of her that knows she's dreaming sighs in surprise and wonders, *Did I say that out loud? Did I say that in my sleep, wherever it is that I'm sleeping? And where am I sleeping, anyway?*

So many places she might be. She might be in her bed in Joe's cottage, the kitten curled tight and forgiving against the backs of her knees. She might be lying in the tight dusty space at the top of the haystack, where she and Luca will go when it's time to say their goodbyes. She might be back at home, having made the leap forward through time and space past all the explanations and apologies they'll both have to make. Or perhaps all of this is still to come, and she and he are asleep on the floor of the Slaughter Man's workshop, waiting for him to return with Joe and Katherine, because of course he was never going to kill them. He shut them in, not to hurt them, but to keep them from themselves.

It doesn't matter. All that matters is that she's glimpsed the future, and seen something worth walking towards.

"Ash," she says again, and this time she knows she's speaking out loud. She can feel it, feel her voice coming back to her, the vibration in her throat, the warmth of the air as it moves past her tongue and out into the world.

She's been asleep for a long time, but now it's time to wake up.

ACKNOWLEDGEMENTS

As always, my first and most important "thank you" is to my editor, Lauren Parsons, to Tom Chalmers, and to everyone in the Legend team. Thank you for believing in and supporting me, for welcoming me into your group of authors, and for not making me delete the scene with the baby rats.

Thank you to Rose Cooper for a cover so beautiful, I genuinely squealed with joy when I saw it.

Thank you to Louise Beech, Lynda Harrison, Vicky Foster, Michelle Dee, Julie Corbett, Emily Ottogen and Jodie Langford – my fellow Hull Women Of Words, and my sisters-from-other-misters. You're amazing and inspiring, and I'm so proud to be one of you. Thank you to my daughter Becky and my son Ben, for not minding me going off into my own head for days at a time, for not complaining when I come to Parents' Evening with sinister notes written on my hand, for listening to all my cat stories, and for generally tolerating all my nonsense. You make me so proud.

Most importantly – thank you, thank you, thank you to my lovely husband Tony. You make everything possible.